DISMI

M000025789

Copyright © 2019 by Dick Ault
All world rights reserved

This is a work of fiction. Names, places, and incidents are the products of the author's imagination or are used fictitiously. Any resemblance to actual events or locales or persons, living or dead, is entirely coincidental.

No part of this book may be reproduced, stored in a retrieval system, or transmitted in any form or by any means electronic, mechanical, photocopying, recording or otherwise, without the prior consent of the publisher.

Readers are encouraged to go to www.MissionPointPress.com to contact the author or to find information on how to buy this book in bulk at a discounted rate.

MISSION POINT PRESS

Published by Mission Point Press
2554 Chandler Rd.
Traverse City, MI 49696
(231) 421-9513
www.MissionPointPress.com

ISBN: 978-1-950659-20-3
Library of Congress Control Number: 2019911945

Printed in the United States of America

DISMISSAL

BUSINESS, POLITICS, THE SEVENTIES AND SEX

DICK AULT

MISSION POINT PRESS

TO PENNIE, FOR ALL TIME

The truth will set you free, but first it will piss you off.
—*Gloria Steinem*

CHAPTER 1

Virgil Cash had no idea of the mess into which he was about to be enmeshed. I presumed I did, but then I was thinking only of the present mess.

As I drove to pick him up at Melbourne's Tullamarine airport, I struggled to keep one eye on the voluminous Melbourne Street Guide and the other on the road. I knew better than to go my usual way through the city center. I had left the office early, and, as a Yank expat of a few years, worked my way through and around side streets as best I knew how, only glancing briefly at the guide when absolutely necessary. It took me through close-in suburbs like Richmond and Carlton, past the brewery, a route I had never followed before, but one that avoided the downtown madness and got me to the airport in time.

A colleague and friend, Virge was as innocent a spirit as his Huck Finn looks suggested. Smart to the point of genius, he was often naive in the ways of the world. As Managing Director of the Australian branch of Brock & Case Consulting, I wanted his analytical brilliance for a major project. As his friend, I loved his sweet disposition and looked forward to some hang time.

His Qantas flight was suspiciously delayed, suspicious because so-called "work-to-rule" strikes (what we called union "slow-downs" in America) were threatened in every enterprise, particularly public services. Was the delay a matter of Qantas employees or air traffic controllers adhering strictly to the letter of the rule book or merely a normal late arrival? For the moment, no telling.

Why was I not shocked when he emerged from the customs door with a dazed look and an unfamiliar smiling woman at his side? Both showed the effects of the painfully long trip from the States and had obviously taken advantage of the complimentary first-class booze. Their clothes were more than a little rumpled, Virge's tie off and stuffed in a side pocket of his tan summer suit coat. His tried his best to smile when he spotted me but lost the struggle, finally letting me know with his eyes and his drooping lips that he was worn out from the ordeal. When we shook hands and gave each other a cautious male hug, he broke into a laugh smelling of liquor and fatigue.

The woman with him teased both of us with a rowdy laugh and introduced herself: "You must be Cooper Houghton. Virgil here and I met over a match, didn't we, sweetie?" She patted Virge on the arm before giving another guffaw and turning back in my direction, grabbing my arm to steady herself. At least that's what I thought she was doing. She too was in a suit—blue pinstripe, with her white silk blouse covering her ample bosom, but tugged partway out at her waist. "I'm Fran Lawson. My husband, Gerald, is sales manager for WM-A, one of your clients, I understand."

She had that right. World Motors-Australia, a subsidiary of the American car company in Detroit, was not only one of our clients, but our biggest and most important. She went on: "I've been in the States on home leave and had the pleasure of flying back with my friend Virge here. When I needed a light, I saw him smoking across the aisle in my row. He was nice enough to light my cigarette and I think we made an instant connection." She gave his arm another pat and laughed again. "He's so funny. I grabbed the seat next to him after we refueled in Fiji and we had a wonderful time the rest of the way, didn't we, sweetie?" Virge smiled unconvincingly.

With that, her driver appeared from customs with her luggage on a cart. As she started off with him toward their waiting car, she looked back over her shoulder at me and smiled but spoke to Virge: "Don't forget to call, Virgil."

She was not at all a bad-looking woman but even her perfume smelled of trouble. Even *I* knew better. "What was all that about?" I asked.

"Oh, gosh, I don't know. She was all over the place. Believe it or not, I don't think even *you* are ready for my 'we met over a match' friend. She was reading a book called *The Female Eunuch*."

"No worries about me with her, my friend. By the way, Germaine Greer, the woman who wrote that book, is an Aussie, you know."

"So I heard more than once."

"She lives in England now, but she and it are still hot items around here. As far as keeping things stirred up locally, we have Muriel Mitchell, as this year's all-Aussie feminist."

As I pushed the cart with Virge's luggage to my car, I was ready to change the subject but he continued on about the Lawson woman. He told me that she had also mentioned Muriel Mitchell and had read passages from the Greer book out loud to him, some of which he found boring, some spot-on and thought-provoking, and some embarrassing.

"Some of it was funny and a few parts were pretty explicit," he said. "I couldn't believe she would read that stuff to a guy she just met on a plane. But she was slurring the words more and more as the flight wore on," he said, "and I suppose my listening skills were slightly under a cloud, so I may not have understood all I should. She laughed at my reactions and flirted at the same time. She gave me her phone number but I'm not interested. And I'm not passing the number on to you either."

"Please don't."

We laughed and agreed that it would probably prove suboptimal in the short time he was going to be here to have any further contact with a horny client's wife, drunk or sober. I was ready to move on, and as we got in my car, I said, "So, anyway, how was your trip otherwise?"

"Slept some, drank some and listened to her some. Before that I watched a movie from New York to LA, and tried again to Honolulu, but don't ask me what they were about because between the drinking and eating, I slept through both. Then she took over on the way to Fiji—it *was* Fiji, wasn't it? I'm pretty fuzzy about that too. I think you're right. About her I mean. Forget her and tell me what's going on with you and Brock and Case?

"All hell's breaking loose is what's going on. I'll fill you in some in the car but I know you must be wiped out from the trip. I won't try to give it all to you right now. We'll get you settled at the Hilton and hit it tomorrow. "

"No, I feel great, now that I'm off the plane and away from her. Vodka beats jet lag every time."

"We'll see about that."

I did fill him in some on the political scene, since we might be driving into it at any time.

"So, your timing is beautiful as always," I said. "To paraphrase FDR from another time and very different context, yesterday, November 11, 1975, is a date that shall forever live in Australian infamy." I did my best to explain that the country, after several years of political turmoil under the Labour government of Gough Whitlam, had just suffered the greatest constitutional crisis in its seventy-four years as a Commonwealth federation.

"There's a constitutional position here, Governor-General, an appointee of the Queen of England, an anachronistic leftover from the days of British rule. The guy in that job right now is Sir John Kerr. Historically, up until yesterday, the duties of that position were almost totally ceremonial. So guess what: he goes ahead and fucks everything up by *doing* something. He exercises his constitutional but obscure, never before used so-called 'reserve powers' and officially 'dismisses' the Labour Party which has been in power—voted in by the people in two straight elections—and which held a comfortable majority of seats in the House of Parliament. Officially, I guess, he 'prorogued' them."

"Say what?"

"Prorogued. Other people just say he fucked them. Still others— many of our clients for instance—take the opposite view. They will tell you that the old bloke rightly sacked the socialist blaggards and ratbags to make way for the Liberal Party to run things."

I could tell Virge was toggling back and forth between trying to understand and trying to stay awake. Poor bastard. His normal curious self straightened up when I mentioned the Libs. "You mean our firm's clients like the liberals?"

I was trying to focus on retracing my circuitous route from the airport, but I had to laugh at his question. "You're down under now, mate. Everything out here is upside down, don't you know? The Liberal Party is actually the conservative party."

Virge punched in the cigarette lighter, shaking his head as he lit up.

"Anyway," I said, "about the time you were landing, mobs of labor protesters were scheduled to strike and take over the streets of all the major cities. They obviously are on the side of those who believe they've been royally fucked—and I mean royally in the literal sense. The bum they want out on *his* bum is the Governor General himself, Sir John Kerr, not Prime Minister Whitlam."

Virge, as I would expect, found it both horrific and delightful. Finally he said, "Like you say, my timing is impeccable once again. Seems like only yesterday we got rid of Nixon."

"But that dragged on forever, and by the end, felt inevitable. This was sudden and shocking, took everyone by surprise, leading to this chaos. Look, you aren't going to be able to take this all in right now. You'll get more over the next few days after you've had a chance to rest up and get your feet under you. Just try to relax while I catch the latest on the radio. I just don't want us to get tied up in the traffic from all this."

Bob Hawke, the head of the Australian Council of Trade Unions and a Labour Party leader, was speaking from the capital in Canberra. He was pleading for calm and for his fellow unionists to proceed in a peaceful and orderly way to right the wrong wrought by the Libs and the Governor-General. "We are Australians," he said, "and we must not resort to violence."

There were reports that the stock exchanges were moving in a positive direction with the news and businessmen were quoted as delighted to be rid of the socialist Whitlam government.

The broadcast then switched live to the intersection in front of Melbourne's Flinders train station, always a hubbub even in normal times, but at this moment apparently jammed with angry, striking workers. Speaking into an amplified megaphone over a boisterous crowd, Ted Ball of the dockworkers union called out that they had walked off all the ships in Port Melbourne as well as other major ports around the country. His call for unity was greeted by loud cheers.

Then John Halfpenny, the firebrand leader of the AMW (Amalgamated Metal Workers) took over: "Now is the time if ever there was a time, for the people of Australia to rise up in anger. There has been a lot of talk about restraint. What does that mean? Does that mean we should lie down and be raped? Or does that mean we should respond to this provocation in a wave of action that will make the history books of this nation burn with the anger of the Australian people?"

The radio commentators let the roars take over without attempting to add anything. Virge was wide-eyed when I glanced his way.

"That's Halfpenny for you," I said. "He's communist by the way."

"For real?" asked Virge.

"Yeah. Quite openly, in fact. Virge, there's a lot about Australia that seems very American, easy for us to fit right in. We Yanks can't help but like it here. But some things are very different. A personnel executive explained to me that, although the communists are a small minority and he personally detests them, Australians aren't as paranoid about them as we are. They're just another political party."

He put out his cigarette and sat back as if to absorb everything while I managed to avoid the street chaos and found my way to the Hilton near the Melbourne Cricket Ground. I told him that the MCG, as it was known, could seat 100,000 for a game of cricket or Australian Rules football. "Mel and I were there with friends just a couple of months ago for the Aussie Rules Grand Final, tailgate party and all, just like the Super Bowl." Virge was not much of a sports fan but I gave him points for at least pretending to be impressed.

"Speaking of Mel, how is the 'Wicked One'?" he asked.

I smiled. "Pure and sweet as ever." This was a standing joke. Virge teased Mel that she only appears to be so pure and sweet to disguise a deeply held wicked streak. He called her his favorite "Mystery

Woman" for the same reason. She loved it, but little did he know the depth of her mystery. For that matter, I keep learning all the time.

Out of some need to protect her, I tried to shift the focus slightly: "You may not believe this," I said, "but these days she spends a lot of time on women's causes with the wife of WMA's managing director, Beth Robertson, who's been a good friend to Mel."

"Another Germaine Greer, this Beth person? Seems like they're coming out of the woodwork these days."

"Not at all. A feminist only in the broadest sense. She is a leader when it comes to battered women, poor Aboriginal women and girls and the like. Not a radical at all. Same with Mel."

"Of course."

"We've both loved our time here. Mel misses her graphic job a little but she's loving her time with the boys and she feels good about the work she and Beth are doing, even though it sometimes wears her down emotionally. I have to say, it's going to be hard to leave the friends we've made. Such generous people and Beth Robertson is among the best. She's actually a Yank, Princeton, New Jersey. Lived here for years though, and is deep into the Aussie community. She's adopted them and they've adopted her."

"And, of course, Mel has that friendship knack," he said.

"Even a stranger at checkout in a Safeway," I laughed. "Still feisty when she's backed into a corner though."

"And smart."

"That, too. Sometimes even smart*ass*, especially when she aims it at me."

After getting him registered, I tried to let him go on his own but he wouldn't hear of it.

"C'mon up for a least a little bit," he asked. "I want to talk. It's been a long time since we've had any time to talk."

In his room, Virge quickly found the new mini bar. "Isn't this a lovely invention?" he said as he removed a small bottle of vodka, and without asking, grabbed a scotch for me. He had a view of the Fitzroy Gardens, and some of the city skyline beyond. Melbourne appeared so tranquil from here, belying the fomentation at the street level. I turned the TV on to the public channel, the ABC, for the news before I went for some ice. When I returned, he was he stretched out on the bed, his eyes glued to the scene in the streets. He looked at me with disbelief as I took a seat on the couch.

"What the fuck?" he said.

"As they say here, Virge, 'No worries, mate, she'll be right.'"

"The hell you say."

Despite repeated pleas for a peaceful and orderly process from Labour leader Bob Hawke, things were spilling over into violence. A mob had moved to the Liberal Party headquarters where they were chanting for the head of the state party to show his face, an invitation he did well to ignore. Then, in what was anything but a calm and peaceful manner, people began to throw rocks at the building. When the police tried to restore some modicum of order, the rocks were hurled at them. One policeman was chased until he got to a police car where he had to fight off protesters as he squeezed his way in, the car then becoming the target for the rock throwers. Other police cars were pelted until they drove off to cheers from the crowd.

"What happened to calm and peaceful?" Virge laughed, his eyes wide in amazement.

"This has been building up for months if not years," I said, "but let's not get into all that now. It's complicated in a uniquely Australian way. You'll hear it all, eventually."

"I'm not sure I want to. But what about Brock & Case? What has all this got to do with old B & C?"

Virge needed a shower and a good night's sleep, but I attempted to answer his question. "You'll meet my team tomorrow and you can ask them. For now, let me just say, it's got everything to do with our clients so, it's got everything to do with us. Our biggest client right now, as I know you know, is World Motors-Australia. That guy you heard on the radio talking about rape, John Halfpenny, is head of the metalworkers union. There's a lot of metal in cars."

"OK, I get it. How does WM-A management feel about it all?"

"They're over the top with joy about getting rid of the Whitlam government. Last summer they made overtures toward building better relationships with those people, but it obviously went against

16

their grain. They will be happy the conservative Libs are in government and will be doing all they can to support them in the upcoming election."

"And when is that?" Virge mumbled.

"Hasn't been announced yet, but soon, I'm sure. Things can't go on in this limbo very long."

I took a short break to hit the loo and when I came out Virge was completely passed. One minute taking everything in even beyond his normal high level of curiosity, commenting and asking questions, the next minute gone. No use suggesting a shower. I knew him well enough to know that when he was out he would probably stay out until he woke up in the morning, still dressed, still on top of the covers. I'd give him time to sleep in before I called to wake him and have him delivered to the office.

CHAPTER 2

When I got home from my office, Mel was on the kitchen phone. She mouthed Gregory's name and gestured for me to get on the other line. Instead I noted her glass of red and headed for some of the same. I planned to catch the evening coverage on the ABC, but Brett had finished his fifth-grade homework and was watching Monty Python reruns. I decided their antics were less absurd and more entertaining than the current political reality, so I joined him. Monty Python was part of our family glue, especially with the boys. We never tired of the reruns, laughing at the same throw-away lines as though we had never heard them before. In this instance, Brett didn't disappoint nor did I. Roger was probably in his room doing whatever seventh-grade boys do. I didn't want to think about it.

At the end of the episode, Brett and I exchanged high fives and he went up to his room. I switched over. The news readers were summing up the historic events of the last couple of days, mostly more of the same. No announcement yet of an election date, only speculation that it would be no longer than a month away.

I'd been following the whole series of events for months and was on the edge of burnout, so Mel's voice from the kitchen phone easily cut through my focus on the news. I thought back to Mel on the phone with Gregory that other time—the first time, almost three years ago now, back when we were new to this country, back when we were both smitten by all things Aussie. Like today, I came home from work and she was laughing into the phone. Back then when she motioned for me to listen in, I was very curious about what was going on, so, unlike today, I took her up on it.

He spoke softly but with a confident voice and was going on about how lucky he felt to be talking with her, what a lucky coincidence that he rang an American by mistake. He asked about her marital and family situation and she didn't hesitate to give him the whole story. We were new American expats, she said. Her husband, Cooper Houghton, was in charge of the Australian office of a major international consulting firm. She worked in graphic arts in the states but gave it up when I was transferred out here. We had two sons, ages twelve and nine, whom she loved dearly. We had just moved into a charming old house in Toorak, a well-to-do Melbourne suburb.

Listening in, I was irritated that she would share so openly with someone we didn't know. All kinds of threats ran through my mind. What I didn't know is that he had already done his own sharing. Now he just went on in a quiet, gentlemanly way to congratulate her on her family life.

"You sound so content," he said. "I envy you."

He sounded like an educated Aussie and asked what she, as a Yank, thought about what was going on with the whole crazy political scene. We were new to the country back then, and while I had been briefed and done my homework, Australian politics were already volatile, to say the least. "I haven't studied it the way my husband has," she told him, "But I know things are kind of tense and unstable. That's about all. For now, I'm trying to keep my distance."

"Very wise of you," he said. "Unfortunately, as a member of parliament, I can't do that. All I can say is that there is a lot of craziness going on and the media couldn't be happier about it."

I made special note of that comment and was frequently reminded of it over the ensuing years.

Compared to the last few days, politics two years ago seemed almost placid. So did that phone call. So did our relationship with that no-longer-strange caller. Mel had been charmed by his gentle manner and sense of humor even though she told me it had all started with his dialing a wrong number, which did nothing to ameliorate my worries. He had called our number by mistake but was delighted, he had told her, for his call to be answered by a Yank. Mel, in turn, was intrigued by having a conversation with a member of the national parliament, all of which led them to engage in that long, rambling and friendly conversation. Of course he now had our phone number, and before we all hung up, she got his, and his name as well: Gregory Michel. He represented part of Toorak as well as Prahran, South Yarra and other close-in suburbs. As it would turn out, Gregory was full of surprises.

When that call was over, I purred, "'You sound so content,' and I must add, 'so wise.' So what the hell was that all about?"

Blushing slightly, she sat down on the nubby beige couch which, like most of the other furnishings, were part of my firm's lease when we moved into this gracious but drab old pile that had been inhabited by bachelor brothers for years. I lifted my glass, struck by the rich color and meaty aroma of the shiraz. Ordinarily I might get up and check the bottle label, but now didn't feel like the time.

"What do you mean?" she asked, defensively. "You heard him. He rang the wrong number and got an American woman. He was intrigued, and after my initial reservations, so was I."

I guess I must have smirked at those last words because she said, "Get the dirty smile off your face. I don't want to hear about any more of your kinky fantasies. It was just a phone call and he just seems like a nice man who happens to be a parliamentarian." She was so Liz Taylor beautiful (an observation I had shared with her the night we first met at that party in Soho), that I was always proud for other men to see me with her and desire her.

"Mmm-hmm." This time my smirk was deliberate.

Her dark eyes flashed and I flinched, knowing what might be coming. "I mean it. Stop it. You know better. That's not me," she said. "I'm not that girl." She always maintained that men knew better around her, that she was not one to be hit on. She told me that even as a teen she had no serious boyfriends. She did date a couple of guys but claimed that her group of friends did things all together, girls and boys. She couldn't even remember her first kiss or who it was who kissed her although she admitted it must have happened at some point. "Boys knew better with me," she said. "That is, until you, you bastard. You opened the floodgates."

Now, when she ended this most recent call, Mel came into the lounge with her wine "He's pissed off, as you might imagine," she told me.

"As I would expect?" I said. "What's his take?"

"He's furious with almost everybody. Obviously the Governor-General and Malcolm Fraser and the Libs as a whole. But he's pissed at Gough Whitlam, too—his own party's Prime Minister, for god's sake—for the way he's handled everything leading up to this, and he's even angry with a lot of the other Labour guys who got them into this ditch in the first place. Of course, I didn't follow it all, but I've never heard him rant like this."

"He hasn't been happy with most of those people for a while."

"I know, but I wish you could have heard him. He's over the top now. And what he calls 'those ratbag union rabble rousers' in the streets. He hates that the unions, who are his party's constituents, after all, are only making things worse for him and the party. I think the only one he is not ranting about is Bob Hawke, and he's not even so sure about him."

None of that seemed too out of line if you were in Gregory's shoes, which I definitely was not. Well, maybe some, since his disdain was so universal, but mostly not.

"Is that the way you ended it with him?" I asked.

"Not exactly. When he finally got out all the spite, he calmed down enough to ask about our plans. He wants the three of us to get together before we leave the country. I didn't say no but I didn't encourage him either. I said we'll have to see."

"But what do you *really* want?"

"Like I told *him*, we'll have to see." She happily changed the subject. "How was it with Virge?"

I gave her the brief version to which she said, with affection, that it sounded like the same old Virge. He was always a favorite of hers. I was mildly disturbed then when she hit the off button on the television. How could anybody just turn off such sublime theater of the absurd? I was such a fan.

"Enough of that crap for now," she said. "Let's all get out of the house and have a nice dinner."

"If the cooks and the servers aren't on strike, you mean."

CHAPTER 3

I checked the news on the telly first thing the next morning. Nothing much new had happened over night but the day promised to be full of more excitement. I left early for the office out of respect for that threat. I didn't call Virge. Let him sleep it off. He had my number.

He finally rang about eleven.

"What the hell happened?" he asked, still obviously half asleep. "I mean really. Don't tell me all that was real. It was all just one of my nightmares brought on by jet lag and booze. That would at least have been more normal for me."

"We should be so lucky," I said. "How are you doing anyway? Have a good rest?"

"I'm not so sure. I just woke up on top of the covers with all of my clothes on. Good thing I had to pee or I probably wouldn't be awake yet."

"Good thing you were awake for that."

I told him to get himself ready and either have a late breakfast at the hotel or come in for lunch with me. His choice.

"Not sure I can eat at all but let's try lunch. That way I can postpone eating a bit longer."

"I'll pick you up at one, OK? Dinner tonight with the CEO of World at eight, remember?"

"Sure. I'll be fine."

He was still a bit bleary-eyed when he got in my car but claimed he had a good rest and thought his body was catching up with the jet lag. I drove to a small Indian cafe in Toorak Road where Kevin Larned and three of his team were to meet us. Kevin was a good bloke, as a consultant, as a manager and as a friend. Youthfully handsome with light curly red hair and a brilliant smile, he was one of the nicest guys I have ever known, and also very capable of taking my spot. My promotion back in New York had me leaving on the first of February. Kevin would be the first-ever Aussie managing director. The Australians in the firm were happy about that and so was I. It was one of my proudest accomplishments in the years there.

Virge would be doing an analytical project with Kevin's team for a few months before he too returned to the home office in New York.

Kevin, Robbie Newsome, Eric Stone and Mary Lou Sand, were waiting for us, having already started in on some of that good Australian beer before we arrived. They stood and greeted Virge in friendly but cautious fashion.

Kevin held up the pitcher for Virge when we sat down. "Care for a glass?"

"I haven't even had breakfast yet, but sure, what the hell," Virge said, prompting laughter from the others.

I had never been much of a beer drinker back home, maybe one after mowing the lawn on a hot summer day, but I found Australian beer to be exceptional. I knew I would miss it when I returned to the States, but perhaps that was for the better. I was gaining more belly than I liked. For the moment, I skipped the offer and settled for a cup of masala chai.

They had already ordered some firsts for the table, Virge had to ask the origin of some and ended only picking at those with which he was familiar, entirely avoiding the curries. In the meantime, friendly get-acquainted questions were exchanged, no heavy business discussions, and more surprisingly, no mention of the chaotic political scene.

Mostly, I sat back and smiled at the interaction. This was the gist of what remained of my job before I was finished here: get Virge up to speed plus—the hard part—letting go of this group. I took pride in every one of them. The guys were easy-going mates in their thirties, smart as any group of Harvard MBAs that McKinsey might boast. Eric was English—a "POM": a Cambridge graduate—but got on well with the Australians. At some point, over a few beers, they had officially decided that while he was not and never would be a true-blue Aussie, he was, nevertheless, fair dinkum. A mate. No higher honor could have been accorded. Robbie was a Melbourne lad, RMIT undergrad, MBA from Monash.

And then there was my friend and mentor, Mary Lou Sands. That name was much too frilly for the person she was and had been changed to just plain Lou long before I knew her. Senior to the others by more than a few years in both age and experience, and holder of a PhD from the University of Sydney, Lou could be a bit prickly, but was probably the sharpest of the lot. In another world she would have (should have) been in my spot, but that time had passed and she had accepted her role as the cranky but respected mother hen of the team. Married to Bernard Sand, renowned author and professor in the social sciences, she had settled for second fiddle in that realm as well, although many believed she had done as much of the writing as he had. She also out-smoked them all. The others, including me, but excluding Robbie, all smoked but Lou went through at least two packs for every one for the rest of us. Unfiltered Camels. She could cite tons of what she called "suppressed research" denying the health risks of her habit. For some reason, she took this Yank under her wing from the beginning. She helped me no end to understand and appreciate the Australian culture, more than once either getting or keeping me out of jams. Not that she didn't shoot barbs my way, as she did the others. Sharp mind, sharp wit, sharp tongue. It wasn't always peaches and cream with Lou but I loved her and would miss her most of all.

At this moment she was saying to Virge, "So I guess you're tagging along on Coop's victory tour."

Robbie saw Virge's puzzled look and said, "You mean you didn't know? Coop is using you as his excuse to travel around to our clients to bask in their hails and farewells. Probably more than a few parties along the way, I'm sure. You'll get introduced and then shuffled off to the side whilst he bathes in glory."

They were all enjoying this at my expense but I was happy to laugh along with them. "Please," I finally said, "show some respect. Virge, don't listen to them. You are the featured player on this trip."

"Oh, I *get* it," he said. "I've lived in his shadow before. I can do it again." After a pause for effect, he added, "If I feckin' have to."

"There you go, mate," laughed Eric. "You'll fit right in here."

Of course, there was some truth in their taunts. It had been a good few years. Much better than the last couple for the Labour Party. While they kept things fascinating for this curious American observer, I had a series of wins to their series of losses. We had been able to fundamentally change the culture of the World Motors Australian subsidiary from a guarded, closed company, afraid of making a mistake, to an innovative, optimistic, hard-charging force to be reckoned with. Even their stance with the Whitlam government had gone from defensive to proactive. Where once they held an attitude of "ain't it awful" toward what they considered government interference, they had changed to "let's find a way to work together." Naturally, they would find that an easier proposition should the Liberals win the next election as predicted.

The change at WM-A took many forms but the exemplar was the vehicle assembly plant outside Adelaide. When I arrived, if you had wanted to give WM-A an enema, the Adelaide plant would have been where you stuck the syringe. They were the worst in the industry in every way possible, by any measure, quantifiable or not. The primary measurable was that they could never make their production schedule. Not ever. On the not so easily quantifiable side, they were just one people-mess after another; a dismal, sick culture. Now they had moved from the bottom slot among the company's four assembly plants, to the top; they routinely met their schedule; they led in quality; and relations with the unions had turned the corner. There was still a way to go in the latter area, but they had already made remarkable strides. Whereas the plant was once an embarrassment, something to be hidden from public view, it was now a showcase. It was the place you took VIP visitors.

No doubt, World Motors was the biggest success story, big in every way, but there had been many others with smaller clients, in several business sectors, from mining to chemicals to consumer products. Our success in the Adelaide plant had even gotten the attention of the Electricity Trust of South Australia, or ETSA, the state-owned electric utility. A win there led in turn to a successful project with the Sydney Water Board in New South Wales. These public sector projects also helped us with our reputation with government officials, regardless of party, and to our status with the general public as well.

For me, it had been a trip, literally and figuratively. I can't say I had enjoyed every minute—there were bad moments, crises of one sort or another—but even those were, in some way, fun to deal with. I compared it to standing at the top of a challenging ski slope. Some people would cringe at the sight, unable to breathe when they surveyed the moguls they would be forced to navigate. Others like myself found them breathtakingly exciting and couldn't wait to plunge down. Developing this attitude among my team took some doing, but now they came to work excited every day, ready to take on the world. Of course, the few ski slopes in Australia were hardly worthy of the name, so I had to revert to other metaphors, but eventually they got the point and joined me on the plunge.

Australia, while comparable in area to the contiguous forty-eight of the U.S., was in fact a much smaller country in terms of numbers of people, with 80% or more of the population clinging to the coastal areas in the southeast. For me, this provided an opportunity to grasp a sense of the whole, a whole country, a systemic whole that I had not yet found possible in the U.S. This despite the political tumult. Maybe that even helped. Everything, including all the warts, on public display all day, every day. Transparently ugly but transparent nonetheless. I enjoyed it. I thrived on it.

Now to collect the accolades and go home. Virge's orientation provided the perfect way to wrap up my richly rewarding stay. There was much I would miss. There were people who had come to mean more to me than I could have imagined. The tour with Virge would force me to deal with some of that, some happily, some not. But I was ready to leave. Cut ties. Move on and up.

No one seemed to notice my short fade out from the badinage around the table. When I tuned back in, the group was trying its best to help poor Virge understand the current events. He was asking questions that revealed his normal sweet naïveté, provoking their further pleasure in bringing him up speed. However, the more he questioned and the more they explained, the more evident became the absurdity. This and the simultaneous attempts to help Virge with the Indian menu. I knew he would be much happier with his pint and a Big Mac but such was his first day of cultural immersion.

Lou pulled me aside as we were leaving the restaurant. "Enjoy your victory tour, mate, you deserve it. But make sure it's a victory tour, not a conquest tour. Use the head that's on your shoulders. You reckon?"

I smiled and gently squeezed her arm. "I reckon," I said.

Back at the office, Virge met one-on-one with the team members on their respective projects, with a few analysts like himself, and the financial department. In the meantime, I made some calls to clients firming up my trips with Virge while I also tried to stay in touch with the coverage of the chaos in Canberra and on all the major city streets.

At 4:30 I pried Virge loose and sent him off with a driver to his hotel. I told him we would pick him up at 7:00 and take him to Kew for dinner with the Robertsons. I was allowing a little extra travel time for protester craziness. Who knows?

CHAPTER 4

Mel was sitting at her mirror in the bedroom getting ready. In her black bra (no push-up for tonight's events, I thought) and her black half-slip, I considered slowing her down but gave her just a friendly kiss instead. "You know I can resist anything but temptation, my love," I said.

"You just say that to all the girls," she said, slapping both my hands away from her breasts as I reached over her shoulders from behind.

"Only some."

"And how is that working out for you?"

"You're here with me, aren't you?"

"Good answer for the moment, but I will still have to give you an incomplete. How was the day with poor Virge? Has he caught up with himself from the trip yet? And how are Judy and the kids?"

"Fine, I guess. We didn't talk much about them." I recapped the lunch and his office rounds and asked, "How about you?"

"I rode with Beth to a WEL lunch meeting." She was speaking of the Women's Electoral Lobby. "Mostly rehashing the big dismissal, as you might guess. That's sucking up all the air time at the moment. But I take good things from it, as always. Those women come from a lot of different points of view, but they're all smart and committed and well-meaning. Almost all anyway. You know how that is. Oh, and Gregory called again."

"So what's going on with him today?"

"He's still ranting, angry with everybody."

"Even you?"

"No, not you either. Except that we're leaving the country, that is. Not too happy about that. They've announced the date of the election, you know."

"I heard. December 13."

"So now he's upset about that too. His seat is very much up for grabs and he has to start campaigning again. He's just sounding more and more desperate. I feel sorry for the poor guy but I am getting tired of his endless whingeing."

"Well, he's going to be busy and we're going to be leaving. No worries."

"Don't be too sure. He's determined we get together before we go."

"'We?' Does that mean you and him or the three of us?"

"Yes."

"Of course. Why would I even ask? What did you say?"

"I made no commitments. I basically dodged it."

We had no trouble on our way to pick Virge up at the Hilton, but it did get dodgy getting around the MCG and Punt Road on our way up and over to Kew: people in diverse clusters moving on foot in messy, anarchical fashion, on and off the footpaths and the streets. They seemed to have no more idea of their intentions than I did. I considered other routes but stuck with what I knew and tried my best to be patient, never one of my strong suits. Mel, always delighted in Virge's company, sat in the back seat with him while I acted as chauffeur.

He teased: "Do these poor, innocent Aussies know that they have a 'Mata Hari' in their midst, that you are a clear and present danger, that, behind this sweet persona is the spy who is the cause of all this current unpleasantness?"

She relished it: "Never. I'm far too clever for them. You're the only one who has ever seen through to the real me." They then went on having a peachy time catching up on gossip from the States, oblivious both to me and the traffic. I was able to concentrate most of the time on the driving. I had long ago mastered driving on the "wrong side of the road" although I still found myself reaching for the blinker lever on the wrong side of the steering wheel, and too often at this point, went to the wrong side of the car to get in. Some of what they talked about seeped in and either intrigued or annoyed me but I let it go. Once free of the mobs around the area of the MCG, things quieted down and we made it to the Robertson's in about half an hour.

The other guests were already there in the comfortable lounge of the large but casually charming and genteel old Kew home of Mike and Beth Robertson. I was ready with my tardiness excuses about the traffic but the conversation was all about the general topic of driving difficulty anywhere around the city so we obviously weren't the only ones. The traffic discussion became tangled with the politics of the moment, a risky party topic at any time, the riskiness only enhanced by the current volatility. However, the relative political homogeneity of the group that Mike and Beth had put together for the evening made this less of an issue.

They had the rare talent of creating engrossing dinner parties. Mike, the Managing Director of World Motors-Australia, was a bit of a stuffy and puffy English Sandhurst grad who moved into industry after a short but promising stint as an army colonel in India. His rise in the auto company had been equally rapid, but for some reason stalled out for some time in his current role as M.D. of the Australian subsidiary. Full of himself and full of bluster, he had nevertheless been kind and generous to me. This no doubt was less a result of my consulting contributions for his company (he barely paid attention) and more because Beth really liked me and had practically adopted Mel. As the top company executive out here, he served mostly a figurehead role when it came to operations. His ego, however, caused him to remind you of his status from time to time. All in all, he was a harmless bloke.

Beth, on the other hand, was the most gracious lady I have ever known, an American from Princeton. Whenever I think about her, the phrase "effortless grace" is what pops up. She was always busy with community projects while never rushed, a gourmet cook without the least fuss, a low-key but effective feminist while still a loving wife to a blustery cartoon of a husband. The only real contributions

Mike made to his organization were his outside contacts, his positive relationships with other business and government leaders. Ninety per cent or more of that could be attributed to Beth, a public relations weapon he was smart enough to deploy at every opportunity.

The guest lists at their dinner parties were a key to their success. Tonight it included Kevin, my offsider and soon to be successor and his wife, Diane, Bill Pawley, Mike's offsider and heir apparent and his wife, Isabelle, and Jon Berry, a strategy analyst at WM-A. Jon was single, which made the party count come out to an even eight including Virge. Beth thought eight the magic number for lively dinner conversation. Dinner at eight for eight was her custom.

Jon Berry's presence was also critical to tonight's special treat. He and Beth were the co-chefs for the evening, having jointly planned the menu. They were busy in Beth's kitchen when we arrived. Mike met us at the door wearing a white apron with a waiter's linen serving towel draped over his left arm. He laughed at our surprised expressions and gave us the rules for the evening. The plan was for Jon to be the guest host, with a major assist from Beth, while the men were expected to be the servers, each to go directly to the kitchen to greet our co-hosts and be given an apron and towel. Jon had selected a matching wine for each course. He, like Beth, was a gourmet cook but also a trained and passionate wine lover.

I had been introduced to Jon, a WM-H personnel staffer in the central office, soon after we first moved to Melbourne and began work with World. It was he who chose the first case of wine for Mel and me, each bottle a unique example of the country's viticulture, with a few European wines thrown in. In those days, Australian wines were a well-kept secret, very little if any was exported. Most Aussies were very proud of their wines, as they had every right to be. Most also made efforts to educate their palates but Jon was at the head of the class.

As Mel and Virge and I were a little late, the aperitif course was already underway with a sparkling Victorian white, refreshingly chilled, to accompany the small appetizer bowls of olives and nuts on tables around the comfortably furnished lounge.

Waiting for my call to duty, I relaxed with Kevin and Diane on the couch while Mike invited Virge to sit in the easy chair that was usually his own. Mike's ample glutes draped over the seat near the newcomer and he began to quiz Virge about his journey, his work background, his hobbies and interests. It was as though Beth had given her husband lessons on how to make small talk and a list to follow. Between answers Virge lifted his glass to his lips while shooting a quizzical glance my way.

Inevitably the conversation in the room turned to politics but not in the sensitive, divisive manner that one might fear at a dinner party. There was very little disagreement that the demise of the Whitlam government was long overdue, the general sentiment going something like this: "It's not just the recent agro over supply [the national budget]. They should have been tossed out at least a year ago for general incompetence." This along with the consensus that the street protesters were ratbags. Only Bob Hawke provoked any small amount of quibbling. Some praised him for his calls for calm and stability while others simply tossed him in with the other ratbags. "It's all show," Mike Robertson declared. "He's a politician, one more socialist, just like the rest of the Whitlam mob but worse: a union ratbag." I was not surprised in the least, but it did make me think about all the union leaders and members who worked in Mike's plants. We had managed to help smooth out and/or smooth over "industrial problems" (what Americans would call labor relations problems) in locations where they were severely damaging to production and quality, but tensions still existed and the current national upheaval was likely to exacerbate them, at least until the dust settled.

I joined the other men in serving the next course, some version of what I might call shrimp but which Jon described as Yamba king prawns with lemon aspen sauce. I left the prawns to the other "servers" but made a show of pouring the semi-sweet riesling with my right hand over my linen-covered left sleeve. The ladies were having a great time observing our awkward attempts at gallant subservience, gushing forth with ironic praise. Jon and Beth joined us, white aprons and all, as we savored the dish and heaped sincere compliments on their efforts.

The dinner continued to delight through a small serving of South Australia whiting fillets with another riesling, this one crispy dry, followed by a most memorable rack of lamb with a big shiraz. While I was fully expecting Lamingtons or a special Pavlova for dessert, Jon served poached pears with a delicious white dessert wine, the best pairing I have ever experienced (not that I have all that much experience with wine pairings).

I was doing my best to fully appreciate the food and drink while following the conversation, with Virge on my right and Diane, Kevin's wife, on my left. Mike was at the host end, with Beth to his right and Jon to his left. Both Jon and Beth frequently had to go off to tend to something in the kitchen. Mel was next to Jon, another of her favorites.

Isabelle Pawley was commenting on the latest feminist blast in *The Age* from Muriel Mitchell. Isabelle was a chunky little Greek/English/American, her accent an admixture exclusive to her. "That Mitchell woman is giving us girls a bad name," she said with a laugh.

Beth overheard the comment and came back in defense of Muriel Mitchell in her usual kind manner. "Oh, Isabelle, Muriel's not really so bad. She can be abrasive in public, I know, but that's just her way of making a point. I have had occasion to work with her on some women's projects, and she can be so sweet and compassionate."

"That's just you, Beth. You are far too tolerant," Isabelle replied.

"Funny you should say that," laughed Beth as she sat back down, still wearing potholders on both hands. "Muriel tells me the exact same thing. She thinks I should be out there on the street with feminist banners bashing men. I tell her I'm happy working with the Women's Electoral Lobby, working within the system with both men and women, to change things. She and I were both there at Beatrace Faust's home when WEL was first formed a couple of years ago. But we were too patient for her. She preferred a more confrontational approach. She is generous with her time and money for vulnerable women though, and we are still friends and work together from time to time."

Mel said, "I can second what Beth is saying. I don't know Muriel as well as she does, but the few times I've been around her, she seemed perfectly nice. A bit too serious, maybe, or should I say intense, but friendly. Doesn't come across as a 'radical libber,' he said, using air quotes. "Those women put me off."

Virge innocently stuck a toe into that conversational thread. "What about Germaine Greer and *The Female Eunuch*? I understand that she's Australian."

"Oh, dear," Isabelle Pawley said, "I won't even let my husband read that book. I don't want him getting any funny ideas."

Everyone looked at Bill Pawley and laughed. His head snapped up in surprise. "First I heard of it," he said. "I haven't been the least bit interested up to now, but I guess I had better get reading."

"I hid the book," Isabelle said and laughed along with everyone else. "Greer gets so, shall I say, unambiguous about women and their bodies and sex drives. I would be happy with a little more ambiguity." She laughed at herself. Like her husband, I made a mental note to check into the book. Isabelle was not finished with her book review. "But she really has it in for men, doesn't she. Really hates them, I reckon."

Mel gave me a smile and shook her head. Isabelle often made her laugh. "I'm just nicely started into it, Bill," she said, "but I find her quite entertaining. As Isabelle says, she goes a bit overboard against males, but I think there is some truth in what she says. Don't get me wrong. I *like* the men in my life but…"

She was interrupted by some titters around the table. I didn't know exactly where she was going, but I caught her eye before she continued. She got a bit befuddled by the reactions, including mine, and blushed. "Oh, my," she laughed. "I'm referring to Coop and my sons," recovering her usual poise. "But she is right about inequality, don't you think? And that we women are sometimes conspirators in that crime, if you want to call it a crime, which the author certainly does. I believe she's right about that. And that women can finally own their sexuality? I think I am just beginning to discover that."

Again, some nervous giggling.

Mel went on briefly, "Like I said, I'm just getting started with the book, so maybe I know just enough to be dangerous, but I am learning things, plus I enjoy her use of humor."

This was all a surprise to me. I had no idea. "Bill, we're in the same boat. I didn't know we even had the book." Laughter. "Are you hiding it, too? What is this, some kind of feminist underground secret pamphlet or what?"

"It's right there on my nightstand, dear, all out in the open. It's been keeping me warm nights when you've been gone." More laughter, this time more raucous. "Time for women to treat *men* like sex objects after all these years the other way around."

"Hear, hear!" Diane said as she patted my arm and moved her leg next to mine, the first gesture visible to all, the second not. I hoped. I made sure to look at anyone but her.

"I hate to miss any of this fascinating discussion," Beth said, "but we need to get the fish out of the oven, Jon."

I got busy serving the fish course. When I sat back down, my focus was diverted once again by the press of Diane Larned's leg up against mine. She just smiled as I gave a quick glance her way. She left her leg where it was, as did I.

CHAPTER 5

Diane was a beauty. She always reminded me of another pretty blonde Aussie, Olivia Newton John (who got me every time at "I honestly love you"). Diane and I had a flirtatious relationship almost from the beginning, a smile here, a discreet touch there, but it had never gone beyond that. Kevin was my friend and my protege, which, I think, may have somehow contributed to her fascination with me but also caused me to take care that it not go too far. There was a popular humorous ditty playing on the radio those days, "The Parthenon Milk Bar," in which a horny group of teenage blokes were trying to pick up girls. The chorus insisted that guys should "Never let a chance go by, go by, oh, never let a chance go by." In most circumstances, I could relate.

I had just decided to relax and enjoy her leg against mine without indulging my proclivities any further when she put down her fish fork and laid a warm hand on my thigh. I checked to see if Mel had taken any notice, and then looked around at the others. No one, I was sure, could have seen the move. It became difficult to concentrate on listening as people gave Virge his second orientation of the day to the sport of cricket. Despite my weak resolve, I moved my left hand to her leg and found a bare thigh above her stockings. She opened her legs slightly to invite further exploration, but I called upon all my willpower to refrain, taking care to focus on cricket before rising to serve the next course. Diane smothered a grin with her napkin as she watched me walk to the kitchen. Mel gave me a brief, quizzical look but refocused on the conversation. I had no idea of what she had picked up on but it concerned me. When I sat back down, I was relieved that Diane's leg stayed in its lane, as did mine. So much for that, I thought.

The men took the dirty dishes to the kitchen, where Jon and Beth were busy washing up. Virge, who had not been required to do any of the serving, urged Beth to join the others in the lounge while he helped Jon. "I'm kind of a foodie myself and I would love to talk with Jon while we clean things up." Our hostess protested mildly but bowed to his firm wishes. Virge and Jon could be overheard laughing and carrying on while the rest of us settled in the lounge, the women sitting and talking at one end of the room, while Mike, Bill Pawley and I turned to business at the other. Kevin and Diane were left by themselves on the couch, engaged in serious conversation carried on in low tones.

Mike left for a moment and returned with three bottles of his favorite local bitter. His next line was totally predictable: "Time for a little cleansing ale." With all the wines we had already enjoyed, including the final port, I was more inclined to a cup of coffee but Mike always preferred a cleansing ale. "Ask him, Bill," he said to Bill Pawley. "What we talked about."

Bill Pawley was WM-A's director of marketing and sales, a sharp man who thought more strategically and innovatively than most of his colleagues. "Coop," Bill began, "needless to say, we're not altogether happy about your leaving. You must know how much we value your help the last few years. I, personally, have a special appreciation since we worked together so closely. Mike and I realize the importance to you and your firm of your move to your new position in New York. Both you and Mel must be very excited about the prospects of going home."

"We are," I said.

"But," he continued, "the fact remains, Mike and I and many others in WM-A, don't want you to go. You are too important for us to just let you go without a fight."

"A fight?" I asked; I had no idea of his intent.

He was quick to clarify. "I can see you're confused, mate. Not to worry. What I am saying—what we are saying—is we want to keep you here, here in Australia, here with WM-A."

He and Mike both leaned in my direction, and Bill lowered his voice. "This is all strictly confidential for now, OK? Here's the scenario. Mike is ready to retire and the powers that be in Detroit have approved my moving into his job as Managing Director."

"That's wonderful. Congratulations to you both. I can't say it is entirely unexpected, but it's the right move and I'm happy for both of you. But what does it all have to do with me?"

Mike leaned back, smiling, but Bill came even closer. It was obvious that he was working me.

"We want you to take *my* job, Coop. Director of Marketing and Sales for World Motors of Australia. And I want you to be my go-to guy. My offsider."

I moved from perplexed to dumbfounded and Bill sensed it. "What about Gerald Lawson?" I asked. As Director of Sales he seemed like Bill's logical successor in Sales and Marketing.

Mike said, "We can't really talk about that at the moment. If you accept our offer, you will have that information and might even want a say in regard to his future with the company." I was now even more in the dark.

"Of course," Bill said, "we're prepared to make it worth your while. We will not only match what they are going to pay you in New York, we will go 20% over that to help with the fact that you won't be going home, and obviously, to help you persuade Mel. You know all about our package of bonuses and perks. We're ready to roll out the red carpet for you, Coop. That's how much you mean to our company."

No way was I expecting this. I was ready for a flattering farewell from the two of them, but nothing like this. I reached into the giant glass punch bowl on the end table next to me and took out one of the hundreds of matchbooks there, matchbooks collected by Mike and Beth from every corner of the world. This one was from Galicia, Spain. The fact was, I wasn't much interested in their offer, but I was sane enough to consider it. More importantly, I knew better than to insult them by simply blowing it off.

"Wow!" was my initial response. It felt stupid as it left my lips. Mike and Bill were now both leaning back and laughing. I laughed along but was not comfortable being a source of entertainment. I returned the matchbook to the bowl and collected myself enough to say wow, again. "Thank you. Both of you. This is all a giant surprise, a very pleasant surprise, I must add. I had no idea. I confess you have pretty much knocked me for a loop. What you're offering is beyond generous. I don't have the words. But you know I have to think about it some. More than some. And I have to talk with Mel. She'll probably say 'Wow' just like I did, but then we'll have to have a serious discussion about it."

"No doubt," said Bill, still grinning at my initial bemusement. "No worries, mate; she'll be right. We will be delighted if you accept our offer. Take your time, but not too much time. Mike's announcement is imminent, and we need to fill in the rest of the blanks for our people. I won't push you any further for now, but at the end of the day, what we're saying is we need you here, Coop. "

Mike raised his ale. "Hear, hear!" he said. "Let's drink to that."

I took a sip and stood. "I'm afraid you guys have surprised the piss out of me. I need to find the loo."

"You know where it is," Mike said.

I walked into the long, dim hallway and saw that the door to the bathroom was closed. When Diane Larned emerged she said, "Coop! You surprised me." She obviously had refreshed her perfume. She smiled and touched my arm. "Were you waiting for me, I hope? By the way, you were the cutest waiter I've ever had."

Before I could answer she looped her arms around my neck and kissed me, a simple flirtatious peck on the cheek. I looked around nervously but it seemed we were alone in the semi-darkness. "We don't want you to leave, you know." Then she pulled me to her, grinding her pelvis into mine, her next kiss on my lips followed by her penetrating tongue. For a moment, I returned her fervor but quickly caught myself, pulled out of the kiss and removed her arms from my neck.

"You know I can't do this, Diane."

She looked at me, frustrated and embarrassed. "Oh, I know. I'm sorry. Wine makes me horny. But it's true, we don't want you to leave. *I* don't want you to leave."

"Kevin means too much to me," I said.

She squeezed my hand and walked away laughing. "I look forward to more of your service," she said.

CHAPTER 6

Mel seemed a bit unhappy with me the rest of the evening and I was afraid of the reason. She stayed polite and engaged with the others but kept her distance from me. On the way back, she rode in the rear with Virge again, the two of them rehashing the party and laughing a lot. Nary a word in my direction.

When we dropped him off, I said, "A driver will be by to pick you up at 7:30."

"You're kidding. Good luck with that."

I smiled. "See you at the airport."

I waited for Mel to join me in the front seat, but she stayed put. I finally drove on. I wanted in the worst way to tell her about my conversation with Bill and Mike about the job offer, but I knew now was not the time. It was an ominously quiet ride home.

I paid our sitter, the nice young girl next door, and poured Mel and myself each a glass of wine.

"I've had too much already," she said. "I'm going to bed."

She allowed me to put my arms around her in a standing hug, but she did not reciprocate in any way. I pulled her even closer and moved a long, dark black curl aside so I could speak quietly into her ear. "Honey, what's going on?"

"You tell me." She eased her way out of my grasp and sat on the couch.

"I don't know what you mean."

"Diane, you ass."

"What about her?" But I decided to stop playing naive and innocent and said, "Okay, so you know Diane. She's a big flirt. We have always flirted with each other, you know that. But that's all, I swear.

41

I was leery when Beth seated us next to each other but what could I do? Diane insisted on a little footsie action just before I had to get up to help in the kitchen. I didn't respond but I also didn't move my foot away. That's it, though." Obviously I omitted the hand action under the table and the encounter in the hall.

"Don't shit me," she said. "You're a dong-waver and always have been."

She had used that expression all too often in the past. "I was not waving anything. I don't even know what you mean when you say that, but I promise, I wasn't waving anything. I've told you every-thing that happened. But listen, I have other news to fill you in on, a big surprise."

She obviously was not satisfied with my Diane story but took a sip of wine and let me go on. I told her about the job offer and she tried her best to remain impassive but I knew better. She reluctantly began to ask questions for which I didn't know the answers, which in turn allowed her to remain disgusted with me. "No way," she finally said. "We need to get home. We need to get the boys back to a more normal life, not to mention ourselves. We need to end the whole Gregory thing. We need to get out of here now. I suppose you found it very flattering but I don't give a damn."

"Funny thing," I said, "You and I are in total agreement on all points. I just wanted you to know."

"So what did you tell them?"

"I couldn't insult them by turning them down flat at that point, not at Mike's party, sitting in Mike's living room. I told them that, as you said, I was flattered but would need time to think about it, talk it over with you."

"So now we talked."

"And now I can tell them exactly that, in a more appropriate way, in a more appropriate setting."

"Soon," she said.

"Soon," I answered.

She stood and I gave her another hug to which she now gave a somewhat reluctant hug back. "You dong-waver," she said as she squeezed my crotch area.

I put a record on the stereo and waited for the rich sounds of Shearing's "Foggy Day" to fill the room.

Back in our courting days while I was in the MBA program at Columbia and she was an undergrad arts major at NYU, we bought a HI-FI player together for about a hundred dollars, a substantial joint commitment. We also jointly purchased a few albums, among them an LP called *Velvet Carpet* by the George Shearing jazz quintet, with lush accompanying strings. That night we celebrated in my Columbia-subsidized apartment by snuggling to our new music. It was all loving and pleasant, but when Shearing's "Foggy Day" came on, Mel virtually swooned in my arms. The rest of the night was history-making. From that point on, that song and Mel never disappointed. When we made our marriage plans, there was no quibbling about where we would spend our honeymoon. The British Museum had its charms but it seemed the sun was shining down on us no matter where we were, even as we forced ourselves to take in Egyptian mummies and the Elgin Marbles.

Now, in our Toorak living room she couldn't resist a smile. "You dong-waving bastard," she said as we began to dance. We fell to the floor and made the sweetest kind of married love possible given minimum clothing removal and an unforgiving carpet floor.

Later, when we were upstairs getting ready for bed, we shared a laugh comparing the rug burns on our backsides.

CHAPTER 7

Virge and I both still suffered from mild hangovers when we boarded the plane to Adelaide. Moreover, he was not an early riser. We barely spoke as we waited in the first-class lounge. I managed to get some paper work done in the silence.

It was not until we were airborne that he said, "Kevin's wife, eh?"

Wary, I replied "What about her?"

"The clinch in the hallway last night. I saw."

"You saw what?"

"Come on, Coop. It was not a complete surprise. I thought something was going on on our side of the table during dinner."

"Kevin's not only my subordinate and my successor; he's my friend."

"I understand that."

"Did you see me push her away?"

"Not really. I only caught a glimpse and ducked back into the kitchen. Good thing it was me. Anybody could have walked in on that action."

"I know, and I pushed her away."

"When I saw you, 'away' was not the way you were pushing."

I explained Diane as summarily as I could and tried to downplay any involvement on my part. Mostly the truth. Virge just smiled. I knew he would be fine with it, whatever it was. He was just giving me a poke. I may have protested too much.

The plant manager, Orrin Webber, met us at the Adelaide airport and drove us just outside the city to his Vehicle Assembly Plant. Normally we would have been picked up by a regular driver, but Orrin wanted to greet me on my last visit as he had on my first two years ago. It was on that trip that, on the way to my hotel, he confided that in his short time on the job, he found just one disaster after another under every rock he had so far been able to turn over. These days he was in a much better mood as a rising star who had transformed a perennial losing operation into the company success story.

"I teed up a meeting with my team this morning," he said. "They want to meet Virge and make a presentation to the two of you. I hope you don't mind. Then, you'll have lunch with Reggie Peters and Lawry Moretti. I believe you know Reggie," he said with a knowing grin.

"Reggie has entertained me in the past, yes. A good man, Reggie." Reggie had often been assigned as my guide and he had managed to find some amusement for me along the way. He said he was dedicated to turning me into a fair dinkum Aussie.

"He and Lawry have a plan for the afternoon that I'm sure you'll appreciate. Tonight's the big farewell dinner, as you know."

"Impressive planning," I told him. "Can't wait."

"The difference is," he said, "I don't have to worry so much about running around to put out fires the way I used to."

"Boring, isn't it?" I teased.

"I'll take boring, mate."

I remembered reading the esteemed management guru, Peter Drucker, in my early days consulting with manufacturing operations. Like me, he had to learn how to tell a good plant from a bad one without knowing anything about manufacturing. With experience he concluded that a good one "looked dull." And he was right. WM-A's Adelaide organization was anything but dull when I arrived, shortly after Orrin took over. A walk through the production aisles was always an adventure—a breakdown in the line here, there a foreman screaming at a fellow supervisor as they ran past each other on their way to the next screwup. Sometimes even an actual fire. Union stoppages or work-to-rule strikes were common. Every day was a struggle to meet schedule (or "shedule", as they say here) and every day that struggle was in vain.

These days a walk-through definitely would look dull. Not that it really *was* dull. Not to the people who worked there. Not to Orrin and not to me. It was an exciting operation to be a part of, a winner. Everything ran smoothly (almost always). There was time for the foreman to meet in an aisle for a problem-solving discussion with a fellow supervisor or wages worker. The schedule was now a doable challenge, not quite routine yet but a regular accomplishment. If that was boring, I agreed with Orrin: I'll take boring.

His secretary had coffee ready for us as she ushered us into the meeting room to applause. The top managers of the plant rose from their seats around the conference table, laughing at our reactions.

"Oh, it's going to be one of those kinds of days, is it?" I said. "I thought we were here for business. Please meet Virgil Cash, the least likely numbers guy you will ever know. He actually knows how to have fun. Not that any of you can relate. He also knows his business better than anyone you'll ever know, and he can help you in ways you never even knew existed."

Virge made his way around the table shaking hands. These were good blokes, good at their jobs and good at enjoying life outside of work. I have held business retreats with American managers who thought they were having a good time together in their off hours but it was nothing compared to these guys. A travel article appeared in the Saturday edition of the Melbourne Age, the "paper of record," about the christening of a new Australian cruise ship. The captain was quoted as saying, "We can just place a wooden box in the middle of our ballroom floor and tell the difference between American, British and Australian tourists. The Americans will sit around the outside of the room and watch it. The Brits will sit around and discuss it. Aussies will use it as an excuse for having a party." My experience in a nutshell.

The team (which is what they had become) presentation was a total review of the progress that had been made since Kevin and I started working with them. They concluded with some challenges they still faced on which they hoped Virge's expertise might be of help.

When we met for lunch, Reggie Peters had some bad news. Virge and I were scheduled to fly to Sydney the next day for a visit to the plant there, but our headquarters transportation office had called to say that they had changed our plans. In protest of the Governor General's actions against the Labour Government, the Sydney air controllers were planning a work-to-rule strike for about the time of our arrival. This meant that planes would still be allowed to take off and land, but at a dramatically slower rate than normal. There was no telling when we might be able to get there. We were now scheduled to fly back to Melbourne tomorrow and wait to go to Sydney the day after.

"God, what the hell is going on?" Virge asked.

"No worries," Reggie said. "You'll get there all right."

"No worries, my ass," said Virge. "I've only been in this country part of three days and I've seen riots in the street, chaos in the government, strikes and threats of more strikes, angry headlines in the paper and continuing news bulletins on TV. All anybody ever tells me is 'no worries.' I want to know when in the hell somebody's going to start worrying?"

The three of us cracked up. "Spot on," Lawrey told him.

I said, "True, but you'd better learn to go with the flow."

"What flow?" Virge asked. "Please show me some flow."

After we called the home office to verify the schedule changes, we rode with Lawry and Reggie out to the Barossa Valley, the Australian Napa, for a lunch of yabbies and salad with a small sampling of whites at the Brauhaus Hotel, an old but well-tended pub in Angaston.

I had been on wine treks in the valley a few times, but these blokes knew their way around. After lunch, they took us to a few of the lesser-known chateaus for tasting. Virge, of course, thought Christmas had arrived. At one spot, Reggie followed a sip of shiraz with the comment: "That's a big, ballsy red." I stowed it away as my all-time favorite wine tasting commentary.

On the way back to Adelaide I told Reggie we would see him at the party that night. "Not me," he said. "I'm not part of the top management business team, you know."

"Oh, yeah" I said. "I knew better. Sorry about that. Wish you could make it."

"No worries. What hotel are you blokes staying at?"

"The Park."

"Maybe we'll catch you there later."

"We'll have to see about that. Thanks to you two blokes and all that wine tasting, I don't even know if I can get through the party."

As it turned out, I forced myself and Virge was just getting started. The party took place in a private room at a convivial suburban restaurant. Not surprisingly, the conviviality of the Aussies perked me up but I tried my best to take it easy on the beer. They made it difficult with frequent toasts to me and my "Yank friend."

I was genuinely delighted with their gift of a coffee-table book of photos of Australian scenes and people, specially bound in leather with the WM-A logo embossed in silver on the tan cover. They recognized my love for the country and for themselves, the people who helped establish my professional credibility out here and showed me how to have fun at the same time.

My farewell "speech" began with a simple expression of gratitude. Then I reminded them of the Monday early in our work together. I was in my Melbourne office when I got word that they experienced an industrial relations crisis early that morning. Not their first by any means, but because the turnaround process was in its early infancy, it threatened to put an end to any hopes they and I had for changing their culture and performance.

"I met Mike Robertson and Bill Pawley right away that day," I told them now. "Mike was angry and asked me, 'What do you think about your project now?'" He said it in a sarcastic tone.

"'It's stuffed,' I said in the same tone and mostly meant it. I thought we might be finished. Mike quit smirking and looked seriously surprised at my response. I think he thought I would try to defend things, including my own ass. I told them that I wanted to get over here as soon as possible but that wouldn't be until Friday. I thought all week about what I could do to cheer you blokes up, give you a pep talk or something. I was sure you would be down and about ready throw in the towel. But when I got here, it was just the other way around. You cheered *me* up. You were so positive you didn't leave me anything to say. I knew then that you were the team that could and would do it. Of course, I took credit for it." We laughed together.

At that I took off my suit coat and tie and began to unbutton my shirt. Their eyes gradually widened and their laughter grew as I slowly revealed the Superman T-shirt underneath.

"You are really something," said Orrin Webber, while others laughed, some with tears in their eyes.

"My son gave me this for Father's Day," I said, "and I knew right away the only other people who would appreciate it."

That was it. They stood and applauded and came to shake my hand. I mingled a short while longer and then told Virge our driver was probably waiting to take us back to our hotel. He was having a good time with some of the managers. A superintendent said, "No worries, we'll get him there." Virge did not protest so I left him and went out to the car.

CHAPTER 8

Reggie stood grinning at a table in the hotel bar when I walked in for a cleansing ale. He was at a table with two women. "You know Nicole, I think," indicating a cute, dark-haired young secretary I had met at the plant once before.

"Sure, I remember Nicky," I said. She stayed seated and smiled shyly in my direction.

"And this is Suzanne Cooley. She just came on board in our personnel department. She's going to handle staff benefit matters." She stood and shook my hand. She too had dark hair and a more mature look than Nicky, though she was attractive as well.

The three of them had already started in on a pitcher so Reggie ordered a new pint glass for me and poured it even as I gave mild protest. We chatted about the party and I got better acquainted with Suzanne, who told me to call her Sue. She had recently gotten her master's degree from the University of Adelaide but had worked a variety of personnel-related jobs in the past. She was excited about this new opportunity and eager to pick the brain of an American management consultant. I was flattered but wise enough to realize that the party had left me with my consulting powers somewhat under a cloud. I told her that I would be glad to meet with her sometime but she shouldn't count on me for much at the moment. She struck me as a bright young woman with a lot of promise.

Reggie kept coming back to the party, wanting to know who said or did what outlandish thing. Through it all, Nicky sat smiling and nodding but almost totally silent.

When the pitcher was empty, I offered to shout for another round although I would do my best to avoid drinking any of it. Fortunately everyone was ready to move on. Sue said, "I don't know about you guys, but I'm hungry." Reggie agreed but I begged off.

"Ate too much at the party. How about you, Nicky?"

"I'm okay," she said.

Her mostly silent smile was now focused on me. She was a petite young thing, early twenties, I guessed; dark hair, cute, slim but curvy body. I knew her only from the one day I needed an office while working in Adelaide. Her boss, Peter Boles, the regional personnel manager, was away for the day and I was given his office to use. Nicky, wearing very tight pants, was so sweet and appealing but young that I thought it best to behave myself. At the same time, she appeared shy but interested. I had to ask her for a few office materials during the course of the day and could overhear the other secretaries giggling as Nicky smiled back at them before walking into my temporary digs, looking as though she was keeping a secret. May have had nothing to do with me, but my imagination was stirred.

Sitting with her in the bar now, just the two of us, I wasn't sure where things were headed, but I had been partying enough since early afternoon that my inhibitions were easily put aside. I simply forged ahead and asked if she wanted to go my room. She smiled her shy smile, nodded and got up from her chair. It seemed like this was what she had in mind all along, only waiting for the invitation. We clinched on the lift to the fourth floor, tongues engaged, pubes grinding. Most clothes came off the minute we got to the suite—all of mine, in fact, while she kept her black bra and tiny black knickers on as we fell onto my bed, where we resumed the clutching and grabbing. My hand was in her knickers when she lurched out of the bed and ran for the bathroom. I listened to her vomiting. Definitely a discouraging sound.

She was on the verge of tears when she returned to the bedside. I stood and put my arms around her to comfort her vulnerable yet still desirable little body. She was shaking and full of apologies. "That's okay," I said, "No worries. Do you need to eat something?"

"Ugh, no," she said, pulling away. "I just need to get dressed and go home."

"No, please." I held her again and eased her to sitting on the edge of the bed. "This could be our one and only chance. I'm leaving for the States soon."

"But I'm sick."

"Do you feel any better now that you've done that?" I asked.

"Sure, but I vomited. You can't kiss me anymore."

"No worries." There it was again. "Use my mouthwash or even my toothbrush."

"Ugh."

"Please. I can't stand the thought of ending our one night together like this."

"Where's your mouthwash?" Oh, man, was I relieved.

Back in bed, I took it more gradually. I stroked and petted and kissed lightly with closed mouth for a while before testing with a bit of tongue. When she tongue-tested in return, I rolled slowly and gently on top of her. Our bodies began to move together but then she pushed me away, gently but with serious intent. I rolled off and she apologized again.

"I'm sorry but I just don't feel right."

I put one arm around her and pulled her head into the space between my neck and shoulder. "I understand," I said and let things stay as they were: a quiet, empathic pause before I once again reached my hand into those cute little panties before finally taking them off, throwing the covers away, giving me a nice view of her dark triangle, what some Aussie wags called "the map of Tasmania." I couldn't tell if she was really into it or just going along with my program when she began to move sensually with her hips. I chose to go with the latter and continued with my fingers. We kissed with mutual intensity just as there was a knock on the door.

I heard Reggie identify himself and I jumped out of bed naked and opened the door. Reggie and the young woman, Sue. I was surprised at seeing her but hesitated only a moment before letting them in as I turned, bare bum and all to find my way back under the covers, covers which poor Nicky had pulled over her head. Sue leaked an embarrassed snicker but came into the room anyway. Reggie just laughed out loud. The two of them moved away to the far side of the room and sat down, Reggie in the desk chair, Sue on the desk itself.

"I guess this means you've had dinner," I said.

"Pie and sauce on the street out front," Reggie said.

"Mmm-mmm," I said.

"It was good," Sue said, giving way to a snigger despite her best efforts at appearing calm and unfazed by the situation. Nicky and I lay under the covers, including her head, my hand surreptitiously finding its way back to where it had been at work. Still wet, hips moving in spite of any obvious mortification. I loved that girl.

The other three of us attempted small talk, my hand still busy, but it was just not a workable situation for anyone. Sue said, "I think I need to go home and these two need to be alone."

They left with little more ceremony and Nicole came out from hiding. She didn't say a word but I could tell she was not real happy. I apologized and we lay there and talked about the general awkwardness of everything since we left the bar. I tried shifting to a less charged subject.

"Your boss, Peter, seems like a good man. He is well respected by people I talk to. How is he to work for?"

She immediately showed more enthusiasm than at any time that night. "I *love* Mr. Boles. He is the nicest man I have ever known in my whole life."

"Really?"

"Oh, yeah. I would do anything for that man."

"Anything at all."

She caught my snark. Once again, she sat up and began reaching for her clothing. "Please, Nicky," I said, "I was just joking."

"I don't care. Don't insinuate anything about that man. If I could choose my father, it would be Mr. Boles."

"Wow, I can tell you mean that. I'm impressed. Sorry I tried to make a joke. Please stay. And I'm sorry I don't measure up to Peter."

"That's ridiculous. That's not what I was hoping for tonight, I can tell you that. That day you were in his office I thought, for a big shot, you were cute and hot. That's all. That's all I was looking for."

She had to go to the loo, she said, and I watched her naked butt as she walked away. Sweetest little ass ever.

When she came back into the room, she started to get dressed, starting with her bra, but soon ran into a snag. "Where's me knickers?" she said, as her hands scrambled through the bedding.

I spotted them on my side on the floor but left them there for a moment, undecided; maybe I wanted to keep them. Nothing much else to show for the night. I guess she caught on to my doubts because she moved over me to see what I was looking at, putting Tasmania right over my face in the process. I reached up and made contact but she was having none of it and moved on to retrieve her underwear from the floor. She stood and finished dressing.

"I need to work in the morning," she said.

I tried once more to talk her into staying but the night was obviously over. I made one last apology for all the evening's hassle. Nicky brushed it off gave me a final polite kiss on the cheek.

"Never let a chance go by, go by, oh, never let a chance go by." Now *I'll always be once chance behind. Oh, well.*

CHAPTER 9

Virge and I were supposed to meet at eight for breakfast in the hotel dining room but I ended up eating alone. I didn't worry. He was not a morning person. However, when our car arrived at nine, he was not in the lobby and I grew a bit concerned. Our driver came in to check on things and he and I went to the front desk to ask if Virge had left any messages but there were none. Our all-business Aussie driver then inquired as to whether we could check the room. The day-manager of the hotel, after asking our reasons and checking our identification, went off to see what was up, or not up, as the case may be. When he returned, his face showed signs of distress.

"Come with me, please," he said to me. "I'm afraid there's a problem."

"Is Mr. Cash okay?" I asked, now worried.

"You had better ask him."

That made me feel a little better. If I could ask Virge, then at least he was alive and conscious. I found that was the best that could be said. He was sitting on the edge of the bed in his underwear, head between his knees, the bedding torn up and reeking of piss. He lifted his head and looked at me and groaned. "Shit," he said. "I feel like shit."

"What the hell happened? Never mind right now. We have to catch a plane. Tell me on the way to the airport. Jesus Christ, man. Whatever it was, throw on some clothes and let's get out of here."

"I need a shower."

"You're damned right you do, but you'll have to do that later. We have to leave right now. I'll let you brush your teeth but that's it. Get your ass moving."

As it turned out, we missed our flight but got the one an hour later. Virge was in terrible shape and couldn't tell me everything about the night before because he couldn't remember. All he knew was that he went from the party to a pub with a group, "a school," he said. He explained that was what one called a group who regularly drank together, an explanation I didn't require. "And we started shouting," he said. "That's the custom. You take turns buying a round and that's called shouting. Your shout means it's your turn to buy."

"Yeah, I know all that," I said. "So get on with it."

"Well there were a lot of guys there."

"And a lot of shouts. I get it."

"And I had last shout. Then they all took off except for me and one other guy. That superintendent who said he'd drive me back."

"Neil Hanshin," I said.

"Neil, right. Anyway, Neil shouted then. 'Just one more for the road,' he said. But naturally, as a guest, and I couldn't let him have last call. So I shouted."

"And?"

"And, I don't know. That's the last thing I remember. I'm sorry, Coop. I fucked up and I feel like shit for it."

"And look and smell like shit," I said. "I hope you didn't fuck things up with our client."

"You think?"

"Maybe. Since you don't know what else happened we don't know if anything will come of it or not. I'll check when we get to Melbourne. These blokes like to party so maybe it will just go down as another drunken night and will quickly be forgotten. Let's hope so. But Jesus Christ, mate."

"I know."

"Well, get some sleep now if you can and get a good night's rest before we go to Sydney tomorrow morning." It didn't take much for him to fall off, his head on a pillow pushed up against the plane's window.

Our Melbourne driver did his professional best to keep a straight face when he saw Virge at Tullamarine and looked straight ahead as he dropped us off, Virge at the Hilton, me at the office. Since we had expected to be in Sydney today, I was planning to get in my car and drive directly home, but I felt a strong need to check on any fallout from Virge's late night activities so I stopped in.

Sure enough. "Please ring Bill Pawley," my secretary, Louise, told me. "He's been ringing here all morning."

Somehow some news must have leaked out to our firm as well. I got some funny looks as I walked through the halls and Keven Larned asked if he could listen in to my call with Pawley.

"What the hell happened?" he asked.

"I don't think it's a big deal," I said, "but Virge spent last night getting drunk with a plant superintendent, not to mention pissing his bed and oversleeping so that we missed our scheduled flight this morning."

Kevin just laughed. "Sounds par for the course to me. Does he have a problem?"

"He sometimes has trouble knowing when to stop, but I don't think it's anything more than that. He's just a fun-loving guy who's easily taken advantage of at times."

"Seemed like a nice guy to me the other day, but I can see a little of that naivete."

"Yeah, well, I don't think—at least I hope—it shouldn't be a huge issue. Let's hear what Pawley has to say." I hit the speaker button on the phone.

Bill Pawley laughed when he gave us the version he had heard. "A little too much mateship, maybe," he said, but then turned serious. "We've had to discipline our superintendent, Neil Hanshin. He came to work with a bad hangover so we sent him home. It'll go on his record and he'll be on probation for a while. I feel bad for him, because there but for the grace of god and all that. But we had to do something. How's your guy?"

I told him about missing our flight but didn't give him the hotel room details, although I guessed he would find out some time anyway. "He's in pain at the hotel right now," I said. "Look, I'm sorry this happened. Virge is a top guy, a good friend."

"I know. Let's hope he's learned something about life in Australia. We'll chalk it up as a cross-cultural lesson and let it go at that."

"Thanks, Bill."

"And, so you know, the work-to-rule strike with the traffic controllers in Sydney has come and gone and everything's back to normal. No worries." I told him about Virge questioning when someone was going to start to worry and he got a big laugh.

"Our new normal," he said.

I hung up and saw Kevin smile and take a deep breath. Me too. I looked out at my view of the Yarra River and downtown Melbourne.

"Bill's a fair-dinkum guy," Kevin said. "I look forward to working with him when he's got the whole show."

"You should. He will make good things happen for his company and ours, I'm sure. I envy you the opportunity."

"You've had a great run, mate. Time for your next big thing back home."

"I have mixed feelings. On the one hand I'm looking forward to it. It's good move for me. But you know how much Mel and I love it here. We could happily turn into Aussies."

"Do I have it right? WM-A may have offered you a job if you stick around?"

"I don't know how things get around here so fast, but kind of, yeah. A very nice semi-offer. But it ain't gonna happen, mate. We're ready to go—especially Mel. I told Mike and Bill I needed to think it over and talk to Mel about it, but there's no way. I was just trying to be polite. I knew what she would say before I asked and she said it in no uncertain terms."

"Too bad. You could have been my client, then."

"You'll do fine with the clients you have."

"So how was your party last night?"

"You mean the one the plant guys gave me."

"What other party was there?"

I caught myself. "Of course. Everybody was just great. A lot of laughs. As expected they roasted me a bit but they couldn't have kinder or more flattering. Those guys always make me feel humble and grateful at the same time. I showed him the beautiful leather-bound book they gave me. "I need to take some time with it myself," I said, "but I know we will both cherish it for the rest of our lives. Speaking of Mel, I need to get home now and rest up myself. My night may not have been as long and wild as Virge's but it was quite a night. I could use some zees."

"What's a zee?" Kevin teased.

"Right. I can use some zeds then."

I packed my briefcase, ready to head home, but Lou Sand waved me in as I walked past her office. She took one look at me and laughed. "You look like hell, mate. I guess that means your farewell party went well in Adelaide last night."

"You could say that." I gave her some of the same story I had given Kevin.

"Going to work for WM-A, I hear," she said, giving me a penetrating look.

"Not likely. Mel and I are ready to head home. And I have a great new job waiting for me there."

"Is that what you want? To go home, I mean? You seem to be at home here."

"You're right. I am. We love it here." I have learned that Aussies love to hear Yanks tell them how much we love their country, but I wasn't faking it. I meant it.

"So what do you want, really?" It was so Lou. She wasn't just making conversation. She offered me a cigarette as though she expected this conversation to go on a while. I accepted.

"I'm not sure what you're getting at," I said to her, and sat down in one of her two "guest" chairs.

"Let me put it this way. You're looking forward to the next stage in your future. What I want to know is where are you going to be a hundred years from now?"

Still unclear, I laughed and said the first thing that came to mind. "In Oslo, I guess, picking up my Peace Prize."

Lou smiled but didn't seem to get as a big a kick out of my answer as I thought worthy. She took a final drag. The smoky smell of her office was beginning to get to me. "Think about it," she said, "and get back to me."

CHAPTER 10

It was a silly Sunday-supplement kind of question but it haunted me all the way home. A hundred years from now, I would be dead. That's it. Dead as a doornail. I realized that a Nobel Prize was probably not in the cards. A hundred years from now no one would even know I ever existed. So where does that leave me? My thought train slid from work to Mel and the boys, and from there to Mel and Gregory and me.

Our deal was that I loved to watch her have sex, to see her face lost in passion, and sometimes to join in with the two of them. It was a fantasy I had for years before it was realized, even before I first dared to tell her about it. Then whenever I dared bring it up, she accused me of just wanting an excuse to screw other women. Eventually I think she started to believe me. I convinced her that my pleasure was strictly in enjoying hers. I had no interest in other women. At the time I said those things, I meant them. But she wasn't having any. She just got mad if I mentioned it and I gave up and stopped.

After that original 'wrong number' conversation Mel had with Gregory, nothing happened for a few weeks. I reminded her of my fantasy. "This may be the opportunity we have been waiting for."

"Bull," she snapped. "There's no 'we' in this thing. It's all in your sick head. Don't waste your time for waiting for something that's never going to happen."

Finally, Gregory called again and we arranged to meet him in a pub in Waverly, out of town, where he would be less likely to be recognized. He said they were known for their good fish.

Mel wrote down the name and directions for the restaurant and hung up. "Don't get any of your weird ideas," she warned. "We are having dinner with a member of parliament and that's all. It will be nice to actually meet him. He seems like a nice guy."

The restaurant was more than a pub, which is what he had called it. It had an old Aussie hotel look on the outside but both the interior (slick contemporary) and menu (standard plus ethnic fare) were right up to date. We spotted a man standing and waving to us from beside a booth. Tall and slim with razor cut blonde hair, he was dressed in a black blazer and well-pressed khaki pants. He remained standing to greet us before Mel and I took seats opposite his. Younger than I expected for a national parliamentarian (I put him in his early thirties), it turned out that he was as charming as one might expect from a politician. That he could charm the pants off Mel was yet to be determined.

Fortunately he knew it was a BYO, which had not even occurred to me. He handed both a dry riesling and a shiraz to our waiter for corking. I opted to start with the white while Mel went red straightaway, as did Gregory, making me feel a bit wimpy.

We three made easy polite chat, filling in some of the unknowns of our backstories. Gregory was obviously witty and intelligent. He and Mel connected on the special if skittery attraction of Prahran, especially the outdoor market on Saturday mornings. They exchanged their favorite stories about everything: the food smells, their special veggie vendors, the kangaroo meat, and the eccentricities of the people shopping there. I could only sit and smile at the connection.

In time, I inquired about the political scene to get his thoughts. He was devoted Australian Labour Party (ALP) but confessed some doubts about the competence and/or conscience of some of the cabinet.

"How about Jim Cairns?" I asked. The Cairns/Junie Morosi gossip was just beginning to make waves back in those days and I thought, with his Canberra and party connections, he may know more than what we could read in the tabloids. Crass gossip, I know, but at least it was front-page political gossip. Jim Cairns was serving as both Deputy Prime Minister and Treasurer for Whitlam but had lately come under scrutiny for his relationship with Junie Morosi, whom he had appointed as his principal private secretary. Considerably younger than Cairns with what the tabloids referred to as "exotic" good looks to go with her "exotic" ethnic background, they ignored her varied work experience and smarts. The media were more interested in the titillating questions about their personal relationship, about which neither Cairns nor Morosi revealed much.

"Jim Cairns is one of the smartest and most innovative men I know," Gregory said.

"And Junie?" I asked.

"I knew what you meant with your first question," he said. "But I don't really know anything about their personal life. I don't really know *her* either, haven't met her, but she seems to be very bright from what I can tell."

"Oh, darn," said Mel. "I was hoping to get in on some of the juicy stuff."

The waiter came to take our order and we hadn't yet looked at the menu. "Give us a minute," Gregory told him. He held up his glass for a toast and said, "May they live happily ever after."

I clinked without really being clear about his implications. "Do you mean Jim and June?"

"If that's the choice they have made. They're both married to other people, of course, and I hope their spouses are happy too. Whatever arrangements, in whatever combination that suits them, I wish all of them happy ever after, don't you?"

"How broad-minded of you," Mel laughed.

"And you?" he asked her. "Don't you agree?"

"I haven't really thought about all that very much," she said. "Just what I read in the papers."

"Like the *Daily Telegraph*, you mean."

"I never even see that rag except in the news boxes on Sundays. But something about the two of them has been everywhere including *The Australian* and even *The Age*. Pretty hard to ignore," Mel said. "Besides, it's fun."

"And you, Coop? How do you feel about such relationships?"

I didn't think it wise to come clean with my private fantasies, especially with the glare from my wife. I dodged: "Looking at it in a less gossipy or should I say a more serious way, what effect if any has it had on his performance that you can see? That seems the more important question. Does he seem at all distracted, whether from the relationship itself, whatever it is, or from all the scandalous publicity?"

"Jim is Jim, as far as I can see. He'll hold his own. He's not among those in my party who worry me."

We ordered and the food came as we chatted on: my favorite South Australia whiting, Mel's lovely looking prawns, and Gregory's manly cut of steak. Mel put one prawn on my plate and I sliced off a small chunk of fish for her. "Nice," said Gregory and smiled at each of us in turn, his eyes lingering a bit longer on Mel's. Just being a gentleman, I assumed.

After the pause in political talk, Mel came back out of the blue with, "I'm afraid I'm just a lowbrow. I would still like to know the juicy bits."

Both Gregory and I whooped and he patted her hand. "You're wonderful," he said. I was surprised to see her blush. I left for the loo just as the live band was finishing up their sound tests.

When I came back, Mel had moved over to his side of the booth and was laughing at something he had said or done. She slapped his arm playfully. "So what is this?" I asked.

Mel got up and slid back into my side "I just had to move over there for a minute so I could hear him over the music. He was talking so low." Indeed, the band was loud, especially the lead singer. He was doing his best knockoff of Gary Glitter's "Rock and Roll, Part 2."

"Just more gossip," he said to me.

"So tell," I said.

"It was nothing important," Mel said.

None of the food had been touched in my absence.

Gregory said, "I don't want to speak too loudly on the subject." I leaned in as he continued. "I just mentioned that perhaps Junie and her husband, David Ditchburn, were open minded enough to enjoy a pleasant polyamorous relationship." Ditchburn was a successful British businessman, now living and operating in Australia.

"Pleasant?" I asked, speaking loudly. "That doesn't feel like the right word for it, does it? And what about *his* wife, Cairns' wife, I mean?"

"Gwen? I don't know, to tell you the truth. I'm not even sure she's in the picture. Look, Jim's a friend of mine, his district borders mine and we have often had occasion to work together on policy matters. He was the leader of the Anti-Vietnam War movement in this country and I was one of his most ardent followers. He has been a mentor to me, so I am not about to say anything against him. He remains a counterculture figure, and I must say, a brave one at that. He wouldn't care what you or I think of his personal choices and I really don't get into his personal life much, but I trust him as much as any man I know. And he's smarter than the rest of my colleagues combined."

My clients wouldn't believe that I could even sit here with this raving socialist let alone find him quite a fascinating personality. I shared their doubts about his politics but who cares? He was a unique and entertaining bloke, and I was enjoying testing his boundaries and he mine.

We could both sense Mel beginning to tune out of the political talk. The band, which had been playing some blues, had now shifted to a techno sound for an American tune they said was called "Popcorn," a lively disco number. Gregory stood and asked Mel to dance. She had always loved to dance and I was never much into it, nor very good at it. She never bugged me about it but I know it was a bit of a disappointment for her. Now she looked at me and I smiled and nodded in the affirmative. She couldn't get to her feet fast enough and off they went. Since this was the first real dance number, there were only a few other couples on the floor, but the number grew as the up-tempo beat even got my foot tapping. She was in her element, having the time of her life, smiling at Gregory as they both seemed to improvise with perfect tempo and timing. He was not a one-dimensional bloke, this one.

They did not return to our booth when the music morphed magically into "The First Time Ever I Saw Your Face." The girl singer was no Roberta Flack but that didn't stop Mel from reaching up with her arms around his neck as his moved to her waist. Her smile turned into contentment as she looked at me over his shoulder and gave me the V for victory sign. I'm not normally a jealous person, but I'll admit I felt a pang. And a twinge in my pants as well.

When they returned to our booth Mel was smiling at me and waving her hand in front of her face as if to ward off the heat. She slid in next to me and squeezed my thigh. She obviously was feeling the effects of the wines.

"Gosh," she said, "that was fun."

"Fun, indeed," said Gregory while I poured myself a glass of their red.

"This has been nice," Gregory said. "I need to get some sleep, what with all the agro I know I'll have to deal with tomorrow. But I hope we can do this again soon."

"So do we," said Mel, without a thought of consulting me. I could only hold my glass up for one more toast.

The three of us walked silently to the car park, Mel firmly holding my hand. When we got to Gregory's Mercedes convertible, he turned. As if on cue, Mel gave him a hug and a soft kiss on the cheek.

On the way home she moved across the bench seat to nuzzle my ear and rub my groin. I said, "We need to talk."

"OK, but maybe in the morning?" She laughed as she unzipped my pants and lowered her head to my lap. "Can't talk right now. Maybe in the morning."

In the morning. She was busy getting the boys off to Melbourne Grammar while I got myself ready to go to the office. As usual, we had maybe fifteen minutes to sit together over coffee and toast.

"How are you feeling this morning?" I asked.

"Fine, why do you ask?"

"Last night."

"What about it?"

"I thought we were going to talk about it."

"Dinner was very nice," she said. "That's a nice place, good food, good service. I liked it. We'll have to go back."

"And?"

"And Gregory was very charming, don't you think? He was funny."

"Yes, he was. And?"

"And what?"

"We were going to talk, remember?"

"What's to talk about. We had a nice dinner in a nice place with a nice new friend. What else is there to say?"

"About what happened?"

"Nothing happened and I don't want to go into it."

I had to leave for work. So much for let's talk about it in the morning. I was in the car and driving. What did it all mean? Just like last night, I was still feeling some combination of anxiety, jealousy, lust, and yes, love—a kind of tenderness for Mel that I had never felt before. And a resentment.

The memory of that night occupied me all the way home. One might say that things progressed from there but what did all that have to do with where was I going to be a hundred years from now?

CHAPTER 11

My reverie was interrupted when I saw Gregory's car parked at our curb. I drove through our gate and left my car in the drive. Thought he'd be in Canberra dealing with the disruptions there.

Mel and he were sitting at the kitchen table with a pot of tea and a plate of biscuits. Although it was midafternoon, Mel was barefoot and wore only a light short robe over my yellow T-shirt with "Carna Hawks" on the front for Hawthorne, our favorite Aussie Rules Football club. Gregory was fully dressed in a gray summer suit, minus a red tie, which protruded from the side pocket of his jacket. It seemed they were a little surprised too. I was put off my feed a bit by the obvious situation. I had never tried to impose any rigid ground rules, but the three of us had always made love together and Mel knew I liked to watch. However, I was determined to stay calm and display sophisticated tolerance.

Mel jumped up and threw her arms around my neck and gave me a quick kiss. "You're supposed to be in Sydney," she said. "Welcome home, honey. What's going on?"

Gregory stay seated but smiled and reached out to shake my hand. I explained the air traffic strike and the plan to go tomorrow.

"Yes," said Gregory. "I heard that. Worrisome times, mate."

"Finally somebody's worried," I said, and related the Virge "no worries" story. They laughed, especially Gregory, his laugh more ironic than hers.

"So how *is* Virge?" asked Mel, pouring me a cup of tea.

I put down my briefcase and took a seat at the table. All so civilized. "That's a whole other story," I said. "He's at the Hilton sleeping off a bad night."

"Not the first time he's had to do that," Mel said. "I worry about him sometimes."

"Who's this Virge bloke?" asked Gregory and we explained.

"Well, I don't know your friend but he's right about one thing. It's time to worry," said Gregory.

"So what's going on in Canberra? Shouldn't you be there dealing with all this chaos?"

"Too late for that, mate. I have to be back here to start campaigning for my seat. And I'll tell you, it won't be easy this time."

"But you won by a landslide last election," I said.

"I'm afraid you don't understand what's going on."

"So enlighten me."

Mel must have already heard some of this because she left the room for the loo.

"So, my Labour party is in the shitter, that's what's going on. Yesterday Gough had his campaign committee and a few MPs like me over to the Lodge. We were supposed to start planning the campaign but he left us there forever, without him, twiddling our thumbs. Finally after what seemed like an hour, he comes downstairs in his pajamas and a short dressing gown. He's pacing around the room and cursing the Governor-General. He kept calling Kerr a cunt, over and over. That's all he said for a long time before he just walked out. We were left to do the planning on our own and the best we could do is come up with a campaign slogan."

"Which is?"

"'Shame, Fraser, Shame.'"

"That's it?"

"That's it. See why I said it's time to worry?"

Mel was back. "Not much to go on, is it?" she said.

"We can never win an election with that," said Gregory.

"But you do have a lot of angry people on your side. Look at what's happening in the streets, or as a matter of fact, at the Sydney airport today. I heard Whitlam say that the election is about what he called 'the survival of Australian democracy.' Doesn't that give you some votes?"

Gregory lowered his head and slowly shook it in the negative. "Rod Cameron..."

"Who?" I asked.

"Cameron. He's our party pollster. He says we're delusional if we think we can hang our hat on that until election day. He says the anger over the way the dismissal was handled won't translate directly to votes for Labour. Two different things, he says. People doubt the competence of our government and it will be damn near impossible to overcome that in six weeks."

"But maybe you can," I said. "You're seen as a solid performer for your district."

"Past tense, Coop. We'll see, but it's to worry. Now I'd better get out of here and back to work."

"First things first," I said, smiling. Was he blushing?

Mel walked him to the door where they embraced and kissed, his eyes opening wide as he looked at me over her shoulder. He then winked at me as his hands moved to her hips then gave her bum a slap. She broke away and slapped his hands playfully. "Get out of here." she said, "or I'll give you even more to think about."

"Promise?"

"You're cute. Now go."

"So that was a surprise," I said when he was gone.

"For me too. He just dropped in about noon."

"For a nooner then. He didn't spend the night?"

"Of course not. Never when the boys are here, you know that."

"So how was it?"

"'It' was fine. The truth is, after he told me about all his woes, I wasn't much in the mood. But I thought 'what the hell, the poor guy.'"

"Always being kind to others, aren't you? So you gave him a pity fuck."

"But it didn't stay that way. I got very demanding and it turned out fabulous."

"Fabulous?" Despite my misgivings, she was beginning to turn me on.

"Mel, you know I like to be there, at least to watch. I'm not sure I can handle your doing this without me."

"This is the first and only time, I promise. Like you said, a pity fuck."

"But fabulous."

"It just happened that way. Not much to start with but then fabulous. I wish you would have been here, I really do. I know you. You would have enjoyed the view and probably joined in." She was laughing at me as she said it, teasing me.

I pulled her to the floor. As she unzipped me she said, "You perv. You like this so much, don't you? I probably smell like sex."

I didn't last long.

What Mel didn't know was some of my speedy orgasm may have been a result of the incompleteness and frustration of the previous night with Nicole. She didn't know and I wasn't about to tell her.

CHAPTER 12

We had a normal evening at home with Roger and Brett, but that night, tired as I was from the trip to Adelaide, not to mention the other events of the day, I had a hard time sleeping.

The buzz of thoughts and emotions carried over when my driver picked me up for the trip to the airport in the morning. At some point, however, I realized we were in rush hour traffic on our way to Virge's hotel. A few protesters holding signs on a few corners: "Shame, Frasier, Shame," "Crucify Kerr," "Save Our Democracy," "Goodbye Goph," "Good Riddance." Otherwise the drive was normal. I was going to work today. I had to get my head ready to deal with Virge's issues and our work in Sydney. Phone messages from my office on my seat beside me. An appointment slip for an initial consult with a new client. Need to do some research first. *The two of them slow dancing at that pub that long ago evening. His more recent slap on her nearly exposed bum at the door of our house. My sloppy seconds. How far we have come.*

The fact that Virge was out and waiting for us at the hotel entrance was reassuring. Morning was not his usual strong suit but he was smiling when he got in the car.

"Any strikes or slow-downs today?" he joked.

Our driver chuckled and said, "No worries, you'll be right." Virge sat back and smiled. "Looking forward to seeing some of the Sydney sights I've only admired in photos."

Boarding was also routine. Once aloft, Virge told me he needed some advice. "That woman called me," he said. "The one I flew over with. You met her at the airport when you picked me up."

"Yeah, I forget her first name but her last name is Lawson. Married to a World Motors client. She was plastered, as I recall. And she…"

"Fran Lawson. She's been calling me and says she'd like to get together for a drink while I'm here."

"You need to stay away from that."

"No worries, as they say. Not the slightest interest. She strikes me as needy and troubled."

"And she's married to a client."

"That too. But that's part of the problem. She called me three times last night when I needed some big-time sleep. She won't give up. So how do I get her off my back?"

"Well, it shouldn't be a problem for very long. You'll be long gone soon."

"She knows that and it seems to make her urges all the more urgent."

"I don't know what to say, man, except to ignore her calls when you can and wait her out. Maybe she'll eventually get the message and give up."

"I don't want to alienate our client. She keeps reminding me that her husband is the manager of sales."

"Gerald Lawson. He's an okay guy. Poor bloke. He must not know what's going on."

"Or doesn't want to."

"Anyway, hang in there, be patient, try not to get her mad and maybe she'll just go away."

"No worries, right?"

"No worries."

The flight attendant brought our coffees. "I'm so sorry about what happened in Adelaide."

"Speaking of that, I won't say no worries. I *am* worried about *you.*"

He admitted he was concerned himself. "Do I need some help, you think?"

I attempted to express both empathy and support as he sat back and listened. He was his usual open self. Finally we shifted our focus to the day ahead in Sydney. I hadn't spent as much time in the plant there as in South Australia because it wasn't in as much trouble. It ran okay, if not great. Management there had been asking when it was their turn and I was expecting we would have to deal with some whingeing.

"Whingeing?" Virge asked.

"Complaining. Whining."

"Oh, my god. There it is, beautiful."

Sydney harbor and the opera house were in full aerial view, still a thrilling sight for me even now. And the Coat-Hanger bridge.

Noah Gates, the plant personnel manager, met us when we got off the plane. Fleshy with a pink face, he took pride as a gracious host. He was a member of the best clubs including serving as the current president of a championship golf club. My first trip to Sydney, Mel and the boys came with me the weekend before to tour the area. Noah provided us a road map on which he had personally noted sites and drew recommended driving routes that took us from Bondi Beach to Palm Beach, from Kuringai National Park to Hyde Park. We crammed a lot into the day without feeling cramped at all. The next day, Sunday, he himself drove us to some of his other favorite spots including Circular Quay where we caught the ferry to Manly. We were his guests for lunch at his golf club where the boys enjoyed his snooker lesson. After my visit to the plant the following Monday, I thought I could detect his disappointment when I made no firm commitments for follow-up work.

Now, with Virge, he was at it again, much to my friend's delight. He drove us past the opera house and over the Coat-Hanger without ever backtracking before making our way to the plant, a route unlike any I had ever taken.

Our afternoon at the factory consisted of standard fare. A plant tour led by department managers followed by a conference room meeting with the top team. Virge impressed them with some quickly formed but spot-on analyses meant to establish his know-how without scaring them off with criticism. He was on his game and they were easily pleased.

Noah once again took us under his wing for the evening, starting with beer and bickies at his boat club in Darling Harbour. He also had us scheduled for a dinner cruise in the Sydney Harbour. I'd had enough celebrating and being hosted in the last two days and the cruise promised to be boring. My experience with "boat rides" is that they tend to be pleasant enough for a short while but go on long after I am ready for them to be over.

The touristy glitter of the boat itself, along with a surf and turf dinner of a small fish filet with an even-smaller cut of leathery beef, only reinforced my resistance. Noah was his usual unctuous self, rehashing the day, still working Virge and me to give the plant the attention it had been missing. My guess was that he was only interested in order to make himself look good to the production guys, delivering them the "Brock and Case treatment," not that he really saw a need for our help. Other than that, we made small-talk on the pleasantness of the weather, the lovely air for an evening on the water. I was ready for it all to be over as the boat turned gently back from the Heads at the harbor entrance and came around to the face the city.

Jaw dropping! The rosy sky over the Sydney skyline took my breath away. It grew slowly more breathtaking as it became more intensely red with each minute. The romantic Chet Baker standard playing through the sound system—I hadn't even noticed any music at all before—moved me to sadness. I left my two dinner mates at the table and walked by myself to the bow and stood there, wine glass in hand, and watched and listened. It was clearly one of the most romantic settings I had ever experienced, and I was alone. I missed Mel desperately. Oh, how I wished that she was with me. That we could have this to share. Tears were just behind my eyes. The captain took his time, gliding under the harbor bridge, prolonging the ache deep inside me before he rounded back to Circular Quay.

I knew I would never be able to tell her of that moment. Nor even try. Words couldn't do it, and even if I could adequately describe the scene and the emotions, she would only feel justifiable resentment that I was there without her, ostensibly at work, spending another boring evening at another boring business dinner with boring business acquaintances, before another boring night alone in another boring hotel room. She often had to listen to my whingeing about my travel woes. This would only confirm her worst suspicions. Almost the worst, that is.

I would tell her the three of us had a nice dinner and went to bed. That was it. Still, I felt the love and longing even as the boat docked at the Quay.

As Noah drove us to the Regency, he and Virge waxed on about the evening. Virge said, "You're being awfully quiet, Coop. What did you think?"

"Beautiful," I said and returned to my silence.

They decided on a final nightcap in the hotel bar. I begged off and went to my room.

CHAPTER 13

How could one complain about being forced to travel when staying in a luxurious suite like this, with an enchanting floor-to-ceiling glass view of Darling Harbor and the Opera House?

I thought of calling Robin.

Robin was the bartender at another hotel where Kevin Larned and I stayed one of the times we were in Sydney. Sitting at her bar, I tried my usual charms, all that I could muster, to no avail. Like a good barmaid, she laughed at our clever flirtations, but didn't return them with her own. It was clear she wasn't having any. She only broke down enough to tell us of her recent divorce, her husband's infidelity, his leaving her for another. She had learned her lesson with men she said, and she was convincing.

Eventually, though, with enough trips back, and enough empathy on my part, I was able to flatter my way through her thick armor. We met three times, first at her house then twice in my hotel rooms. That first night at her place in the Sydney suburb with the quintessentially Aussie name of Woolloomooloo, we had to improvise, since she hadn't had sex since her husband left her. Therefore she was not on the pill and I brought no protection. But where there's a will there's a way. The second get together was more conventional. The third and last was just that. She was having her period, and after she was down to her underpants and I was naked, we decided that maybe it would be nicer if we just cuddled. We really did like each other and both knew it was our last time before I left for the States. Our parting took on an agreeable glow.

Now, as I turned out the light in my luxurious suite, and buried my head in my pillow, I didn't want to devalue that night with Robin nor the one tonight on Sydney Harbor, missing my missing wife. I was content in my choice.

I was startled awake at 2:30 a.m. by the phone in my room. A doctor informed me that Virge was in serious condition at the hospital and that, as he had given my name as his contact person, I should come immediately. She wouldn't tell me any more before I arrived except to say that it was serious, that Virge was in trouble. I scrambled into some clothes, skipping a shower. I was there in mere minutes by taxi.

A middle-aged woman with short white hair met me at the ward station in her scrubs. Her polite smile quickly took on a more sober look. "How do you do, Mr. Houghton. I'm Mrs. Lawton, one of Mr. Cash's doctors." It is normal for Australian physicians to drop the doctor title, but *one of his doctors?* "I'm afraid you can't see him just yet," she said. "We're doing some tests."

"What the hell happened? 'Doctors' plural? What's wrong with my friend?"

"At the moment," she said, "we only know what a Mr. Noah Gates was able to tell us. That and the little we've heard from Mr. Cash himself. Apparently, Mr. Cash was having drinks in a Kings Cross pub tonight with Mr. Gates. As I understand it, they were physically attacked by some pretty rough mugs. That can happen in that part of our city, unfortunately. We treated Mr. Gates for some minor injuries and released him but poor Mr. Cash is more serious, I'm afraid. In addition to some broken ribs and other bumps and bruises, he suffered a serious head injury."

"Head injury! Oh my god. Just how serious?"

"That's what we're trying to determine right now, but we do know his skull was fractured. It seems to be what we would call a 'Battle's sign fracture,' which can cause brain damage but we just don't know yet. We're administering a cranial CT scan right now. That should tell us more about the extent of his injury. In the meantime, we have used sutures to stop the fluids from flowing from his nose and ears."

"Fluids. Jesus."

"It's quite common in these cases for there to bleeding from those areas."

"Oh, my god, oh my god. Why the hell did they beat him up?"

"All we know is that Mr. Gates told us he and Mr. Cash weren't doing a thing, just sitting there drinking beer, when these no-counts started yelling rude things at them. When the men were ignored, they surrounded your man's table and began beating on the two of them. The head injury probably occurred when one of the men bounced Mr. Cash's head on the floor."

"Ya think?"

"We really don't know. Mr. Cash was conscious and talking but could barely remember anything at all. The men ran off but the police have a good idea who they are and are investigating."

"A skull fracture! Jesus!"

"Skull fractures must all be taken seriously but usually heal themselves. Unfortunately, with this one, it is down behind the ears, a Battle's sign fracture, as I said, which can cause neurological damage. But as I say, we won't know until we've done further testing."

I was still very confused. "I think I heard you say something about some kind of scan." I made it into a statement but all my statements were questions at the moment.

"A CT scan, yes. Some people call it a CAT scan. It is a very powerful diagnostic tool but very new to us. We only recently got our machine and it takes a long time to develop the data. We may not know anything definitive for days. He will have to be hospitalized."

"Days? Days. Oh, my god."

"Mr. Cash asked that we first contact you but he also mentioned his father. Apparently his father is a surgeon in America, is that right?"

"As a matter of fact, his father is Dr. Norman Cash, a world-renowned brain surgeon at Johns Hopkins University Hospital in Baltimore, Maryland. I can see why Virge, Mr. Cash, mentioned him.'

"Indeed. Now that I hear the name, I am somewhat familiar with his work. Unfortunately he is a long way away, as you well know. In distance, that is, and even in terms of what day it is. We have not known how to contact him, but we will get right on it now. Still, I'm not sure what help he can be to his son way out here. But be assured we will find him and talk to him."

"Yes, please. Maybe I can help. Maybe I can find a way to reach him."

"Please do what you can. You can use a phone at the floor station. It will be greatly appreciated. We'll continue to work on it as well."

Jesus!

CHAPTER 14

A nurse found an empty desk with a phone for me. I was too frazzled to do the exact math, but I knew it would be sometime tomorrow in the States, probably daylight. I started with a call to our New York headquarters. They were as stunned as I was—maybe more so because they had no context—and they assured me that they would do whatever was necessary to get Virge the care he needed, including flying him home if that was what was best. They also dug out some contact information on his father.

My next call was to Johns Hopkins. I had to go through several people to get to someone who could help me. Dr. Cash's assistant listened to my story in horror and immediately had him paged. When he got on, he seemed remarkably calm as I filled him in. He sounded like a doctor talking to a patient: me. He asked a lot of questions, most of which I couldn't answer. When he found out all I could tell him, he said, again calmly but with full certainty, "I will need to talk with the medical people there, obviously, but he will have to come here as soon as is feasible. I want him to be cared for by the medical staff here at Hopkins. There will be no question about that. Do you think you can arrange his transportation?"

I assured him that would be not problem. I reviewed my previous conversations with our New York headquarters and gave him their assurances as well. Then I worked with a nurse to get him hooked up with Mrs. Lawton.

I paced the waiting room, happy when the tea lady brought me some coffee. I had not eaten since the boat ride the night before and she gave me directions to the canteen on the main floor. I finished another coffee as I stood at the daily menu board checking meager breakfast choices: eggs, baked beans on toast. Mrs. Lawton found me there as I was about to get in the queue behind nurses and what I assumed were a few family members of patients. Visiting hours had not yet started.

"I talked with his father," she said. "He was very thorough and asked all the important questions, but I'm concerned about his request to fly his son to America. I certainly understand it, but it can be such a difficult journey under the best of circumstances and we don't even know the status of his condition yet."

"But you can do it?" I asked.

"Do you mean, can we let him go? I suppose, but I recommend against it."

"Perfectly reasonable of you, I'm sure, but I am not about to get between Norman Cash and his son. Especially on medical matters."

"Yes, he was very clear in his request."

"You call it a request. My guess is it was a demand. My experience with most surgeons is that any requests are really meant as demands, and Dr. Cash is among the most demanding."

Her laugh struck me as both knowing and rueful. "As a surgeon myself, I am inclined to order that he stay here. We can give him care the equal to anywhere in the world. We know what we are doing, we are good at it, and we always put our patients first."

"But you will do it."

"Only because it's Dr. Cash. Otherwise we wouldn't consider it. If we must, we will prepare your friend for the trip as best we can, make him as safe and comfortable as we can."

"How soon will that be?"

"We'll start the preparations immediately, but we must keep him here until we have the results of the scan so we know of any neurological issues that we can act on right away as well as pass the information on to his father. I told him that and he agreed."

"No worries then. We're all on the same page. I will see to it that first-class travel arrangements are made as soon as we know the exact timing."

"Mr. Houghton, you have flown out here and back more than once, I presume. You know about those flights—plural—the stopovers, especially when traveling that direction, the confusion of days and night traveling through so many time zones, the jet lag. The pure endurance required even for a perfectly healthy person."

"Believe me, I do know, and I dread it every time. Especially in that direction, as you say."

"But we will do what we must do."

"Thank you and I'm sorry you have been put in this predicament. I don't like being there either."

"It's Mr. Cash, the son, my patient, your friend, that I am concerned about."

"Granted. Me too. Can I see him yet?"

"I'll check but I don't see why not. Don't expect too much though. He's still pretty much out of it."

I ate my eggs, beans and toast and went up to Virge's room. He was asleep. The only tubes were for monitoring his vitals. I sat there for some time before his eyes opened. He didn't seem to know who I was or where he was for a moment. Then he smiled.

"No worries, mate," he said.

"No worries," I replied.

"This has been one helluva trip for me, hasn't it?"

"So what happened. Nobody can tell me much."

He tipped some ice chips into his mouth from a small paper cup. "I know what you mean. They can't tell me either and I sure as hell don't know. I remember leaving the boat. I remember dropping you at the hotel."

"Dropping me?"

"Yeah, I mean we let you out at the entrance, but Noah had already suggested he and I go on for a 'cleansing ale.'"

"No shit. He gets that from his big, big boss, Mike Robertson, his managing director."

"So I remember going to the bar with Noah. Said he wanted to show me the Kings Cross section. A little local color, he said. And that's it. Nothing after that. I guess some guys beat us up pretty bad.

I know my ribs hurt and my head aches. So that's it. What else can you tell me?"

"That's all I know too. The cops seem to think they can find the guys and have started an investigation."

"Oh, crap, an investigation?"

"You have a problem with that?"

"I guess not, but what the hell, it was a bar fight."

"Do you know how or why it started?"

"Not the slightest idea. I don't think we did anything but have a few beers, but I'm telling you I really don't know. And my head is starting to feel worse just trying to think about it."

"Okay, I'll leave you alone. Anyway, I need to get working on your flights back home."

"Not home, Coop. Johns Hopkins."

"Right."

"My dad," he said, sinking back into his pillow.

"Your dad."

"No worries, right?" he said.

"No worries."

"I wish."

The test results came in the next morning. There were no clear signs of brain damage but Mrs. Lawton said they wouldn't know that for sure without several days of careful monitoring in hospital. "The trip is risky at best," she said, "but the good news is that this kind of skull fracture normally heals itself over time. That time will undoubtedly be prolonged because of the travel."

"I can't thank you enough for your diligence, doctor," I told her. "I know you did everything possible."

When they wheeled him out to the car later that day, I was taken aback by the cast he had covering his whole head with openings only for his eyes, nostrils, mouth and ears. It was braced in a metal frame to protect it from being jostled, or for that matter, from his being able to move it. Mrs. Lawton was there with orderlies to help him from the wheelchair into the car. She may even have had tears in her eyes, but her no-nonsense instructions were very clear to both me and the driver.

I helped him into a wheelchair at the airport and pushed him out to his gate. Neither of us were much for male hugs, but I gave it my best before he boarded under his own power.

He would be stopping for a couple of hours in Honolulu and again in Los Angeles, before getting on another airline for the final leg to Baltimore Friendship. I could only imagine the terrible grind ahead for him. Still, I wished I could go with him.

CHAPTER 15

It was later the same night when I flew in from Sydney and the driver dropped me off at home. I knew Mel would be upset to hear about Virge.

I could see only a dim light in the living room window as I walked toward our front door. I peeked in to see if Mel was there, and saw Clare, our teenage babysitter from next door, sitting on her boyfriend's lap. She was in her first year at a local university, a pretty girl about whom I admit to having had inappropriate thoughts on occasion. They appeared to be watching television but when I paused a moment, I noticed his hand was in her opened jeans. She closed her eyes as his hand continued to move. I couldn't hear, but from her expression I inferred purring sounds. I probably should have gone to my door but I was fascinated and more than a little turned on. It then hit me that they were sweet young kids in love. I didn't want to make anything dirty of it. Instead I made sure to be extra noisy on our steps. I rattled the locked door knob and rang the doorbell as though I didn't have my house keys. Clare seemed flushed and embarrassed as she carefully opened the door to check who was there. She laughed a nervous laugh when she saw it was me. Was she relieved or even more embarrassed or both?

"Oh, hi, Mr. Houghton. I didn't expect anyone at the front door. Mrs. Houghton went out for dinner. She should be home soon."

"Thanks, Clare. I'll take it from here. Paul, nice to see you."

Her boyfriend was down in a crouch in front of the easy chair they had been sitting in. My chair. I surmised he may have been hiding an erection and I smiled to myself. Oh, to be young again. I paid Clare, and when Paul was able to stand up and come to the door, I shook his hand before it dawned on me where it had been. The two of them were quick to get out of there.

It had been a long hard week. After seeing Virge off, I went back to the hotel to shower and change clothes before stopping in briefly at the plant to check in on things. Noah had returned to work after missing a day or two. Turned out it had all been a surprise to the management there until the police detectives showed up unannounced the morning after the event. All plant management knew was that Noah had called in sick. They knew he had been entertaining us the night before. Thought maybe he was hungover. There was nothing he or they could add to what the police already knew. The detectives, in turn, were not very forthcoming about what they had learned in their investigation. They did say they thought they had one of the culprits and were confident of bringing in the others. Seemed there were four of them. When I got there, I was asked if Virge had told me anything that would help them bring charges. I said he had basically told me he remembered nothing after arriving at the pub. I described his injuries as best I could and my conversations with the hospital medical people. "All I know for sure," I said, "is I got him on his plane and he's in for a torturous trip."

Mel was shocked when she got home and I told her the news about Virge. She actually had tears in her eyes. "Poor, poor guy. Are you sure he's going to be all right?"

"Not at all. I'm not even sure *I* could survive that trip." I told her what the doctor had told me: that in most cases this sort of fracture heals itself over time. But I could offer no further comfort.

She had been out for dinner with Beth Robertson, a charity affair. She said Gregory had called earlier. He was home from Canberra, campaigning. He did not sound optimistic and was still pissed at Goff. "He said there were back-door efforts to get Queen Elizabeth to undo Sir John Kerr's decision but Gregory says it's pure rubbish. Never happen. He wishes he had a closer relationship with Bob Hawke. Hawke, he says, has a more realistic handle on the issues and what Gregory is picking up about the mood of the people as he moved around the district. But that's all we talked about. Oh, and he always asks about you. I told him all I knew was that you were probably having a nice time in Sydney."

"You have no idea," I said, and left it to her to fill in the blanks.

We then watched a little television ourselves. I took my usual place in the easy chair and tried to coax her into sitting on my lap. She laughed and pleaded fatigue. "Me too," I confessed and soon fell asleep with the TV on.

In my office the next morning, I checked in with the plant manager in Sydney. He seemed reluctant to go into much detail. Legal and personnel issues he said. He did tell me that there was a small page two article in the *Morning Herald*. Police reports confirmed four men had been involved. They claimed after they exchanged insults with "those two poofters," they told them they had better leave if they knew what was good for them. When the two men refused and continued the verbal exchange, violence ensued. One of the men apparently admitted to pistol whipping "the Yank" in the back of the head. (So the fracture wasn't from getting his head pounded on the floor or could both things have happened?) Charges ranged from simple assault to assault with a deadly weapon, to assault intended to produce great bodily harm. I was relieved to learn that the victims' names were not revealed. The plant manager wouldn't tell me what was going to happen with Noah.

Right away I called Mel with the news.

"Oh my gosh," she said. "I can't believe it. Did you know?"

"Know what?"

"About the poofter business. Did you know Virge was homosexual?"

"Never. And I still don't. Just because some mugs in a bar fight said that doesn't make it so."

"Poor Judy and their kids, if they find out."

"Mel, don't jump to any conclusions. We don't know any more about that than we did before."

"Coop, you know him and so do I. Haven't you ever had any suspicions?"

"Maybe a little. But he is such a devoted family man, I always just dismissed any thoughts along those lines."

"You're right. But sometimes people lead double lives, you know. You do know about that, don't you?"

She had me and knew it. "Let's not go into that right now," I said, and she laughed and said, "G'day, mate," and hung up.

CHAPTER 16

Gregory had the December election campaign figured rather well. His party, to his chagrin and thanks to Whitlam's obdurate stance, banked its hopes on the continuance of people's anger over the Governor-General's abrupt and unprecedented interference into electoral politics: "Shame on Frasier." On the other hand, Frasier's Liberal/National Country Party Coalition, pounded away at economic issues, inflation, suspicious loan deals, the general incompetence of the Labour government, and even got some play when they revived the alleged Junie and Jim sex scandal. Because of the economy and the Whitlam government's policies, it had become common among many of my colleagues and clients, even before the dismissal, to coin the expression "Would the last businessman leaving Australia please turn out the lights?" The Libs very effectively turned it around into their campaign slogan, "Turn on the Lights, Australia." My own sympathies were torn between my political and economic principles and my feelings for Gregory, our friend and comrade in arms, pun intended.

While he tried his best to overcome these handicaps and stay optimistic, he told Mel and me that at the end of the day, he had little realistic hope. He begged the two of us to join him in Canberra for election day on December 13. At his suggestion, we booked a room at the Travelodge, a mid-range chain, not my usual more luxurious accommodation. "More anonymous, under the radar," he said. He saw himself as a relatively unknown backbencher anyway, not likely to draw much attention, but one couldn't be too careful these days. Better, too, that we don't use the flat he kept for his capital stays.

Mel and I arrived late that afternoon and settled our things before going out for dinner on our own. We tried our best to stay away from television screens and election night coverage until we knew the polls would be closed. We dragged it out until after nine and then went to our room. Gregory knew our room number and said he would make it as soon as he reasonably could. We changed into jeans and turned on the telly.

Since voting is mandatory in Australia, there was no question of voter turnout, as there may have been back home. Bob Hawke was the main TV commentator on behalf of Labour and a bland, easily forgotten official spoke for the Liberal/Country Party coalition. Obviously I have forgotten his name. Since the counting hadn't officially begun, Hawke did his best to demonstrate hope, but his skepticism was apparent. The coalition bloke had no doubts at all about the eventual outcome.

I poured wine for Mel and me as we settled in on the small couch. I was having difficulty keeping my eyes open when Gregory tapped out our agreed-upon knock on the door. He wore a larger smile than fit the circumstances as he hugged both of us and gave Mel a quick kiss.

"How's it looking?" he asked as he took a beer and stretched out on one of the two standard beds. "Never mind," he said. "I know." He had been at Labour Party headquarters, which he reported was a pretty gloomy place to be despite sporadic cheerleading efforts by various party officials. Gough had not made an appearance. Polls were indicating a major trouncing. Only the final official vote tally remained to confirm it. Hawke's commentary clearly pointed in that direction, despite the moderator's attempts to keep things in suspense. He also did his best to make a partial case that, if indeed Labour came out the loser, it may only be a one-time aberration brought about by Whitlam's personality and the unique circumstance of the dismissal.

"We could only wish," Gregory said to us.

Hawke was having none of it as the dismal results poured in, the size of the slaughter growing by the minute. He stated in no uncertain terms that the people had spoken "in all parts of the country." That Labour needed to listen and change its ways, its policies and practices if they were ever to regain the confidence of the people. No use making excuses, despite the despicable act of the Governor-General.

The final result was that the Liberals and their coalition partners won the greatest parliamentary majority in the country's history. Liberals. I still found it hard to grasp the fact that, in this country, they were really the conservative party.

However, long before we knew those results for sure, Gregory had passed out on the bed, fully clothed. I was not far behind, my eyes closed while I was still sitting up on the couch. Mel had changed into a nice but not naughty nightgown when she woke us both and told us to change and get into bed. Gregory stayed where he was, just undressing down to his underwear. Mel and I shared the other bed after she gave each of us a minimally friendly kiss goodnight. So much for the illicit delights of polyamory.

The next morning, Sunday, December 14, I woke to Mel in Gregory's bed, apparently naked and cuddling under the covers, speaking in low tones so as not to wake me. Obviously they had sex during the night, but I was not aware. When they saw that I was awake, Gregory got out of bed and took a shower.

"Good night?" I asked Mel.

"Mmm. Nice but kind of sad," she said, moving her small but creamy body under the covers with me. "He has invited us to help him clear out his Parliament House office this afternoon."

"Would that be safe? For him, especially?"

"He thinks it will be pretty dead around here today. A dreary hangover day, he thinks. He's going to go change and clear out his flat and then call and let us know if the coast is clear. He says, even if we were spotted, he could just claim we were friends from back home. Which, in fact, we are."

"What do you think? You want to do that?"

"Sure, why not? It might be interesting to see what's going on over there. And it will probably be sad for him. I'd like to be there for him if we can."

"OK, by me, I guess. I do have my own reputation to protect, you know?"

"And mine?"

"And yours obviously. But everyone already knows you're a slut."

She slapped me hard on the arm and got out of bed. "I'm joking," I said. "You know I'm joking."

"It's a bad joke, then. I was even thinking of letting you find out just what kind of slut I could be after he leaves, but you can forget that now."

"What's going on with you two?" Gregory chuckled when he came out of the bathroom wrapped in a towel. Mel hugged him as he made unsuccessful efforts to hold up his towel.

"Absolutely nothing." she said. "And I don't think there will be for a while. You don't look very ready yourself."

"You know I'd love to, my dear, but I have to get moving."

I tried my best when he was gone. She giggled some as she pushed my roaming hands away, letting me know I might be forgiven. She also let me in the shower with her, but it was pretty much all about the business of showering.

We were dressed in our "work clothes" when the breckie lady brought our breakfast, me in jeans and a polo shirt, Mel in a short denim skirt and white tee. Ready to pitch in where needed. Gregory called and confirmed that Canberra was virtually emptied out. Almost no tourists. Few reporters that he could detect. We set one o'clock to meet him in his office. In the meantime we took a sparsely attended guided tour of the Australian War Memorial, followed by a quick sandwich in the museum canteen. It was surprising to me that this city had been the center of so much action and turmoil over the last month and more, right up to and including last night. Now it looked like a ghost capital. I was half expecting to see old newspapers and other debris swirling around the empty streets as in the old movie *On the Beach*. This hadn't been a world war as in the book and film, no threat of nuclear fallout from the northern hemisphere flowing down with the winds to wipe out the Australian population, but the deserted streets and buildings had the feel of something big come and gone.

Parliament House—officially called the Provisional Parliament House for over fifty years as plans plodded forward for building a Permanent House—was dull and quiet and sad as well. The newly elected MPs would not be seated until February so this was strictly a moving out day for the losers. Many offices were already empty. We saw a few men alone, leaving with boxes in their arms; boxes they had packed themselves; boxes, I presumed, filled with files and memorabilia from their terms in power. So much for fleeting power.

We found Gregory with his office door open, sorting the wheat from the chaff, or, at this point, was it all chaff? Files were stacked on the floor, files he would arrange to have shipped to Prahran. He was now busy merely stuffing other files and miscellany into black plastic bags to be thrown out by the custodial staff. He laughed when we entered and said, "'Look on my works, ye Mighty, and despair.'" Mel gave him a hug and asked how she could help. He gave me a rueful smile and said, "Dig in, mates, it all has to go. If you could, just set some of these bags out in the hall." He began to remove personal items from his credenza, photos of the better days with Goph and their Labour cronies, a photo of a Labour convention with Bob Hawke at the podium congratulating Gregory on his electoral victory, even a picture of Gregory with Jim Cairn and Junie Morosi at some gala, the three of them dressed in beach gear with their arms around each other, laughing. Mel stood by and watched sadly as he took the items down and placed them in a smaller box.

"How about the things on your desk," she asked, lifting his official wooden nameplate, holding it lovingly, running her finger over the words carved there, reading it aloud:

"Mr. Michel/Prahran."

He looked at the nameplate and then at her, a stunned and angry look. He ripped it from her hands and hurled it across the room, creating a gash in the wall.

His angry eyes turned to me. "Close that fucking door," he said. He took Mel by the shoulders and roughly moved her until she faced his desk, her back to us. He pulled her short skirt up and her white panties down, unzipped his pants and rammed his hard cock into her. She scarcely knew what was happening but made no protest, bending over more with her elbows on the desk.

Normally I loved to see Mel in the throes of passion, my greatest sexual thrill, my primary fantasy come true, my voyeur's dream. I would usually sit and watch for a while, my erection aching until I began to masturbate, sometimes then joining in, Mel satisfying the both of us at once.

But what I saw now was passion of a whole different sort. I fell limp into one of the chairs, too confused to be aroused. At first I felt fear for Mel and anger at Gregory but sat paralyzed with no notion of what to do.

"Mel, are you ok?" I murmured.

Her answer: "Fuck me, Gregory, fuck me."

It was over in minutes. Gregory pulled away and put his limp penis back in his pants. Mel just continued to lie face down on the table, her pussy dripping. I couldn't tell if she was crying or laughing. For his part, Gregory now slumped into the chair next to me and put his head in his hands.

"I'm sorry," he said to no one in particular. "I'm sorry," he repeated, perhaps to Mel or to me or to God. Or to Gough Whitlam.

She turned and sat on the desk facing us with a serious look on her face, pulling up her white panties. "Coop, honey, come here, please." She moved the crotch of her knickers aside as I crawled to her on my knees. I was in completely unexplored regions now but I knew exactly what she wanted me to do. My tongue found her and I did my duty. She moaned until she thrust her hips in orgasm, just the way I would have hoped.

"I love you guys so much," she said later, smiling, holding our arms when we left the Parliament building. He headed off to finish up in his flat after we agreed to meet him that evening for dinner.

On the walk back to our hotel, I asked Mel, "So what the hell was that all about?"

She tugged my arm closer to her and then stopped and faced me with an intense expression. She reached out to me and folded me in her arms. "I don't know, Coop," she said, and started to cry into my chest. "All lust, I guess, but it feels so humiliating now."

"To you or to me?"

"Both of us. Maybe all three of us. He was obviously feeling humiliated by his situation. He was so angry and rough I guess, and I just let myself get caught up in his mood. It felt good at the moment, I'm sorry to say. Then *I* was the humiliated one. Which I then dumped onto you, I know. What can I say? I feel so shitty about it."

"And, of course, I jumped in myself. It was all so confusing and intense. Now I feel all dirty and I don't like it."

She continued to hold me close. "I know. I know. It's not us, is it?"

"I hope not."

"No more, okay? I don't want to think we're going to be those people. And to be fair, it was not like him to be like that either. But I think we have to call a stop to the whole thing before we sink even further into some sewer."

I let her go. She wiped her tears and we resumed walking. "Good thing we're leaving this country soon, don't you think?" I asked.

"Yes, that should make it easier, but I want to stop things even before that. The three of us deserve better closure than that before we leave."

We held hands on the way to our room. In a lighter mood, I teased with "What would your Germaine Greer say about what happened?"

She jerked my hand in mock displeasure but laughed. "Good question. She might even have approved of the sex part but ... "

"The power dynamics," I interjected with a smart-ass smile.

"Exactly. I don't know exactly where she would stand there. More importantly, I don't know exactly where *I* should stand. Now between you and her, you've both got me thinking too much. So, what's the deal? Have you been reading my copy of the book?"

I gave her a pat and said, "Not really. Just what I have overheard from you and others."

By evening, she and I had rebounded enough to be ready for a quiet dinner in Gregory's favorite Canberra bistro. After apologizing again, he seemed to be content. We toasted to our new lives, whatever they may be.

The three of us carried a vibe of loving forgiveness with us from dinner to the Travelodge. Mel emerged from the bath in a long, sheer, white lace negligee, taking Gregory's and my breath away while effectively erasing the afternoon's strange encounter. The three of us made a much gentler form of love, a kind, compassionate form of make-up sex. Perhaps farewell sex as well.

CHAPTER 18

Christmas is a different matter in Australia. It's summer. It's hot. We had a low-key morning exchanging gifts from under a small artificial tree, then ate breakfast, after which all four of us watched and laughed at Monty Python reruns in our lounge.

In the early afternoon we drove to Kevin and Diane Larned's in Brighton for Christmas dinner. The Larned's home was one I always envied. Plenty large enough without the stuffy Toorak mansion ambitions: one story, simple, clean red brick exterior, more modern than anything in Toorak. I suppose in some ways it was just more typically American suburban. Perhaps it was my short timer's syndrome beginning to click in, ready to go home. The brick garden wall was modestly low, allowing for an unobstructed view across the road to Middle Brighton Beach on Port Phillip Bay. The minute we got out of the car, our boys joined their son and two daughters giving their new Christmas gift trampoline a tryout. Nearby was the moderately sized in-ground pool, ready for use on this sunny day.

The interior of the house was equally up to date, but I was amused to find traditional English Christmas decor: larger than life Christmas tree, decorated with red and gold ornaments and white garlands suggestive of snow; a white angel at the top; a few traditional gift boxes underneath where Mel and I placed those we had brought. The piéce de rèsistance, for me, was the dining room sideboard, on which a mirror was laid flat, bordered in white wool snow, miniature ice skater figurines in gliding poses around on the glass.

"Beaut," I laughed as Diane gave Mel an enthusiastic hug and me a more perfunctory one.

"My skating rink, you mean?" she said with a smile. "Fun, eh?"

Kevin came into the room with mugs in hand. "Mulled wine," he said. "Just what you need on a summer day."

Dinner was in the same mode: platters of both roast beef and turkey, Brussel sprouts (never my favorite) and all the other traditional trimmings. There were two amazing desserts: Colchester pudding and profiteroles, which we took to the lounge to enjoy with our port.

The mood was generally festive, our kids and theirs keeping up an ongoing chatter, provoking frequent laughter in us parents. I was grateful that Diane took the seat at the base of the table, far from me, far from temptation for either of us.

While we carried things to the kitchen, the conversation took a more serious turn when Diane asked about Virge. "Kevin says that the official company version is that he is out of his father's hospital and healing at home. I thought you might know more as his friend, Coop."

"Not much. I did speak with him once. Not that he said anything, but he sounded pretty depressed to me. He did tell me that he knows he has a problem and has started attending AA meetings."

"He seems like such a good bloke," Kevin said. "I didn't take him for a poof."

"I know nothing about that," I said. "I've known Virge pretty well for a long time. I know he's devoted family man. His wife, Judy, is great—really smart and fun. They dote on their three kids. So is he a poofter? Not that I know of."

Mel interrupted, "Coop, you know it's possible. I always thought it was possible. He could be bi, you know."

"Anything is possible," I said. "He's always been a bundle of ambiguities. A delightful bundle most of the time; frustrating some of the time. Keeps you on your toes."

Mel added, "But a great dear, sweet friend."

"I love the guy," I said.

"So sad," Diane said.

We followed the kids across to the beach. It was summer but the late-day breeze off the bay made us wish we had worn a light jacket or sweater. The adults sat on a blanket that Diane brought while Kevin opened the Eski and pulled out four cans of beer. "A little cleansing ale," he said. Jesus, now everybody's doing it.

The kids were having a good time chasing, cartwheeling and drawing their names in the sand. "Bring them tomorrow for Boxing Day," Kevin said. "Much more low-key. They can swim in the pool and I'll do a three-way on the barbie."

Mel looked at me and smiled a private smile. He actually meant he would be doing a mixed grill of lamb chops, steaks, and sausage.

Diane looked a bit surprised at Kevin's invitation but quickly recovered: "That will be fun. Good idea. Boxing day is much more relaxed. We'll have a good time."

When we left, she gave Mel another big hug and looked away from me. It made things simpler than at the Robertson's party, but it also caused me to wonder what was going on. We had had such a good family outing that I put it out of my mind on the drive home. "That was nice," I said to Mel.

"Wasn't it, though," she answered. "Didn't you think so, boys?"

"So we're going back tomorrow?" asked Roger with a discernible eagerness. "I heard we might go for Boxing Day and a swim?"

"Would you like that?" asked Mel.

He punched his little brother who whinged but laughed. "He'd like that," said Brett.

Mel and I exchanged side glances and smiles. I inferred some kind of budding relationship between Roger and one of the Larned girls, probably Bindy, their 13-year-old.

My smile lingered as I reflected on the day. Such an ordinary family holiday—"wholesome" was the word that emerged for me. Strange how good it felt. So quotidian yet so gratifying. I could get used to that, I thought. I looked forward to tomorrow.

At home, the boys went to bed and Mel and I sat on the couch in the lounge, turned on the telly and held hands until Mel got up to answer the phone.

"Yes, let me put Coop on. He knows more than I do. Just a moment." She waved me to the phone and said, "A Mrs. Lawson, asking about Virge."

I struggled to place the name until I heard her slurring her words. Fran Lawson, the woman who got off the plane with Virge that first day. The one he said had frequently called him.

"So did you have a nice Christmas?" she asked. "I hope you had a nice Christmas."

"As a matter of fact, we did, thank you, Fran. It is Fran, isn't it? Do I have that right?"

"Fran it is," she said. "How about our boy, Virgil? Was he with you, I suppose? He won't return my calls." She was obviously in her cups.

"I guess you haven't heard," I said. "He's gone home to the States."

"Oh dear, no wonder. Why so soon? He was supposed to be out here longer than that. I do know that much. I was hoping he and I might meet for a drink sometime. He seemed so sweet on the plane. We met over a match, you know."

"Yes, I remember you said that when you got off the flight. No drinks with Virge this time I'm afraid. He was in accident and badly injured. Had to go back to his father's hospital in Baltimore. He's out now and I spoke to him once. He's doing OK, recovering at home. That's all I know."

"Oh, shit," she said. "I had no idea. Poor guy. No wonder he didn't return my calls." I let that pass. No need to go into the real reasons. No need to warn her off stalking him any longer.

"So, I'll miss him," she said. "How about you? You and your wife, I mean. I think you said you knew my husband, Gerald, sales manager at WM-A."

"We've met once or twice, yes."

"He said he saw you recently at his hotel in Adelaide."

I felt a jolt. My stomach tightened. "Really? I don't remember."

"Oh, he didn't want to bother you. He said you were busy with a cute little girl from the plant. You two and another couple. I guess they work at the plant there too. He said something about a party for you that night."

"Was he at the party?" I knew he hadn't been there but it was all I could think to say.

"No, he wasn't. Didn't know anything about it, he said."

"He missed a good one. We had a lot of fun."

"And then continued it at the hotel bar, I guess."

"Oh, that wasn't part of the party."

"Really, Gerald said it looked like you were having a good time."

"Just some friends from the plant having a nightcap."

"A cleansing ale?"

"You could say that, I guess."

"Gerald said you and the girl looked like more than friends."

Where the hell was she going with this? I checked around me to see if Mel was in listening range. "No, just friends for a nightcap."

"You like to meet friends in a bar, then." She was still slurring. "How about me? How about you and me meet for a drink sometime."

I was struggling. She was the last person I was interested in meeting for a drink. "Sure, that would be nice sometime," I said.

"How about tomorrow? It's a holiday. We can celebrate Boxing Day over a drink at lunch. Maybe at that place out in Waverly where you and your wife had dinner with the MP." She guffawed when she said it.

Jesus Christ, that was a long time ago. A year ago at least. Way before she ever met Virge.

"Gerald and I were there that night too. Nice place, I thought. Very romantic. The MP is a good dancer." She laughed again.

My stomach flipped. What did she want?

"Look, Fran, tomorrow won't work, I'm afraid. We have family plans to visit some people for the holiday. Maybe another time."

"I have an idea," she said. "We have season tickets for the Australian Open tennis. Actually, we have four so Gerald can entertain customers. The people who were going to go with us for the quarter finals had to drop out. How about you and your wife join us at Kooyong? It will just be a nice day with one of your clients. What could be better than that?"

She had me completely off guard. And by the balls. "I don't know. What day is that? We'll have to check our calendars. Is that a work day?"

"It's New Year's Day. That's why Gerald's clients dropped out."

I couldn't think of a good enough reason to say no. I could only stammer, "New Year's Day? Hmm, I will have to let you know."

"Gerald would love to see you, I know."

I guess that could have been true but I took it as a threat.

Naturally Mel wanted to know about the call right away. "That was Fran Lawson. She happened to be on Virge's plane the day he got here. Apparently they had a few drinks together. She keeps saying they 'met over a match,' whatever that means."

"Interesting." Mel said it with a smirk.

"Married to Gerald Lawson, the WM-A Director of Sales. Said she called to find out how Virge was doing. Hadn't heard about all his troubles. She assumed he was still out here. Anyway, she invited us to the quarterfinals of the Australian Open. They have four season tickets and use two of them each day for his clients. The people they had lined up for the quarters dropped out, I guess because it's on New Year's Day. So she invited us."

"New Year's Day? I don't think we have plans. It might be fun," Mel said. "What do you think?"

"Not sure, really. The tennis might be fun, but I'm a little leery of that woman. She seemed kind of clingy to me the one time I met her. Of course she was sloshed. She sounded a little that way on the phone too."

"No wonder she and Virge hit it off."

"So I'm not sure we want to get involved in that."

"It's just tennis. Outdoors in a tennis stadium. Kooyong, right? That doesn't sound too involved to me. Besides we'll be out of the country soon. So what can go wrong?"

"I guess. So it sounds like we're going. I almost feel obligated anyway. Because of her husband. His position, I mean."

"Okay. Let's do it. Sounds like fun. I've never been to a big tennis match. And Kooyong. Never been there either."

So it was settled. But not me. I went to bed with a nervous ache in my gut. So much for the end of the kind of wholesome family Christmas day I so longed for.

CHAPTER 18

When I tried to sleep that night, the call from Fran Lawson swirled in my brain and ached in my gut. Who knew what about what? What would they say/do about it? Mel and I had this understanding when it came to Gregory. We had come to accept it as part of our love for each other. And Gregory was a charming good friend. But who else would see it that way? And Mel, herself? Our deal was based on my having persuaded her that I had no interest in sex with other women—that my kink, if you think of it that way, was simply that I enjoyed seeing my wife in a state of passion with another man. I had finally, after some time and effort, convinced her that it was not a rationalization for me to have sex with anyone else. Now what if she finds out about Nicky in Adelaide. Evidently we were spotted in the hotel there by Fran's husband, an executive with my firm's major client. So far no word about Robin in Sydney, but with the way things were going, who knew when that would surface? Maybe somebody spotted me driving out to Woolloomooloo, for god's sake.

I loved Mel with all my heart, but certainly she would feel betrayed, and why not? My story had been a lie. As I saw it, and as she would see it, she with Gregory was not cheating, but I was. Then covering it up with lies. Would I lose her now? And the boys? As I lay there in the night, knotted up, tears formed. I got out of bed and went into the lounge, where I paced and sometimes sat in my chair, churning, a few times weeping.

Nor was I oblivious to the potential career impact, my promotion, my whole relationship to my firm? Would I lose all that as well? That painful muddle was further entangled with Mel and my family, separate but closely linked domains.

I had brought it all on myself, I knew. Who did I think I was that I could get away with it, something I didn't consider at all during the times I was indulging my desires, ruled by my libido and my ego? I won those women over. I was charming enough, good looking enough, smooth enough, and horny enough. A good lover, maybe. They were attractive enough, coy enough, challenge enough, sexy enough. They were not even particularly good lovers. The sex was not great. But it was sex. With a woman. A conquest, I suppose. And let's face it, I was horny. I have never not been horny. Not since I was old enough to be aware of girls. Not since the scene with my second cousin, Eric. Not since my first masturbation. Not since my first glimpse of porn in the old Tijuana Bibles even before puberty. Not since my first gropings with my first serious girlfriend, a sweet girl in junior high, a girl whose reputation I destroyed by my locker-room boasting.

Oh, Jesus, I was digging now. Nothing left out of the seething surge. I felt nauseous. I made it to the bathroom and tried to throw up but nothing. No chance of a purge. I was stuck with it until morning light, which couldn't come soon enough in that endless night. Morning? Then what?

As it turned out, Boxing Day dawned a glorious summer day, taunting me. My first coffee instantly burned a hole in my raw innards. I gave up on breakfast. When Mel came out of the bedroom tying the belt of her robe, she took one look at me and visibly blanched.

"Coop, you look like shit. Are you sick? Too much Christmas stuffing?"

I told her it was probably just "short-timer's syndrome." It was about work, I said, and feeling guilty about leaving Kevin and the team with so much up in the air. I told her that I had been up for hours worrying about it. I told her I felt ill but that it would all be okay once I could start in again, working, taking care of things.

I was actually relieved when Kevin called with a change of plans for Boxing Day. Mel and the boys were still invited for a swim and to hang with their kids but Kevin and I needed to meet Mike Robertson at WM-A headquarters. He had some sort of special request for us. Kevin didn't know what it was but said Mike didn't sound like it was any sort of emergency, just something he needed us to look into while I was still around. I managed a deep sigh. Something to do. Something to occupy my brain, quiet my churning bowels.

Mel said she would take Diane up on her offer. The kids were so looking forward to another day in Brighton. With the girls, I thought.

Our meeting was scheduled for late morning but I immediately got myself ready and headed for my own office, hoping that someone or something would occupy the time before I was due across the Yarra in the Melbourne WM-A headquarters.

Fortunately or unfortunately, my lame duck days had now fully arrived. Almost no one was around; it was a holiday after all and I shouldn't have been there either. Most of my own office work had already been passed on. In other circumstances, I might have been pleased and proud. The way I was feeling, though, it merely made me feel irrelevant. They wouldn't miss me a bit if my worst fears burst to the surface. Would everything I worked to build now come crashing down around me? Coming in here early did nothing to relieve those fears, merely amplified them.

I checked the time and decided to try calling Virge. It was not a holiday there but I was pretty sure he would be home, still recovering.

"How's it going mate?" he said when he heard my voice. I knew he was putting on his best Aussie to assure me of his good spirits. It worked. At least a little.

"I'm a short-timer is all." I answered. "The world's lamest duck."

"Not as lame as me," he said. "We should form a club. The truth is, I'm doing quite well. Physically that is. My recovery is way ahead of schedule. Mentally/emotionally? That's a different matter."

"Tell me about it," I said. "We may both suffer from a similar syndrome."

"I don't know, Coop. Sitting around here by myself—Judy and the kids are gone during the day—it gives me too much time to think. I'm almost at the point where the doctors will be releasing me to go back to work. The people at the office—my boss, my secretary, my old office mates—have been great. They call all the time. Some come to visit. They tell me my chair and my desk are just waiting for me to get back into action. They say how much I am missed."

"That all sounds right to me, Virge. That's great. I'm sure they mean it. I should be so lucky."

"You are. You will be. It's waiting here for you too. But I don't know."

"Know what?"

"I'm not sure I'm ready to push that same rock up that same hill."

"I always thought you loved your rock."

"That's just it. I did when I was all involved in getting that damn thing up the slope. I enjoyed both the process and the results, even sometimes when it rolled down again and I had to start over. I looked forward to wrestling that same rock. For better or for worse, now that I am forced to get away from it, to sit here and read or watch television during the day, or to just sit and look out at our pond, I'm not so sure. I want winter to hurry up and be over so I can get out and work on my roses."

"Roses?"

"Maybe they're my real rock now, Coop. I sit here and think how I would love to spend all my time with my roses. The trouble would be like now, too much time in the winter to think about it, about starting all over again in the spring. So I sit here and think about moving south."

"From your beloved Connecticut?"

"Crazy, right? But that's where I am these days. Roses and moving south."

"Weird," I said.

"I know."

"No, what I'm saying is, you may not believe this, but I can totally relate to what you are telling me."

I heard him chuckle. "You're right. I can't believe it. Not you.

You've got a shiny new rock sitting here waiting for you. The kind of challenge you love. You'll be rockin' it in no time and having a ball."

"Don't forget, I don't have a hell of a lot to do here right now, so I'm thinking too. About my own roses and moving south."

"You don't have any roses, man," he said. "And you would hate it if you did."

"So maybe not roses, then. I don't have any thoughts about what my roses might be. But I've had the pleasure out here of being a pretty big frog in a smaller pond. I know my new job is perfect. They've set me up with something that is just the way I would draw it up if I could have it just the way I want it. But even then, I will be one small part of that great big pond. I'm not sure I can do that anymore after being in Australia with this job I have now. It's been the highlight of my life so far, the best years. I'm not sure I want to be back in New York no matter how desirable they make the rock. At least you have your roses to think about. I have only the abyss."

"A little melodramatic, my friend."

"You're right. But then I am staring into more than one of the abysses right now."

"Is it abysses or abyssi?"

"All of the above."

"Remind me, how old are you?" he asked.

"Thirty-nine. Soon forty."

"Mmm-hmm."

"And you?" I asked.

"The same."

"So you are suggesting we are just facing our mid-life crisis."

"Just saying."

"Well, you started it," I said. "You and your roses started this whole conversation."

"So what now? What are we going to do about it?"

"I don't have any fucking idea, you asshole. I suppose we'll just go on with our respective rocks and forget about all this shit."

"Maybe. Maybe you can do it. Hell, of course you can do it. I'm not so sure about me."

"Then sell your house and move south to a house with a big yard."

"I still have a family to support," he said.

"Not really. A trust-fund boy like yourself doesn't have to worry about such small matters."

"I still have a family that I need to support. Me."

"Got it."

"Look," he said, "I'm glad you called. I can't talk to anyone else about all this stuff. Even my wife. All she does is try to cheer me up. Says she knows me, knows I'll find the answers when I feel better. Maybe she's right, but that stops the conversation. So thanks for calling. Wish you and I had talked like this a long time ago."

"I thought we always talked, Virge. More than most guys anyway. But I have learned things about you recently that have surprised me."

"I had hoped to keep it that way, old friend. But things come out when things come out. People too, I guess."

"Ready or not," I said.

"Ready or not. Maybe we're ready now."

"Or not," I said. "I hope we are. There are things that you might be surprised to learn about me that might be coming to the surface. Other than Mel, I see you as my best friend. I will be leaning on you."

"Call again, soon. We'll exchange rocks."

"Love you, my friend."

It seemed somehow appropriately confusing when Kevin showed up soon after that call in a polo shirt and slacks, not the usual office uniform. He looked at me in my navy blue suit and laughed, none of which made me feel better. I was obviously left out of another loop. Things felt more and more absurd.

"Sorry, mate. I only just found out myself as I was about to leave the house. Mike wants to meet us at Huntingdale. Lunch and then golf. I knew you didn't play so I didn't try to head you off."

"What's going on?"

"Mike was going to meet us at his office, but since it's a holiday, he and two of his sales and marketing guys decided to play golf. They invited me but knew you wouldn't be playing and asked if it would be all right if we moved our meeting to his club for lunch. You'll be fine in that suit. Better than fine. You'll fit right in at Huntingdale." He could scarcely contain his glee. If he only knew how it played into feelings already gnawing my innards. "I would drive us both," Kevin said, "but I'm going to be staying for the golf."

"Of course," I said. "I'll head out to your place after lunch to catch up with Mel and the kids if that's okay."

I thought I detected a hesitation before he answered. "Certainly. It hadn't occurred to me but it makes sense. Yesterday was a nice day for all of us. Today's weather seems even more fine for enjoying the beach. While you're having fun at my house, I'll be either chunking or sculling another chip."

"Your choice."

"Not really."

CHAPTER 19

The clubhouse at Royal Huntingdale was a handsome old pile with much more character and charm than the clubhouse at the more well-known Royal Melbourne. That's all I knew about it, never having been on either golf course. Kevin was right that I would fit in with my suit. Even the golfers were required to change into a jacket and tie to come into the dining room. I might have been better off with a blazer, but I was fine as it was.

Mike Robertson was holding forth at the table with Bill Pawley and Gerald Lawson. He interrupted himself mid story when I came in. I was not planning to meet up with Lawson. At least until the Open.

"G'day, Coop," Mike said as he rose to shake my hand. "Kevin?"

"He'll be right along," I said. "We had to drive in separate cars so he could stay for golf."

"Of course," Mike said as I greeted the others. Lawson didn't smile or even make eye contact as we shook hands. I didn't know him well but his reserved behavior was not typical of a sales type. Was he making a statement or was I just being paranoid?

Kevin was soon behind me and we all sat down at the white linen-covered table. The dark wood wall paneling and the black and white photos of past club members spoke of tradition, more English than rough and tumble Australian. The lunch was all Mike's shout and we started with a round of pints.

"So we need you blokes to fly over to Wellington," said Bill Pawley. "We know we need to spend some money there. The plant is in terrible shape. But before we do, we'd like you to take a look.

Performance is bad too. Is that a result of the poor facilities or would we just be throwing good money after bad? You blokes did such a nice job in Adelaide. Just a quick sizing-up, would you?"

"You know I'm a short-timer, right?" I asked.

"Exactly," said Bill. "We hoped we could get you over there once more before you go. You have such a good feel for manufacturing. We would just like your first impressions. Kevin can follow up from there."

I glanced at Kevin. His nod told me he had already agreed to the trip. "So when are we talking about?"

"Monday," Bill said. "This Monday. Just the one day. You can fly over this weekend or whatever. Just a quick in and out."

I looked over at Gerald Lawson who was still not looking my way. I was determined to get a reaction from him of some kind. "So, Gerald," I said, "I guess that means we can still make Kooyong on Thursday."

He only looked down at his menu and said, "Seems like." This was trouble. My stomach took another flip.

We had another pint before we ordered lunch and another pint with our food. Kevin informed me that he had already arranged for us to fly over to New Zealand on Saturday afternoon, take in some of the Wellington area on Sunday and hit the plant on Monday. I didn't argue. Maybe the trip and his companionship would serve as some degree of escape, momentarily at least. The rest of the lunch was spent in idle gossip, golf stories, and the Ashes cricket matches in England. Everyone agreed that Tony Greig was stirring things up for the English side, to the chagrin of the Aussies.

"Let's go in the lounge for some coffee and a nice port," Mike said when we finished our dessert course. I was glad I wasn't going to be playing any golf after all these preliminaries. As bad as I was the few times I had played, I was quite sure I wouldn't even make contact after all the alcohol consumption and this was even before the port.

Bill asked me to stay behind when the others moved to the lounge. When we were alone, he said, "Coop, I must say I'm a bit disappointed in you. We made you a very generous offer at the dinner at

Mike and Beth's, a serious offer, and we never heard a word back from you. What's going on?"

"Oh, my god," I said. "I have to confess I forgot all about it. I can't believe I let that happen. Jesus, I really didn't mean to blow you off. I told Mel right away that night thinking we'd discuss it more the next day. She was stunned and non-committal that night, as I was. I scarcely believed the offer was for real and then, right away, got involved in a lot of other things (some of which I'm not about to tell you). You may have heard my friend Virge ran into some problems."

"Yes, I did hear. Sorry about that. He doing all right?"

"Just talked to him this morning. He's still home recovering. He seems to be doing well physically, but I think he has too much time on his hands. He's thinking of quitting and moving south. Raise roses, he says. I can't see it but who knows. He's such a good guy. I hate that this all happened to him. And then there's just getting ourselves ready to go home. To be honest, I think the whole idea just faded into the background without our realizing it. I am so sorry. I can't tell you."

"And then there's politics, right?"

I paused. What did he know? "Sure, we've been holding hands, so to speak, with our friend, Gregory Michel. He's both pissed and despondent. I guess that's the right word for it. Bill, it's not that my politics are the same as his, it's just that he's been a friend."

"Well, I can't say I'm happy to hear that you forgot about us, mate. Not good."

"What can I say. It's unacceptable, I know."

"Is it just your way of letting us know you're not interested?"

"No. I mean not consciously anyway. Not intentionally."

"So are you telling me now that you have some interest?"

"I guess. We've never resolved it, Mel and me. We still have to have that talk but things have been so up in the air with our whole transition. Bill, I promise, we'll make some sort of decision before I leave tomorrow for New Zealand. We'll talk about it today, as a matter of fact. While you're playing golf."

"Before you do, you need to know we are changing our offer."

"Am I being marked down for bad behavior? I would understand if that's the case."

"Crikey, no, on the contrary. Maybe we should but the fact is we are ready to sweeten things a bit. Make them a better fit, both for you and for us. Instead of my old job in sales and marketing, we want to make you Operations Director. You would be number two in the whole organization. We think it makes better use of your strengths. Naturally our compensation offer would reflect your greater responsibilities."

"Thank you for that, Bill, but compensation was never an issue. You were very generous the first time. And I love the new offer. I agree it's more up my alley and I think I would be good at it. I would love it, I'm sure. The only issues are Mel and the kids, one. We love it here but will they take to the idea of living here on a more permanent basis."

"And you?"

"Me too, I guess. I have to think about it."

"You said that is issue one. How about number two?"

"Oh, just my firm, Brock and Case, and my career there. They have been very good to me, Bill. I've been happy there. Probably part of the reason I let this matter slip—unintentionally of course—is that I was not looking for a job. I already had a new job, a job that I was looking forward to."

I did not reveal that I had just told Virge of my misgivings about jumping back into that huge pond. I didn't yet know myself what that meant. I also didn't tell him about my other current existential panic. Pray he never find out. Then I had a thought that made me ask, "What about Gerald, then? Will he move up to your old job? Seems the logical move."

Bill fumbled with his linen napkin and brushed some crumbs from the table. It was obvious that he was uncomfortable with my question.

"Coop," he said, "I shouldn't even be discussing it with you, but the answer is no. We just informed him of that before you and Kevin got here. You may have noticed his demeanor over lunch—not his usual self. We just don't think he's ready for that job. Maybe never will be. I feel bad for him right now but that's the way it is."

I had indeed noticed Gerald's demeanor, but thought it was directed at me. Who knew? Maybe some of it still was, but no, everything was not about me, no matter my paranoia. I felt some little relief. The fact was this news might only add to Gerald's motivation to blow me out of the water with what he knew or thought he knew.

Bill surprised me when he seemed to read my thoughts: "Again, I shouldn't say anything, but Gerald has some problems at home too. I'm only telling you these things because you may have to deal with them when you come aboard."

"His wife?" I blurted, immediately regretting it.

"She's a piece of work. You know her? I say that hoping for your sake that the answer is no."

I explained Virge's flight with her and the phone calls that followed.

"Quite a guy, your Virge. He managed to find trouble before he even got here." Despite his smile, I thought he was being a bit insensitive—both toward Virge and toward Fran Lawson— but told myself that he meant it in only in a good-natured way.

"Enough with the gossip," he said. "Just a tip: she's a story and then some. Stay as far away from her as you can. Not that he has what it takes for the job anyway, but none of that other agro helps."

"I get it," I said. *Already too close for comfort. I'm already a possible victim.*

"So think it over. Talk with Mel. But I'm expecting an answer soon and I hope it's the right one."

I told him I would let him know the next week. Before or after Kooyong?

We joined the others just as they were starting their second coffee and port. I stuck strictly to coffee. Strange game, this golf.

CHAPTER 20

As I drove out to Brighton to join Mel and the kids, I realized that my conversation with Bill didn't ease my mental and emotional maelstrom. Only made it worse, more complicated, more of a total mess. It's always flattering and nice to be wanted but what if it turned out I would be wanted for all the wrong things.

I did my best to join in the family fun at Diane and Kevin's but found it hard to stay fully engaged. Mel noticed, I think, and Diane continued to avoid eye contact with me. She had always been such a flirt but there now was a coolness, a distance. I no longer understood my world at all, as if I were blind, reaching, flailing about, grasping but finding nothing solid to grasp. *Oh, how I long for more days like yesterday.* We had such a wholesome Christmas here just a day ago. It felt like another lifetime.

But I forgot. Diane had already been a little on the cool side yesterday as well. I was losing any ability I ever had to read my life situation, constantly either under or over shooting. Or both.

When Mel brought up my odd behavior later at home, I fell back on my short-timer syndrome story, and how busy and guilty-feeling I was as I prepared to leave. Then I dropped the bomb: the offer from Bill Pawley and Mike Robertson to stay and take a position, a very nice position, with WM-A.

She was beyond stunned. She was staggered, momentarily struck dumb. I poured us some wine and took it into the lounge where she sat on the couch, flummoxed. "My god," she said. "This can't be happening. I mean are they serious? I know you would be wonderful at that job. I can see they would love it. But you? But us? Our plans?

Home? Roger and Brett? Even good old Brock and Case? What will they say? What will they do?"

I could only confirm that I had all the same questions, the same misgivings. I dared not admit to even more gut-wrenching ones than those.

"No wonder you've been acting weird," she said. "Why didn't you tell me sooner."

It was as difficult to explain that to her as it was to Bill Pawley. Who would just forget such an offer, let it slip their mind? It was patently ridiculous. That I had other things, even more fundamental to our lives things, was the only true way to justify it and I couldn't tell anyone about that, least of all Mel.

She was quiet for a while and I was not about to interrupt her silence. After draining her glass of wine, she asked if I would please pour her another. She was wiping away tears when I came back into the room. She took another sip and looked helplessly into my eyes. "So much to think about," she said. "You know, if we stay, that leaves Gregory in the picture."

Jesus, I had forgotten all about Gregory. As intense as that relationship was for all three of us, we also all knew there was a clear point of closure. I confess, I wanted that closure. It was nice while it lasted, more than nice. Exciting. Passionate. Even loving. A fantasy fulfilled. A thrilling clandestine adventure.

And I was ready for it to be over.

What was the alternative if we stayed? A painful break-up? A boring, gradual tapering off? Or worse, a boring sameness over years.

"Jesus, Mel, I confess that question—about Gregory, I mean— did not even occur to me. All that other stuff you said, yes. But I never even thought of him. Him and us, I mean."

"Coop, I love Gregory but I'm not in love with him, not the way I am with you. I went along with it at first mostly for you, for your fantasy. But it turns out it has been a wonderful experience for me too. Beyond the thrill, that is. I have found a new freedom and a more powerful self and I like it. In most ways anyway. Not always. I have had my guilts along the way, some regrets, but the love and passion and even friendship always pushed those negative feelings out of the way. But I'll be honest. I'm ready for it to be over. We had our adventure and it was lovely, but I have been ready to get home and close this chapter. Ready for a normal family life again."

"My exact feelings. Maybe I even grew to love you all the more because of that adventure, but now I just want to love you alone and you to love me alone. All I want are the people in this house right now."

"I long for that. This is crazy, but while I was quiet there for a while and while you were getting my second wine, you wouldn't believe who I was thinking about."

"A lot of candidates. I don't think I could guess beyond the obvious."

"I was thinking of Beth Robertson. Can you imagine?"

I finished my first glass and was ready for another, but I couldn't wait to hear the rest of that story. Why Beth? Why now?

She pointed to her head and laughed. "Coop, I realized something just then that's probably been in there for some time, but now it just popped out so clearly."

"And?"

"And I realized that when I grow up I want to be Beth."

"Beth is a wonderful woman," I said, "but I don't…"

"Me either. Not fully. Yes, she's a wonderful woman, but it's more than that. I don't know exactly what I mean yet, but I know she never had and never would have had a Gregory."

"I'm sure you're right, but…"

"I don't just mean having a three-way affair either. It's not as simple as that. I think it has something to do with the fact that she's a wonderful woman because of a kind of clarity. She can do all the things she does, for others and even for Mike and herself, because she has this clarity about her. I can't explain it any better than that. It's who she is."

"I think I know what you mean and you're right. And we don't have it, do we. You have more than I do but neither of us comes close to Beth. Neither does Mike, it goes without saying."

"Mike? You gotta be kidding me. But that's just it. You know she must know what a shallow man he is. She would even be clear to herself about that and yet he doesn't even make her flinch. She loves her life. She just seems to love life itself. I want to have that clarity, Coop. Gregory is not the only thing in the way and neither are you, my love. I can't have it with the two of you in it, not the both of you anyway. I'm almost positive I could have it with just you. But what I know now is that it has to be something in me—not you, not him, not the kids, not anybody but me. I need to clear some obstacles first, but then I need to find it in myself, by myself."

"I want to help."

"I want you to. I need to find it myself, but I love you and I would love your help."

She finished her second glass while I got mine. When I came back, she was smiling and said, "That was nice. Thank you for listening. Now what the hell are we going to do?"

If only she knew how much more confused the dilemma facing us was. Based solely on what she did know, it was a doozy. She didn't have an inkling of the abyss beyond.

Diane had told her before I did about Kevin and my trip to New Zealand. I said, "After ignoring them for as long as I did, I owe them an answer soon. I told Bill I would let them know as soon as possible after I get back."

She stood and looked out toward our back garden, invisible in the dark, and turned on the outdoor lights. "It's lovely here," she said, "but I can't process any more right now. I need to try and sleep on it if I can."

"Will you sleep with me?"

"If it's just you and if we just sleep."

"It's a deal."

CHAPTER 21

I didn't hesitate long after Kevin and I were airborne for New Zealand before inquiring about Diane. "She seems cool toward me the last couple of days. You know how we normally are. We both have fun flirting, all harmless, I hope you understand. But something was different both for Christmas and again yesterday while you were playing golf."

"That's my doing. Sorry."

"Your doing? I hope you know you have no worries from me. You're not just my colleague, you're my fair dinkum mate. I know you told me she has strayed a few times, but not with me. I swear to that. I would never…"

"I hope not, I really do. But she mentioned something to me about the Robertson's dinner party. And you know I've seen your powers of persuasion at work on our road trips. You're a master."

The flight attendant brought us our ginger and ryes. I was blindsided by Kevin's comments and looked out my window at the sea before I could even take the glass in my hand. "My god, you must be able to see the difference. I don't mess with wives of my friends. I like Diane and don't want to hurt her. Or strain my friendship with you."

"Meaning?"

"If I must, I guess. Yes, there was some footsie between us that night at the Robertson's dinner table, but you have to believe me, it was initiated by her. I pulled away as soon as I knew what was going on."

"And the meeting in the hallway?"

"Oh, man, I even forgot about that. What did she tell you? I was right there when she was coming out of the bathroom. She put her arms around my neck—not the usual innocent hug, either—and I pulled them away and explained, as I am doing with you, that I couldn't get involved that way with the wife of one of my closest friends and colleagues. I wish Virge were here to back me up. He happened to catch the whole thing and asked me about it later."

Kevin took a long drink and looked away from me, toward the windows across the aisle. He then put his hand on my wrist and said, "The damn trouble is, I believe you. I believe you and not my wife. That's a hell of thing to have to admit, isn't it?"

While relieved, I was by no means happy. "Christ, mate, I'm sorry but I'm telling you the truth."

"Naturally she has her own version of the same two incidents, and you were the initiator. I had my doubts right away, given her track record, but again, you have a record of your own. How could I know for sure? How do I know even now?"

"I can only hope, for your sake, let alone my own."

"In either case, I felt I had to ask her to cool it. Like I said, that was my doing."

"I understand completely."

"And, like I say, experience tells me that your version is at least closer to the truth."

I held my glass up, to which he responded with a clink from his. "It's the truth, Kevin. The whole truth and nothing but."

"Now where the fuck do we go from here?"

"We? Which we are talking about? You and me or you and Diane?"

"I mean me and Diane but it makes for a problem for you and me, too, I guess. For your family and mine in the future. Except that you're leaving soon and that could be the end of the issue for you and me. She and I will still be here with the elephant always in the room. Let me tell you something. This sexual revolution business has not been good for my marriage. Diane has taken it to mean she can have sex whenever she wants and with anyone she wants and I'd better not have anything to say about it."

"It can cut both ways, can't it? This sexual revolution business. Remember when we were younger, like in secondary or tertiary

121

school, we used to have to struggle for it, fumble in the back seats of cars, try to get past first base, get elbows in our ribs when we did."

"I guess first base is a baseball thing, but yes, I know what you're saying."

"Then came the pill and women's lib and all— Germaine Greer and her mob, for instance. All of a sudden, women seem to think sex is a good thing and they should go for it."

"Maybe that's been your experience."

"I'm not proud of it all but in the last few years I have experienced what you could call an embarrassment of riches. At some point it seemed like promiscuity was just part of the zeitgeist, part of what we call the sixties, but it's still going on now. I basically stopped asking questions and tried to enjoy the ride."

He smiled and lit another cigarette but it was obvious that he was uncomfortable.

"I'm sorry, but like I said, it cuts both ways. Turns out it's not all peaches and cream. They—women, I mean; some women, I mean—want to set their own rules now. They want to be the aggressors, the hunters. Who was that Greek goddess of the hunt?"

Kevin laughed at me. "Artemis," he said. "The limits of your American education are showing. Artemis was a dedicated virgin and anybody who tried to mess with her came to a violent end."

He was right, I forgot that part. "I admit I was not a mythology major, but you also help make my point. Today's woman—and to be fair, I don't mean all of them—want what they want when they want it or else they're after your balls. It puts men in a double bind."

"Like my wife, you mean."

"Look, I'm sorry, mate. I wasn't thinking of anyone in particular, just a general observation." I touched his glass with mine. "Cheers."

"Cheers," he said, not smiling. I hadn't seen his great smile the whole flight. I could tell he had enough of this topic and I managed to refrain from commenting on how it all impinged on my own marriage. It dawned on me, however, that this whole conversation about Kevin and Diane added another complication for Mel and me and the whole WM-A job offer, making it harder to accept and stay here. And then the whole thing with Fran and Gerald Lawson and what they know or don't know, or at least what they think they know, and what and who they will tell. How does that relate to this thing with Diane, if at all? Yes, they are both about me; me and sex, me and infidelity, me and loyalty, me and Mel, me and WM-A, me and the truth. Jesus, it's getting harder and harder to breathe.

Kevin could see I was stewing. He clinked *my* glass this time and offered me a cigarette. He said, "At least it will be out of the way for you and me soon, so let's put it aside for the rest of this trip. Let's enjoy Wellington and do our usual good job at the plant on Monday. Maybe we'll have some clarity by the time we get back home."

"No worries, she'll be right," I said, and made myself smile.

"Fair dinkum," he said. We both laughed at our Aussiness and waved our glasses in the direction of the flight attendant. She soon brought us two more.

The Melbourne to Wellington flight is not all that long for this part of the world. Some Aussie had once offered me the observation that, at that time, Australia was about ten years behind the States in terms of trends and popular culture, and New Zealand was ten years behind Australia. I didn't know what to make of that. Australia did seem to be a tad lagging, but I wouldn't say ten years, and some might say that was even a good thing. My guess was that the same could be said about the New Zealand assessment. All I knew for sure was that Americans typically yearned to visit both places and loved them if they got there. Maybe they were simply seeking out a simpler, more placid time, consciously or not. I could identify.

Wellington airport did seem a bit dated, your basic functionality. We were met by another plant personnel manager, an older man than Sydney's Noah Gates. Graham Winston was a senior in his job, nearing superannuation status, I presumed. I apologized for getting him out on a late Saturday afternoon but he brushed it off as his pleasure. "We're just glad to have you here. We have some problems and we know it. We know we need some outside help. There is only so much we can do. You'll see what I mean on Monday. Our manufacturing director is eager to spend time with you."

We seemed to be driving forever, out of the city past graceful low green hills dotted with grazing sheep. We finally arrived at our spot for the night, a plain white, clapboard country motel. The Personnel Manager had explained that our own WM-A car was waiting for us there for the weekend. He gave us a marked-up tourist map for a Sunday drive around the south end of the north island along with a hand-drawn map to the plant for Monday.

After checking in, Kevin and I met at the bar alongside the outdoor pool. It was pleasant pastoral evening and we could have been happy just sitting there for the night, at least pretending to be trouble free, but we both said as long as we were only going to be in Wellington for two nights and had only been in New Zealand once before, we would drive into the city. We wanted to see what the nation's capital had to offer on a Saturday night.

Kevin took the wheel as the more experienced down-under wrong-side-of-the-road driver, although I had plenty of practice myself after three years. We arrived in the city about eight and looked for a place to eat. To our increasing incredulity we could find nothing open. The nation's capital city, eight o'clock on a Saturday night and not a restaurant to be found, despite our citizen inquiries. We did manage to find one sandwich shop open with nothing to drink except soda.

By nine-thirty we gave up and drove back out to the motel. There was some sort of party going on. We were told that it was a regular Saturday night event for locals, with a small country band, fiddler and all. People of all ages were there having fun, pitchers of beer on tables around the pool, little kids dressed up, playing, running around the dance floor just inside, giggling. It reminded me of nothing so much as an old rural wedding reception I might have been dragged to as a kid myself, one where I ended up having a great time with all my cousins.

By then we were even more hungry, and we were welcomed to partake in the roast beef, mashed potatoes and gravy dinner, washed down by a wonderful New Zealand ale. A few of the locals must have felt sorry for us eating by ourselves and invited us to their table when we finished. They teased the Aussie and the Yank and told us wonderful stories about local life. It did indeed seem like we had gone back in time and it was just what we both needed in order to sleep in relative peace.

As it was, though, I was once again lonely for Mel. I withdrew a few Polaroids from a pocket of my small suitcase: intimate photos of the three of us, Mel and Gregory and me. Mostly the two of them while I took the pictures. I did get a couple of him and me sharing her, but I they were too close up to show much of the story. They didn't make me horny like they were intended, though. With all the talk of sexual revolution alongside the old-time family atmosphere around the pool, the photos just made me feel sick. I tore them into tiny pieces and flushed them down the toilet.

CHAPTER 22

The pastoral tone of the evening before carried over into Sunday. Before setting out to drive back into Wellington, we each got started with a full New Zealand country breakfast brought to our respective rooms by the breckie lady. From there it was just two blokes motoring around the southern end of the north island, Kevin at the wheel, me navigating from the map given to us by Graham Winston, the plant personnel manager. The city was still quiet on a Sunday morning, but beautiful: the graceful arc of Wellington Harbor bordered by handsome hills, the parliament buildings and the new executive offices being built across the street in the shape of a beehive. Out in the countryside were more miles of the green, sheep-sprinkled hills. We drove through several quiet small towns. Somehow it all made me feel like that Christmas Day with Kevin's family in Brighton. I mentioned it to him again.

"It *was* nice, wasn't it?" he said. "The way things should always be."

"Exactly," I said. After a brief pause, as we drove on, I asked: "Did Lou ever ask you her question?"

"Not sure I know what you mean."

"The other day she asked me where I thought I would be a hundred years from now?"

"Truly? She asked you that? Good on her, but why, I wonder? What did you say? I wouldn't have a clue if she asked me. Dead, I guess. That's all I can think of."

"My first thought too. I gave her some glib answer about fame and fortune or such, but I can't stop thinking about the damned question."

"And what conclusions have you come to?"

"Nothing profound, I'm afraid. Still gnawing on it." The gentle green hills were just the right setting for my thoughts. "After all the bollocks about fame and fortune, I decided, like you, that I would just be dead. So then what? I came to the conclusion that I probably would not be a person people would remember or read about in their history books. That's a pretty small sample, when you really think about all of history, so I'm not likely to be there."

Kevin laughed. "You never know, mate. If anyone could…"

"Bull. Don't kid me. We're both pretty good at what we do, but in a hundred years, nobody will care fuck-all."

"So? What then?"

"Not sure, but I'll tell you what I think so far. I'm thinking that the only things that really matter are the very few people closest to you, your family and close friends. Maybe your work. Not your accomplishments. Nobody is going to care much if at all about your accomplishments even *ten* years from now. I mean the work itself, the day-to-day pride and satisfaction."

"You're over-thinking, aren't you? Quite the philosopher. Good old Lou's got you going. She's a stirrer, that one."

"No doubt. Anyway, that's as far I got on her question."

"Thank god." We both chuckled, but I continued to ponder in silence.

Without my noticing, we had moved from pastoral hills to rugged coastline. My mood was such that I was on the edge of confiding things to Kevin that I had never told anyone, even Mel: things from my childhood, from my teens, more recent things from my life on the road, even my night with Nicole, and even with Mel and Gregory. I was in a vulnerable place, feeling a need to share with someone, someone I could trust. Fortunately I held back, realizing that Kevin was a good friend and not a priest.

The charming Lake Ferry Hotel near the coast was open for Sunday lunch. They served the best fish and chips I've ever eaten, an opinion shared by Kevin. It was busy with locals coming from church and a few other tourists like ourselves, but the food was worth the wait. The couple running the place still found time to chat with us and to suggest a stop in nearby Martinborough to sample some wines, a suggestion we were happy to follow. I was feeling back closer to normal. I wanted simply to enjoy the mellowness of the day.

When we returned to our own hotel in the late afternoon, we stopped at the bar for a cleansing ale, and congratulated ourselves for such a nice Sunday without worrying about our mutual troubles or where we would be in a hundred years. At least we had avoided talking about it.

"We'll be okay," Kevin said, raising his pint. "No worries mate, she'll be right." I took it that "she" was not a reference to anyone in particular, just a neutral pronoun, part of a common Aussie expression meaning "It'll be fine." In this instance, we both knew 'she' might have more specific meanings but we didn't explore. We called it an early night and went to our respective rooms. I mindlessly watched whatever was on the telly. When I woke about 2:30 I turned off the test pattern but couldn't get back to sleep, my brain and gut back to their swirling and churning.

Kevin and I were at our old collaborative best the next day at the plant, listening, observing, silently checking in with each other when we heard or detected some symptomatic component of the plant's dysfunctional systems. It was what we were trained for and what we were good at. The manufacturing manager gave us the usual tour, determined to show us how good he was and how much the plant needed investment. On the latter point, he was quite convincing when he took us out to one of the outside walls of the building itself and pushed it with two hands. We could hardly believe it when the wall well and truly sagged under such slight pressure. He invited us to have a push, and fair dinkum, we moved the bloody wall.

"I've done this same thing with Mike Robertson and Bill Pawley," he said. "Just like you, they shake their heads, can't believe it, but here we are. Wonder what the chairman or president in Detroit would say. One of the biggest, most successful companies in the world."

His point was well taken, but Kevin and I nodded noncommittally. We were consultants. We could and would include it in our report but could promise nothing more. It was indeed a shameful situation.

Kevin went to lunch in the executive dining room with the manager and several of the plant's top team. I said I would like to try eating in the staff canteen with the office workers, the foremen, and lower level staff. The manager asked an industrial relations rep to take me. Rollie Wichert, a personable young man, was surprised by the request but introduced me to his lunchmates at his regular table. People were staring at us.

"This is a big deal," one of the tablemates said. "People like yourself usually eat upstairs. That's why you're getting all the looks."

Rollie laughed and said, "They're probably thinking you came out here to sack them all."

We left for the flight back in the late afternoon, our only sighting of the South Island coming shortly after takeoff. I had never been. Even though we were in the midst of summer, the snowy mountain peaks were magnificent, in their beauty and in their indifference. I put a New Zealand vacation with Mel and the boys on my to-do list.

For most of the two and half hours of our flight to Melbourne, Kevin and I became the team we had forged over the our two years together. We intensely, almost passionately, shared our observations, made lists for our report, tried to go below the surface to pull together some underlying threads that would capture the essence of the dysfunctional organization we had just witnessed. Not just the what's but the why's, the connections, the relationships among the symptomatic problems we had observed or heard about. I was pleased to let Kevin take the lead. He had matured: he had always been first-rate at problem solving specific issues but had grown in his ability develop a working theory to put them into a contextual whole. I took some pride in developing that aspect of his skill set as I watched him begin to sketch out a visual diagram showing the dynamics of the intertwined cause-effect cycles in a systemic way. We factored in the nearly collapsed outer wall, but the diagram put it in the context of other sociotechnical issues. The result was a graphic rat's nest of words and arrows and circles. He volunteered to clean it up tomorrow, after he had a chance to sleep on it, but we were satisfied for the moment that the mess on the paper was a valid representation of the mess we had seen that day. Mike Robertson and Bill Pawley may not be happy when we show them, but they would have to take it seriously.

I relaxed with my ginger and rye and cigarette as he finished up. I would miss him, miss working with him, but he was more than ready to take my job.

It was a satisfying day of work in many ways and we sat back in silence for the last half hour of the flight. That's when the doubts set in. Not doubts about the work we had just done. Doubts about what we would each find when we got back.

We were met by separate drivers to take us to our separate homes. I said, "No worries, mate."

"She'll be right," he said.

We shook on it.

CHAPTER 23

Mel was sitting in our lounge with a glass of wine, watching the ABC evening news when I got to the house. Most of the news still revolved around Gough Whitlam, Sir John Kerr and the newly elected Prime Minister, Malcolm Fraser. I plopped myself down without preliminaries and poured myself a glass from her bottle. I took her hand. She smiled.

"So what's new?" I asked.

She gave me a quick smile and turned off the telly. "Same old same old." she said. "How was your trip?"

I gave her a quick summary. "Kevin and I were solid, I think. I will miss working with him."

"If we go home, you mean?"

"I guess that's what I meant. But honestly, I will miss working with him even if we stay. I would be his client. Strange, huh? Have you thought any more about things?"

"'Things' yes. But no answers have popped up for me yet. You?"

"Same. The truth is I tried not to think about it too much. Tried to stay busy and focused on the job at hand. It all leaked in at times, of course. Especially at two a.m. or so."

"Me too. Incidentally, Gregory called."

I couldn't tell from the clench this gave me whether the very fact of his calling was good or bad news. I asked her.

"Good, mostly. He wants to take us to dinner this week. A farewell dinner, he called it, and I didn't go into our issues around that. It was cute when he emphasized it was just going to be a dinner, that's all. He said he had two important announcements he wanted us to hear first from him before they became public. He wouldn't go into them. Wants them to be a surprise. Good surprises, he said."

"Intriguing," I said. "Any idea?"

"Not at all but he wants to take us to the Fiorentino. I thought you'd like that. I said we could make it Wednesday night. I thought maybe you'd like a night home after your trip and I'm going to be out all day tomorrow with Beth at some function. I thought Wednesday was pretty clear."

My favorite Melbourne restaurant. "Evidently," I smiled in response, "he's not worried about being spotted with us in public at this point."

With some dread, I thought of the tennis quarter finals at Kooyong the next day, but that shouldn't get in the way of a dinner with Gregory. I mentioned both to Mel.

"Oh, that. I did notice that on the calendar when I was talking with him. Kooyong should be fun but I can't really say I'm looking forward to it as much as I should be."

If you only knew how I feel about it.

She took a last sip of her wine and stood. "Dinner's almost ready. Will you round up the boys? I think they're out in back playing some sort of cricket game. I've heard some arguments but nothing violent."

I called out to Roger and Brett and then went up to our room to take off my tie and jacket and run some cold water over my face. When I came down, they were all seated at the table, passing the roast lamb. A nice new bottle of claret was waiting for me to pour. My new Modern Jazz Quartet album *The Last Concert*, was playing. I hoped the title was incorrect.

It was good to be home but again sleep came hard. Added to everything else now was the puzzle of what Gregory had in store for us. Was I eager or anxious?

We soon learned. Mel and I arrived at Fiorentino's first and went upstairs. I had been there often enough I barely noticed the huge murals chock-a-block with famous Renaissance figures.

Gregory arrived with one of the prettiest young blondes my eyes had ever beheld. "Pretty," as trite as it was, was the word that first came to mind. Not sexy, necessarily and certainly not what one might call a "tough blonde." Sweet, maybe, with a lovely smile as Gregory introduced us.

"Vicky Markle," he said, "I want you to meet two of my closest friends."

"I know all about you two," she said, as she shook our hands and sat down. "Gregory is always talking about you."

Obviously that gave Mel and me reason to check eyes. Surely not everything. Gregory was quick to clarify. "Not quite, Vick, there is way too much to tell. I could never cover it all." I gave him points for saying that without really saying anything. I found Mel's hand under the table and gave it a squeeze. She told me later that he did the same with her other hand.

Vicky was as charming in a very simple way as she was pretty, dissolving any awkwardness we felt at meeting her this way, Gregory's bolt from the blue. It turned out that she was a former staff member for a Queensland M.P., and that she and Gregory had known each other for some time. "We've been friends since Gregory came to Canberra, I think, but only just started dating since the election. The thing we've had in common since December 13 is that we are both unemployed. Not a good base to start from, is it?" she laughed.

I couldn't help but notice Stan Smith, the American tennis pro, seated with a group at the next table; a larger, round table. Ordinarily I might be tempted to listen in on their conversation but there was too much going on at our own table for that.

"So you know each other from Canberra," Mel said.

"And politics," I added.

"Which brings me to my other announcement," Gregory said. "In my case, I have found work."

Vicky slapped his arm playfully. "And don't think he isn't letting me know every chance he gets. No, I don't mean that. I think it's wonderful and he's been very thoughtful about it, even a bit humble."

"Humility is not usually my strong suit, as my friends here know," he said. "But it came out of nowhere, a wonderful surprise, and I am truly grateful. Bob Hawke, whom you know I admire but who I thought scarcely knew of my existence, called me to come see him in Canberra. The bloke actually said he thought I was an ALP comer, the kind of person he wants to help rebuild the party after the trouncing we took in the election. He offered me a job as his recruiter, so to speak, with other promising back benchers and potential candidates in the future. Said it could lead to big things for me down the road. To tell you the truth, I couldn't have drawn it up any better."

"My god, that's amazing," I said.

"Isn't it?" chimed Vicky.

Mel reached her hand over to pat his.

"So does that mean you'll be in Canberra?" I asked.

"Pretty much. I'll be based there but I'll have to do a fair amount of travel."

I thought I detected relief in Mel's eyes as she looked my way.

"So we've been busy looking for a place for him," Vicky said, "since he had already given up his old flat there."

"Not that that was a great sacrifice," Mel said.

"So you know his old flat, then," said Vicky, causing the other three of us to scramble some. But Vicky went on without fuss: "You're right. It was a bit of a hovel, wasn't it? We'll do better this time."

"We?" said Gregory, breaking out into a grin and taking her hand.

"Oh, you know what I mean. I've been trying to help him find a place," she explained. "Since we've been here the last few days I've also been helping him get his place in Prahran ready to sell."

"Vicky's been great, I have to say. Don't know what I would do without her... I say, isn't that Stan Smith at the next table?"

"Who's Stan Smith?" Vicky asked.

I answered, "One of our best tennis players. American, I mean. Won the U.S. Open and Wimbledon just a couple of years ago. Slipped a little since then, but still a factor here I suppose."

"Oh my, I didn't know. I don't really follow tennis very much. I do know that the Open is going on this week, but I don't follow it at all."

Our waiter took our wine order. Gregory insisted on choosing it and paying for it. "This night is my treat for the two best Yanks ever to grace our gentle and placid shores."

When the wine came, I raised my glass: "A toast to a gentle and placid Australia."

Mel, who had been quiet for a while, said "Don't we wish," and turned to Gregory. "I couldn't be happier for you. And Vicky, I'm just so glad to meet you. He needs somebody like you to keep his feet on the ground." Gregory smiled at the comment. Vicky looked at him, pleased to be a hit with his friends.

I raised my glass again: "Here's to Vicky and Gregory."

The dinner was up to the high standard of Fiorentino and I was in an amiable mood as we drove the short way home.

"Well, what do you think?" I asked Mel.

"About what? So much to think about these days."

"About Gregory, of course."

"What I think is, Vicky is just adorable, that's what I think. And one more thing: I hope he never tells her the whole story of our relationship, for our sake, but even more for theirs. She couldn't be prettier and sweeter, but she has a strength about her too. She's just what Gregory needs and he seems to know it."

"I agree, but how does that make you feel? A little jealous maybe?"

She looked annoyed at the question but said, "If you must know, I did think about that, about whether I felt or should feel jealous. The answer is no. My feeling is it's time, time for him, time for us to get past all that. It was nice while it lasted, and I hope and trust that we can all remain real friends. But it's time. It's a relief, in fact. Whether or not we leave the country soon, it's a relief. Now we can all get on with normal lives."

I was pleased to feel the same way even when I paid our sitter, Clare. No boyfriend this night. When we were alone, Mel and I joined spontaneously in a deep embrace.

When I woke a little after two a.m., that damned Fran Lawson and her husband Gerald took control and wouldn't let go. I could work with Kevin in the office tomorrow. Then Thursday and the Open.

CHAPTER 24

Thursday dawned ominously hot. The forecast high was forty degrees Celsius, about 104 Fahrenheit. Windless. A perfect day to sit out in the sun for hours with Fran Lawson and her husband at Kooyong. Gerald claimed to have something on me from the hotel bar in Adelaide and the two of them apparently spotted Mel and Gregory "close dancing" when we met over dinner in Waverly back two years ago. Fran had virtually stalked Virge and now was after me. A promising day, indeed.

Mel came downstairs looking cool and lovely in her coral shorts and dressy white tee shirt carrying a plastic container of sunscreen and a white visor. I was wearing my khaki shorts and a white polo shirt, my white bucket hat resting on the coffee table in the lounge. At least we were prepared for the *weather-related* heat.

Despite the weather, Mel was eager for a day at Kooyong. Me, not so much.

The Lawson's were not there when we arrived, and not having our own tickets, we had to stand outside the old concrete stadium for some time, waiting, which only added to my anxiety. We bought some iced tea and looked over items at the souvenir stand without buying anything but a program. Finally Fran showed up alone and gave me an inappropriately big hug.

"I'm so sorry," she said, but had a big grin on her face anyway. "Gerald decided not to come. He's been grumpy lately anyway. He wanted me to make excuses for him but to hell with him. He's not here because he's being an asshole. Oh, is this your wife, Coop?" *Implying?*

"Mel, meet Fran Lawson." I said, without responding to the wife question. "I've told you about Fran." I left it to hang in the air.

We took our tickets from Fran who was looking around to see if there was someone else to give her extra to. Someone she might like to sit with I suppose. In the end, she simply left it at the ticket booth.

Our seats were fine, not great, about two thirds of the way up, on the side of the court near one end-line. I was relieved when Fran chose to sit on the other side of Mel from me, but when she explained that she did it "so we girls can chat and get to know each other," my comfort receded.

There was close to a full house when Evonne Goolagong and Helen Gourlay entered the court to begin warming up. Fran and Mel both ignored me when I pointed out the irony of calling it a warm-up in such heat. The two tennis players looked small and isolated down on the grass court. Both women were Aussies, and strangely enough, married to men named Cawley, although not related. I almost felt sorry for them. I had never heard of Gourlay so I kept my eye on the other end of the court, where Goolagong, dressed in canary yellow, impressed me with her bouncy athleticism.

As it turned out, it was not much of a match. Not that I am an expert on such things, but I think it is fair to say that Gourlay seemed rattled to be on such a big stage facing such a formidable opponent. Goolagong won easily in two sets, 6-3, 6-3. I took advantage of the break before the men's match to go out for a pee and a beer. As I stood drinking from my Styrofoam cup, I didn't see Fran approaching from my rear, a rear she actually pinched, causing me to spill some of my beer and her to let out a raucous laugh.

"Tennis anyone?" she said.

"I don't play," I replied.

"That's not what I hear," she said with more horse laugh. "How about you just buy me a beer."

The truth was that I didn't want to exhibit any sign of friendship in any way. I wanted to dump out the rest of my own beer and return to my seat next to Mel. Instead, in self defense, I bought Fran a beer.

Trying to sort out more precisely where she was coming from, I asked, "What's up, Fran? What are you up to and why?"

She took the cup of beer but didn't drink from it until she had given me a stony stare. After pausing for a big gulp, she laughed again and said, "I don't know what you mean. I just wanted us to get better acquainted. I missed out on Virge, poor guy. You were his friend and I thought you and I…"

"What? You and I what?"

Another laugh and another swig. "Oh, who knows what might happen? You know what I mean? Maybe we could just be friends and see what happens from there."

"Nothing would happen from there," I said as firmly as I could.

"Maybe, maybe not. What am I? Not as cute as that girl in Adelaide?"

"Just a work acquaintance, like I said. A nice girl I had a drink with her and two other friends. That's all."

"My husband commented on just how friendly you were in the bar. Gerald is not here because he's a bit pissed these days. Depressed too. So depressed that he's pissed. I don't know what he might do."

"Like?"

"Like anything. He's said he's not going to take things lying down. He's not just going to ride quietly off into the sunset like they do in your movies."

"Look, I don't know much about Gerald's situation. It's not my business and I sure don't know what it's got to do with me."

"Don't you though? That's not the way he sees it."

"I think I hear a threat there somewhere."

Another laugh. She drained her cup of beer and pulled my arm to her side. "Not from me, dear. Like I say, I just want to be friends."

She was effusive toward Mel when we returned to our seats. In turn Mel was friendly but more restrained. I could not have been more uncomfortable.

The men's match only made things worse. Like the women's, it was an all-Australian quarter final between someone I had heard of,

Tony Roche, and someone I had not, Ray Ruffels. The best I can say from my limited experience is that they both were competent, content to stay back and rally. Ruffels won a tight first set, 7-6, but Roche handily won the second 6-2. While it was difficult for me to concentrate to that point, it became impossible when the third set stretched endlessly to another six-all tie, at which point the crowd merely laughed, neither player managing one point on offense. As the ball moved inexorably back and forth across the net as though by machine, Ruffels squeezed out another 7-6 victory. I tell this now with greater clarity than I found at the moment. The sun was so hot, the game so monotonous, that there was little to no escape from my inner turmoil.

What did this woman want? Her husband? What were they prepared to do? What would I do? What would Mel do? What would happen at Brock and Case or the offer at WM-A? Did any of that matter if I lost Mel and my boys? I could not stand one more set of mind-numbing rallies.

I was afraid Mel might object when I suggested we leave, but she said, "Oh, my god, please. I was afraid you would want to stay to the end. Let's get out of this heat and boredom." She apologized to Fran Lawson, who almost leapt from her seat, ready to go as well.

In spite of its being a very tightly contested match in the year's first major, people were pouring out of the exits. In the exodus I hoped we could separate ourselves from Fran but no such luck. She held my arm tightly and talked nonstop to Mel about the crowd, the boring match, the heat and how nice it was that they could get to know each other. As we finally had to split to go to our respective cars, she surprised Mel by embracing her and kissing her on the cheek before approaching me for the same. I did my best to offer a friendly smile and hold her at arm's length but she managed to pull me close enough to, in lieu of a kiss, whisper in my ear: "We'll stay in touch, won't we?"

Mel had kept moving. I caught up to her and she gave me a puzzled look. I looked away as we hurried silently through the crowd to the car park. Even though a tie-breaking quarterfinal of a major tournament was just getting underway, outgoing traffic was dense enough to keep my attention.

When we were finally clear and driving the short way home, Mel asked, "What the hell was that all about?"

I momentarily considered playing dumb by asking to which "that" she was as referring but thought better of it. "I don't know and I don't think I want to know," I said. "I have thought she was a package of trouble since she got off the plane with Virge. I hope we have seen the last of her, if you want to know the truth."

"She said something to you when she tried to hug you."

"I'm glad you said 'tried.' But yes, she said something about staying in touch."

"Really? Ugh. She tried to charm me all day but I didn't trust her from the moment we met."

"Good instincts," I said. It was true. Mel often had quicker, better judgments about people than I did. Over time I had learned that she was more often right than I was.

"Coop, honey, I think we need a break. We're dealing with too much crap right now. Trying to decide whether you take the job here or go back home with B and C. Too many factors in all that for me to get my head around. Then there's the whole situation with Gregory. And then this, whatever it is: this thing with Fran Lawson and her husband."

"What thing with them?" I asked.

"I don't know, but it doesn't smell right. Let's take the boys to Fiji for a few days or a week and clear our heads."

"Fiji? We always planned to go there on our way home."

"Are we going home or staying here? Where *is* home, anyway?"

"Good question."

CHAPTER 25

Only later did we learn that Ruffels won his match and would go on to lose to John Newcombe in the semis. We saw only news highlights of Goolagong winning the women's championship, and we did catch snatches on the telly of Newcombe's victory over Mark Edmondson in Sunday's heat and wind-plagued finals, glad that we weren't there. We were busy packing for Fiji, so we couldn't watch much of it.

I had cleared things with Bill Pawley and WM-A. We needed some time away to make our decision, I told him, a lot to think about. I would definitely let him know one way or the other when I got back. He seemed very understanding and even gave me some tips on what to see and do in Fiji. "I think you're doing the right thing," he said. "Get away. We want you to be fully sure and committed if you come with us, no second thoughts. But let's be clear, we hope you decide to join us." He couldn't have been nicer about it.

It also happened to be Brett's eleventh birthday. We joked that the trip was in his honor, and though he was skeptical, it made him happy. We did share some cake and allowed him to open a few gifts before leaving for Tullamarine.

In the last couple of years, we had made quick middle-of-the-night fueling stops at Fiji's Nadi airport on our flights across the Pacific from the States, but knew little about the island country; however we had learned from friends that it was a popular holiday location for many Aussies. Some had recommended a family resort called The Fijian, which is where Mel made the reservation.

We checked in at Tullamarine and went to the first-class lounge to wait for our flight announcement. To our surprise, the one other couple waiting there was Evonne Goolagong and Roger Cawley, the Brit she had married only the previous June. She was as pleasant as could be as she let the boys examine her Open trophy. They were on their way to their new home in Naples, Florida, she said, as she graciously accepted congratulations from Mel and me. That would put them on our same flight, I said. After the brief chat we herded the boys to the far side of the room to give the couple some privacy. Cawley had smiled pleasantly through it all but said almost nothing.

Once on the plane, Goolagong immediately pulled a blanket over her head ready to sleep, still hugging her trophy. Cawley read. She didn't stir for the whole leg to Nadi or, for that matter, when we landed and got off.

We arrived at night and took a cab to a local Nadi hotel, too late for the two-hour drive to The Fijian. Since we had crossed the international dateline, we had a second small celebration of Brett's birthday and the gift of a snorkel for the resort.

The shuttle ride the next day was long and arduous, over bumpy roads. We were stopped two times to wait for cattle to cross. The Fijian was totally tropical and casual in setting and appearance. We settled into our comfy villa and changed for the lagoon beach, Brett with snorkel in hand, the rest of us using rentals.

The lagoon temperature was tepid, making it easy to get in, but Brett balked. Now that he was faced with the reality of swimming underwater with real fish, doubts arose. We coaxed him until he started to cry. Mel offered to sit on the beach with him until he was ready while Roger and I tried our luck. The fish were there all right, but the water was not as clear as I'd hoped. A storm the day before had made it murky. Like everything else.

When we came out, Mel had persuaded Brett to try out his new snorkel in the pool. He tried but was not entirely happy with the result, tossing the snorkel down on his chaise after getting out. "No worries, chum," I said. "You'll get it."

"I don't want to get it," he said and lay down to stick his head into his book.

"He'll be fine," Mel laughed. "Give the poor boy some time."

All this was typical, banal family stuff, and I wanted in the worst way simply to enjoy it for just what it was, but no such luck. I wrestled with "the decision" in my head while at the same time the whole Lawson matter was stuck in my gut. The old "who knew what when" set of questions, and what would they do with the information? What would *I* do with it? Would all this wholesome banality I was trying so hard to enjoy be gone forever. I longed for the quotidian like never before.

We lounged away the rest of the day; lunch, sunning, swimming—no more snorkeling for the time being. We cleaned ourselves up for dinner in the large main dining room.

The waiters—for the most part big, handsome black men—wore dark green sarong-like skirts called sulus. Our waiter—Mason, he said his name was—was especially attentive to the boys. At one point Mel got up and followed Mason a few feet from our table and whispered something to him. She came back with a smirk on her face.

When dinner was over, a group of husky skirted men surrounded our table as Mason placed a cake with one candle in front of Brett. The men sang happy birthday in deep voices, finishing with "Happy birthday, dear Houghton." Brett appeared to be surprised, confused and happy all at the same time. Mel was delighted and gently patted our waiter's arm. "Thank you so much," she said. "His name is actually Brett Houghton, but thank you so much. He loved it."

Mason looked perplexed but smiled and said, "You're welcome, ma'am. Happy birthday, Brett Houghton."

Brett soaked it up—his third birthday party in two days. May it last forever.

CHAPTER 26

I smiled to myself as I laid my head on the pillow and fell asleep easily. At three a.m., the swirl was back and I didn't sleep again until about 5:30. Brett was awake and active at 7:30. Roger was desperate for more sleep and did his best to ignore his brother, then scolded him to get back in bed and shut up. As obvious allies of Roger, Mel and I exchanged exasperated looks and closed our eyes, attempting to ignore the hullabaloo. All for nothing. The new day was under way.

After breakfast the boys and I were persuaded by Mel to join her on the shuttle into the nearby town of Sigatoka for shopping. It was mainly a town of tourist shops run by Indo-Fijian merchants. Originally brought to the islands from India by the British colonialists as indentured servants to work in the sugar cane fields, these ethnic Indians, after finally gaining their freedom, had moved into other occupations. In Sigatoka, they seemed to have a monopoly on the small shops, where they were practiced bargainers. We followed Mel around and let her be the negotiator.

At one point I broke off in order to find something for her, some kind of jeweled token of our trip. I was working on reaching agreement on a bracelet when I felt a nudge on my arm, only to see the grinning face of Fran Lawson, who followed up her nudge with a hip bump in the manner of the current dance craze. She looked at the bracelet and sniggered, "Is that for me? How sweet." To the merchant she said, "Make this man pay. He can afford it." Why did every word this woman spoke sound like a threat or a warning? And why was she here, in this shop, now?

I told her I was hoping to buy it for my wife. To the Indian salesman I said, "And no, I can't afford your price. This bracelet is not worth that." Without flinching, he praised the piece further and offered to bring it down to half price, to which I agreed.

As he rang it up and wrapped it in tissue before putting it in a small bag, I asked Fran what in the world she was doing there. It was late morning but I could already smell liquor on her breath.

"Gerald and I have been planning this vacation with our son for a long time. Unfortunately, he's stuck back in Melbourne trying to negotiate a buyout with the company. Not happily I might add. Why? Are you afraid of me or something?"

"A little, I guess."

"We should talk, Coop. In fact, we need to talk. Maybe we can work something out."

"Like?"

"Like a friendly pact, something that will help us both find satisfaction."

A threat? A seductive promise? A seduction threat?

"How do we do that? Do you mean here in Fiji?"

"How about this afternoon. I booked my son for a diving tour. I know you're staying at the same resort we are." Exactly how did she know that? "I'll be in building seven, unit three. We'll work something out. Can you make it around two?"

I felt I had little choice and would have to make some excuse to leave the family. So much for my quotidian fantasies.

At two I left Mel and the boys at the pool with a story about needing to walk for some exercise. Still in my bathers and tee shirt, I found the room and knocked. Fran opened the door with a cigarette in one hand and a glass tumbler two-thirds full of what I presumed to be red wine in the other. She too was in her bathers: a neon coral bikini with a sheer white cover up that didn't quite hide a few folds of flesh. Before I could react she gave me a kiss on the cheek.

"I wasn't sure you'd show," she said.

"I guess I thought I needed to," I said.

Without asking she drew another tumbler of wine for me from

a box on the rattan coffee table. Handing me the glass, she said, "You'll probably think this is just some shitty plonk," Aussie slang for cheap wine. "But what the hell, this is not a charity gala. It's just me and my son and I only let him have one small glass a day."

I sat in the only chair. She, on the other hand, ignored the couch and sat on the side of the bed, crossing her legs. "So," she said, "Here we are. I was beginning to wonder about you two."

"Mel and me you mean?"

"I mean you and your pal Virge. What is it about you two? You both seem to be avoiding me. I mean I know Virge is gone—poor guy—but I was starting to wonder about both of you."

"Wonder what?"

"Like maybe you don't like girls?"

"How do you figure?"

"One: avoiding me. Two, I heard he and the guy he was with when he got mugged were poofs. So, I thought…"

"One: we were not avoiding you. And two: I don't think Virge's wife and kids would agree, and I'm damn well sure about me."

"That right? Good to know." She stood and began to strip the Polynesian batik spread from the bed. It was of the same pattern as the beds in our room. "I always pull the covers off," she said. "Who knows who or what kind of shit has gone on on this bed?" With that, she stretched herself out on the sheets and gulped from her glass, again with her snigger as she looked my way. I tried to ignore her brazenness but it did nothing to reduce my nervousness in even being there.

"I do scare you, don't I?"

"Some. Should I be scared? I don't want to be scared."

"Of me? No, of course not. Not if you play your cards right, anyway."

"Meaning?"

She got out of the bed. "If Mohammed won't…" she said as she got up and walked over to straddle my lap. "All I want is a little companionship, is all. I'm easy to get along with."

I moved my head back from her as far as I could. "Fran, you're fun, I know, but I really do love my wife."

"That's what they all say and maybe you do. I'm not stopping you."

"And Gerald?"

"I don't love Gerald. Gerald is an asshole. I never could figure how he could bullshit his way to the job he has now. They should have fired his ass years ago."

"But…"

"But, shit. He's my husband, the father of my child, and most of all, my meal ticket. I hope the hell he's bullshitting his way to becoming a better meal ticket as I sit here on your lap. Which I kind of like, by the way." With that, she took off her cover up and reached behind her.

"Fran, please, you don't have to do that."

Her bare breasts were now at my eye level. Despite myself, I did feel a stirring. The truth was she was an attractive, if slightly older than I, sexy brunette with nice designer boobs. She leaned in and kissed me with open mouth, into which I instinctively inserted my tongue as my hands went to her all-too-firm breasts. In seconds my brain kicked back in and I pulled and pushed away.

"No, I'm not going any further with this. It's already over the line."

Her smug grin turned into a fake pout. "A girl just has to have fun," she said. "I'm alone, Coop. Alone here, alone in Melbourne. All I want is a little companionship."

"And this is what you call companionship?"

"I'm human, Coop. I have human needs. And from what I've heard, you do too. You love your wife, maybe, but you spread it around some too. Just like me. You are not so innocent now, are you?"

I was relieved when she got off my lap, but only momentarily. Next she was on her knees, moving herself between mine. She rubbed my crotch and said, "Mmm." I wriggled to avoid her touch but there was no way to totally escape. I stood but she just reached for the waistband of my bathing suit and began to tug.

That was enough. I am not normally a passive guy. I didn't get where I got in my career, in my life, by being passive, but so far she had taken the lead. Now enough was enough. I was determined to move away, to get out of there. But she wasn't finished. She caught me off balance and shoved me to my back on the bed before climbing on top of me. She ground her pubis into mine. "No," I said, but she didn't stop. She kissed me again, but I kept my mouth closed and firm. She continued to press her mouth aggressively onto mine. Whatever trace of arousal I had felt earlier was long gone. Now there was only confusion and repulsion along with a taste of fear.

I shoved her body off mine and leapt from the bed. She seemed to give up. She stayed face down, her head in a pillow. I thought she might cry. Instead, she began a series of muffled rants. "You bastard, you dirty bastard. You sonofabitch. You motherfucker." Her head rose and she glared at me. "I was willing to play nice. I have no idea what that asshole of a husband is going to tell people—is telling people right now—but I was willing to play nice, be a friend, even to your wife if I had to. I was willing to work on Gerald. It could have been all friendly-like. We could have had a nice discreet affair and you could have gone on with your life like nothing happened. But now, fuck you. Fuck you. I could have fucked you nice, and believe me, you would have loved it. Loved it. But now I *am* going to fuck you and your life will never be the same again."

"Fran, listen…" I was desperate.

"Listen, shit."

"Fran, I like you."

"Shit."

"I do. You're right. I haven't always behaved like a good husband. But I'm trying now and I like it."

"Fuck you."

"Fran, I would have loved an affair with you. I know we could have had a wonderful time of it. But it's too late now. The time has passed. For both of us. We both have problems and we have to move on if we're going to resolve them."

"Shit. You're all bullshit. I've got you scared now and you'd say anything."

I tried turning the tables. "So what if I'm the one to start talking? What if I tell people what went on here this afternoon? What happens to your life then?"

"You wouldn't. Who'd believe you?"

"Believe you tried to rape me?"

"Rape you? Bullshit. I was just trying to be nice. Besides, like I said, who'd believe you? Me raping a man, a prick like you?" She threw her glass of wine in my face, making a red mess on the bed and the floor. It could have been blood. Fortunately, she didn't throw the glass itself at me or the blood could have been mine.

"All I know," I said, "is that we can hurt each other. Bad. Is that what we want to do?" I had been trained to stay calm when the other person was pissed—that the calm one had the advantage. I was trying but it wasn't easy when calm was not what I was feeling.

"You're pissed off at me, I understand that. Maybe it's my fault. But don't you see, it doesn't matter. We'll both be fucked if we start telling people all we know."

"Bullshit. You're just trying to save your ass."

"I am, but I'm trying to save yours too."

There was a knock on the door.

"Mom, it's me."

Fran's eyes showed panic. "Christ, it's my son. He's not supposed to be back for hours." She grabbed her bikini bra from the floor and hurriedly fastened it. I tried to put the spread back on the bed to cover some of the red stain, but there was nothing to be done about the floor.

"Mom, it's me. Open up."

She yanked on her sheer cover up as though that would result in a picture of modesty. I remained standing as she went to the door. As far as I knew I looked the same as I did when I came in, except for my reddened face, which I could explain as sunburn.

"What the hell has been going on in here?" her son said, his wide eyes sweeping the room.

"This is a friend of mine and your father, Mr. Houghton. He

works with your father sometimes as a consultant." She was talking too fast. "It turns out he and his family are staying here at The Fijian this week too. We were just sharing a glass of wine and I spilled mine. Sorry about the mess."

I held out my hand to the boy. "And this young man is?"

Fran said, "Oh, I'm sorry, this is my son, Keith." I shook his hand. He looked skeptical or maybe it was just shy. "So why are you back so soon," she asked him. "I thought the diving trip didn't get back until dinner time."

He continued to look around the room, not at his mother. I got the feeling that this was not the first time he had discovered her in compromising circumstances. His combined air of suspicion, disappointment, and surrender indicated he had been here before. "We tried," he said. "We got part of the way out and went in the water but it was way too rough. Plus you couldn't see anything anyway. The skipper finally gave up and came back in. We all got vouchers to get our money back or to go another time."

"Well, I'm just glad you're safe." She gave him a hug and looked at me over his shoulder with a pleading look. Pleading for what I wasn't sure. There was so much for which to plead.

"Thank you for the wine," I said. "I'm glad we ran into each other in the store. I hope Mel and our boys and I can get together with you and Keith while we're here. I'm sure the kids would have fun. I was sorry to learn that your husband couldn't make it." I was also talking too fast. "I'm glad we had a chance to talk."

With her back to the boy, Fran gave me a dark look but followed it with a polite hug as I left.

Jesus Christ. I walked back to the pool area in a daze. *What just happened? What next? How long have I been gone? It feels like forever. How will I explain it to Mel?*

My confusion was only enhanced when I found Mel and the guys at a table by the pool eating fresh papaya and laughing at something Brett had done or was doing. They scarcely acknowledged my presence. Mell looked up only enough to register my arrival and patted the seat of the chair next to her, still laughing, her eyes back on a playful Brett. They were obviously having a wonderful time without me, as though nothing unusual had happened in the past hour. Or was it hours?

Mel finally turned her smile my way and patted my hand: "You look flushed. Did you have a good walk?"

CHAPTER 27

After another night of little or no sleep, I made myself get out of bed at five a.m. I brewed a cup of coffee to take out to the patio when I noticed the message light blinking on the phone. I dialed the operator and was told that I had a message to call Kevin ASAP. Now what? I didn't dare call while my family was asleep so I continued out with my coffee. It was barely first light but the heat was already intense. Only a very few resort employees were stirring: cleaning tables, washing down the concrete patio, sweeping concrete paths.

I tried to quiet my mind enough to focus on the facts of my situation, to move into problem-solving mode. No deal. How could I solve a problem if I didn't know what it was? With what and whom I was dealing? I thought if I had a pen and some paper I might start by making a list, but I didn't and I didn't want to go back to the room to get it. It was all an amorphous mess, with tentacles in all directions. I pride myself on my tolerance for ambiguity, but this ambiguity came tied in knots of fear.

I left my empty mug on the patio table and began to walk. I had no idea where I was or where I was headed. I just kept walking out the entrance drive until I came to the main road, such as it was. The sun was coming up and more resort employees were walking in to work, all of them black, wrapped in uniform-patterned sulus from the waist by the men and full length by the women. They were all shapes and sizes but many of the men were handsome and the women beautiful. Most gave me a cursory look and smile, others were so absorbed in conversation with a friend that they were oblivious to me. I walked past the little nine-hole resort golf course where two small boys were scurrying around for who knows why. Looking for golf balls, maybe. Sell them later to the tourists. They looked surprised when they spotted me, and stopped running, turning away and walking more slowly up a fairway.

Mason, our waiter from the first night, also showed surprise when we met going our separate directions. "Good morning, sir, Mr. Houghton," he said. "Up so early? Where are you going, may I ask?"

"I have no idea, Mason. I'm just walking."

His face turned from a curious smile to something more serious. "Be careful, sir," he said. "There is much jungle around here. It is easy to get lost. It can sometimes be dangerous for our guests if they don't know where they are going."

I didn't tell him I was already lost and possibly in danger in a jungle of my own making. I said, "Thank you, Mason. I think I understand all that. I'm about ready to turn around and go back. Just waiting for my family to wake up."

"Your pretty wife and those two little boys. I am sure they will be missing you soon."

I didn't tell him that I was learning they may never miss me at all. That they would go on happily without me.

"Thank you for remembering," I said. "You must see so many people coming and going all the time."

"Yes, sir. But some people are special."

"Yes, they are," I said.

"Have nice walk, Mr. Houghton, sir, but remember what I said. Have a nice day today."

We continued on in our opposite directions. Maybe I wanted to get lost. Maybe I wanted to walk off into the jungle. Maybe I wanted to vanish.

The boys were still in bed but yammering at each other when I got back. Mel, in her nightgown and robe, was in the process of making coffee but looked up with a worried expression.

"Where in the world? You didn't leave note or anything. You had me worried."

"Sorry. I couldn't sleep and went out to drink my coffee on the patio, then decided to take a walk."

"Another walk. Like where do you go on these walks?"

"Just out there in the jungle someplace, someplace where I can get lost, I guess."

She came to me, reached for me, pulling me close for a long, firm embrace. She spoke softly, her face close to mine: "That's just what I was afraid of." When she let go, she looked at me intently. "Seriously. You've been scaring me. What's going on with you?"

Now I pulled her back in. "Just a whole lot of shit. The short-timer thing, I guess, plus *The Decision*," I said, emphasizing it like a book or movie title. "It's a whole tangle of things, Mel, and I don't even know where to grab the thread to begin to try to untangle it."

When I told her about the phone message from Kevin, she tried to minimize my concern, telling me that it was just another typical work "crisis," that Kevin tends to panic over little things, that I was always good at dealing with both crises and Kevin. She was right again, of course. At least about Kevin and me. But she didn't know what she didn't know.

I put off returning his call until after breakfast with the kids.

"Sorry to interrupt your vacation, Coop," he said, "but you need to get back here as soon as you can. There's a firestorm going on here. That's all I can say."

"Firestorm about what?"

"About you for one."

"About me?"

"Yeah, mate. We shouldn't go into it over the phone. You just need to get your arse back here before it hits the news."

"The news?"

"Like I say, it's a firestorm and it's just starting. You *could* call it a shitstorm. That's all I can tell you until you get here. You get yourself to Nadi as soon as possible. We'll send a plane as soon as this call is over."

"What the fuck, mate? Send a plane?"

"Get your arse to Nadi."

Mel heard my end of the call and her expression mirrored the feeling in my gut. I filled her in on the rest of the riddle, but it didn't lessen the riddle, only made her party to it.

"I hope you're right about Kevin's overreaction to things," I said.

"A firestorm? What the hell does that mean?"

"Well, he says it could also be called a shitstorm. Does that clear it up any?" She didn't laugh at my joke.

I got busy packing as Mel and I tried to work out the logistics. Was she going to be coming with me or staying on with the kids and taking the return flight that was already booked? She decided they would stay. They boys were down at the pool so I went down to tell them that I was leaving. They wanted to know what a firestorm was.

So did I.

CHAPTER 28

I got curious looks when I walked through our hall of offices on my way to Kevin's—curious looks that to me only conveyed that something was up, not whether it was good or bad. He stood when he saw me.

"Close the door," he said. The look on his face was more informative than those in the hall. He didn't shake my hand. He lowered his head and shook it in the negative as we both sat.

"What the fuck, Kevin?" I said.

"What the fuck, Coop?" he said. It was clear he was not happy with me. As he began to spin out the story, he showed signs of being angry with me, and at the same time, afraid of me. He hit me hard right away with the fact that Bill Pawley had called to cancel our contract with World Motors-Australia.

Despite my forebodings, I was incredulous. "Canceled? The whole thing? The whole contract?"

"We will have no further work with that company. Jesus Christ, mate, what did you think would happen? They say that you and Mel had some kinky sex thing going with that former M.P. from Prahran, what's his name, something Michel."

"Gregory Michel. He's a friend of ours."

Kevin lowered his head all the way to his desk before looking up at me in bewilderment. "Friend? For Christ sake, a friend? Coop, they have photos."

"What do you mean photos?"

"Someone took pictures of the three of you at Parliament House the day after the election."

"Sure, we helped him clean out his office."

"And then?"

"And then we went to dinner."

"They have pictures of that as well."

"So?"

"Some of the photos show Mel and him canoodling."

"Canoodling? Fuck sake, Kevin, what the hell does that mean?"

"Apparently when you left the table to piss, they were making out."

"Jesus, mate, they were saying goodbye. He took us out for a farewell dinner. We were about to leave the country. We didn't know if we would ever see him again."

"The way Bill told it to me, it didn't look like a little farewell hug and kiss on the cheek."

"I know him and I know my wife. That's what it was. I wasn't there, I guess, but I can guarantee…"

"Bullshit. How about the photos of the three of you going into your room at the Travelodge? Not enough farewells yet? And him coming out of that room the next morning."

Bloody hell. Fight or flight. There seemed to be no escape. I had to fight. "We decided after dinner we weren't ready to say our final goodbyes so we invited him to come up for a drink. It got late and he just crashed on the couch."

"Coop, this is Kevin you're talking to."

"The Kevin I worked with for the past two years? The Kevin whose back I always had and who I always trusted to have mine? The Kevin who now takes the word of I don't know whom over his friend, the friend who got him promoted, by the way?"

He frowned. "Not that I want to sound ungrateful, but I got myself promoted, thank you. As for always having my back, as for our mutual trust, when I let my wife in on some of the story, she took the opportunity to tell me that you made some moves on her more than once. You might guess that didn't make me too happy, or ready to trust your word. Not just about this three-way thing or whatever it is, but about anything. You gotta admit that I watched you make your moves on more than one occasion. That bar maid in Sydney, for example. I admit I admired your skills and determination. But I never thought…"

"It never happened, Kevin. Some lines I never cross. I don't make moves on my friend's wives."

"That sounds nice, but that's not what Diane tells me. And do I believe you or my wife?"

"Kevin, you told me yourself that she has not always been true blue. I will tell you now, even though I don't want to, that she hit on me more than once but I made sure she knew that I wasn't having any—that you were my friend and I couldn't betray that friendship."

"That's supposed to make me feel better? That she was the one making the moves on you? Shit man, she's my wife. What the fuck do you think I'm going to do, divorce her because you tell me that she hit on poor little innocent you, the guy who makes out with any Sheila who'll have him and pimps his wife out to some politician? You want me to believe that you observe some sacred line?"

Calm. Stay calm. Time to calm things down.

Obviously we were making things worse. I couldn't believe how he was spinning the facts. Not Kevin. If Kevin wouldn't believe me, how would I ever convince anyone else? Who else wanted to know, anyway? World Motors, obviously. I would have to call or better yet go see Bill Pawley right away. Maybe I could turn things around there. And their job offer. What about that? It was silly of me to think otherwise for even a minute. But maybe. This was all just circumstantial b.s. that they had. A few photos that could be explained away. No silver bullet. And this thing with Diane was, of course, ridiculous. Why would she even try that story on Kevin? Surely, with a little time, he would be able to see through that. I may be guilty of a lot of things but I was true blue on that one. Surely he would realize that. Maybe not right now, in the heat of the moment, but he would come around. I hated the way he was talking to me now but I just need to stay calm and weather the storm. Firestorm, he called it. Maybe, maybe not. Stay calm.

"Kevin, I know you, and I like you too much to take offense at what you're saying to me, the words you are using, as though I would ever pimp my wife. Pimp, for god's sake. I love my wife even more than you know. And Diane. I can see why that would piss you off, but mate, it didn't happen, and I think someday you will believe me. Someday soon, I hope. Let's all just let up on the pedal for a minute. Everybody, including me, including you. Nothing is the way it seems right now. Let's cool it until it all quiets down and then we'll see what's true and what's not? You called it a firestorm, but if we don't pour more petrol on it, maybe it'll flame out."

I knew "petrol" didn't really fit a nuclear metaphor, but it was the best I could come up with at the moment. I just hoped that Kevin, who was smarter at that stuff than I was, would take it for what it was and let it go.

He stood and paced. I took that as a good sign. He was thinking, reflecting, not just reacting. "There's something else," he said, "something about a you and a girl in a hotel in Adelaide."

Oh, Christ. Oh, Christ. Nicole. Nicky, the cute young secretary from the plant.

"Jesus, Kevin, it was the night the plant management gave me a farewell party. I left the party a little buzzed and when I got to my hotel, there she was, in the bar, with a bloke from industrial relations and another woman. I sat and had a pint with them. That was it."

"You want me to trust you," he said, still pacing, still speaking in a lowered volume, but with a tinge of anger back in his voice. "You want me to believe you about everything—Canberra, Diane, all that."

"Yes, of course I do."

"Bill Pawley's people spoke to that bloke, the one you met with the young women in the bar that night. His name is Reggie, the industrial relations rep. They asked him what happened that night. He spilled everything. He wants to save his job. He told them things didn't end in the bar. He told them about things he witnessed first-hand in your room that night. Good god, you had sex with that girl while he was watching? What the fuck is wrong with you? And now you want me to trust you, to believe you?"

My stomach sunk. I felt sick. I knew that the story was not quite

159

accurate in all its details but picking at it would only make me seem even more ridiculous. Reggie had it close enough for a hanging. The best I could do now was plead.

"Jesus, Kevin, I was drunk. I was celebrating. She was a pretty girl. I never tried to hide that part of me from you. Not every detail he told them was true, but it was true enough. I admit it and I regret it. I regret a lot of things I have done, especially about cheating on Mel. But I am telling you the truth. Most of all, I beg you to believe me about Diane. That is, as you call it, a sacred line."

He stopped and looked at me with dead eyes. "And most of all, that's the part I can't let myself believe. Most of all, I need to believe my wife."

I had nowhere else to go. "I'm sorry, Kevin." I got up to leave, not knowing anything else to say or do for now.

"And, Coop," he said, "that thing you said about how you love Mel more than anything, more than I could know."

"Yes, and it's true."

"Good luck with that now…"

CHAPTER 29

I went to my own office to sort things out. When I opened the door to that familiar setting, I was struck by a spine-chilling cluster of thoughts and questions: At least I still have an office and a desk. For how much longer—today? tomorrow? until we leave for home? Kevin never brought up my status here at Brock and Case, just WM-A. How about this company, my own firm? Was I done for here as well? Did it slip his mind or was it because I was leaving soon and he wouldn't have to deal with it? Were they leaving it up to New York to decide what to do with me? Did I, would I, have a job at all anymore? Did I care? What about Mel and the boys? What about the rest of our lives?

I did not sit comfortably in that luxurious office chair, worthy of a senior partner like myself. I intended to slump back and think, clear my mind, make a plan. Instead I sat uneasily on the edge of the chair, my elbows on the desk, my head in my hands, frightened, angry, on the verge of tears, on the verge of throwing things. Fight or flight?

Flight sounded good. Enticing escape. But there was no place to run. At least for the moment, fight was the only option. But how? Or even who?

I rang Bill Pawley at WM-A. I was told he was tied up. I left a message requesting a return call. The same with Mike Robertson. In desperation, I even rang Reggie Peters in the Adelaide plant. Why had he turned on me with the story about Nicole? He was almost as guilty as I was. At that point, I was grasping at straws. All I could do with Reggie would be to lash out at him. It would do nothing to help me out of the mess. Maybe only further complicate things. But it didn't matter. Lashing out was all I could think to do at the moment; lashing out at anybody and everybody, lashing out at the world. No worries, Reggie was not available, I was informed. I told the woman who answered to forget it, he didn't need to return my call. I was running out of people to call. It was too late in the States to call Virge but I tried anyway. No answer.

People walked by my hall window, most without a glance my way. What did they know? Were they deliberately ignoring my presence or just going about their normal business? There goes Eric Stone from my team. Didn't look in. That has to be classified as strange, or at least unusual. I've been gone and the people on my team would normally at least be checking in with me about my holiday. Wouldn't they? Or would they? I can't even work that one out. I don't even remember how to act normal.

Virge rang back. He had been in bed and just missed picking up my call.

"How are things down under, mate? I must admit I'm glad I'm not there except for missing you, my friend. I'm awake now I guess, so tell me what's up, besides me?"

I filled him in as fully and honestly as I could. I knew he would listen as well and judge me as little as anyone could possibly do. He lived up to my expectations, asking just enough questions, only at appropriate times, and expressing empathy with neither phony approval nor pity for my situation. "Geez, Coop, I get the bind you're in. Almost like me."

"Almost?"

"You don't have a skull fracture yet and haven't been called a queer."

"You're right. I guess that should make me feel better."

"Any idea where you go from here?" he asked.

"Nothing comes to mind. I don't know how to fight what's already out there and who knows what's coming around the corner?"

"Maybe you can join me in Decatur."

"Decatur. What the hell is that?"

"I guess I didn't tell you, did I? I took a new job with the CDC in Atlanta."

"No shit, man. No, you didn't tell me. What's that all about?"

"Roses, remember? I'm going south to spend time with my roses," he laughed. "Or maybe azaleas and dogwood and peach trees. Anything to push back the entropy that has taken control of my life. Seriously, I'm going to perform my analytical shtick on health research. As you probably know, the CDC's located near Emory University. They could probably use Professor Houghton in their business school and you could still do some consulting."

"Nice thought, but if things get any worse, I may be as untouchable there as I am here and maybe in New York."

"Sure hope not. I know you know how to find trouble, my friend, and maybe some of this is just karma, but I also know you have found a way out of big messes before. Even messes of your own making."

"Thanks for that, anyway. But listen, you have just given me the best news I've heard in a while. Congratulations. I couldn't be happier for you. How are Judy and your kids reacting to the move?"

"Judy couldn't be happier. She's tired of the winters up here and once saw Atlanta in April when God was there in full bloom. The kids aren't eager to leave their schools but we are trying to persuade them that they will love it down there. And no lie, I'm going spend as much time as I have available growing roses. We aren't even there yet and I joined the Greater Atlanta Rose Society."

"Of course, you did. When do you move?"

"Due on the job in February, in time to get started on the roses. We just closed on a charmer of a house near Emory."

For that brief moment I was experiencing true delight. "Shall I sing the song?" I started in off-key with "Everything's coming up…"

"Please," Virge interrupted, "you know you can't sing a lick. Besides, in your spot, that song don't make no sense."

"Yeah, thanks for reminding me." I sank back into reality. But stored somewhere inside me was the knowledge that delight was still, somehow, a possibility. I took a breath and thanked him for talking with me, listening to me. I told him I was happy for him.

"I'm pulling for you, Coop. Talk to you soon, I hope."

I hated to end the call. Now what?

I got in my car and headed across the Yarra to WM-A head-quarters. What good it would do I had no idea. I was moving in a dark void, desperate to act. I stopped at the security desk and told sergeant Tiller I needed to see either Bill Pawley or Mike Robertson. I had checked in at that desk many times and the security people all knew me. Tiller greeted me politely before picking up a clipboard and checking a list on it. Unusual. "I'm sorry, Mr. Houghton, I can't let you up there. Don't ask me why. Those are just my orders."

What else did I think was going to happen?

Mel wasn't home. Still in Fiji. A small break. I could go home without having to face her yet.

Home felt empty and of little comfort. I dumped my stuff in our bedroom. *Our bedroom.* Downstairs I grabbed a can of Melbourne Bitter from the fridge and sat down in my chair in the empty living room. I lit a cigarette. Some guys might crack a bottle of whiskey at this point and get stinking drunk. I didn't want to get stinking drunk. That sounded awful. I didn't want to make myself even sicker. When I was younger, in college for example, if I was feeling worried or depressed about something, I would just lie down and go to sleep. I knew that didn't work anymore. What was I going to do after I finished the beer?

The phone rang. Maybe Mel's calling, curious to know why I was so urgently called back to Melbourne.

"Mr. Houghton?" A woman's voice. "Mr. Ellingsworth would like to see you as soon as possible." Todd Ellingsworth was the top legal counsel in our Australian office. Why the hell does he want to see me? I asked the woman what he wanted to see me about but she said she didn't know.

I could be back there in about twenty minutes. I paused for a sip of beer and said, "How about first thing tomorrow morning?" I don't know what he wants but it can't be good. Better I sleep on it. Like college.

She checked Ellingsworth's schedule and said, "I will let him know."

I turned on the TV news. More on Frasier's new Lib government but nothing earth shaking. The news reader then said, "Stay tuned for the latest on the Canberra sex scandal right after this." This was the not the ABC but a channel controlled by Citizen Press, the company that put out the Sunday tabloid *The Canberra Mirror*. Both the paper and its radio and TV cousins thrived on the seamy side of things. It seemed like a scandal a day, so I ignored their tease, never for a moment thinking it had anything to do with me.

I turned off the telly and made myself some scrambled eggs and started in on another beer. Mel called from Fiji while I was eating.

"So what was all that urgency about?" she asked.

"Hopefully nothing but we don't know for sure yet," I lied. "Kevin says that WM-A is upset about something and threatening to drop us. I'm going to look into it tomorrow and try to smooth things over. It's not the first time."

"Really?"

"Oh, sure, clients don't always love their consultants. You know that."

"But WM-A?"

"They've been our best client for a long time, sure, but there are always ups and downs. We'll see."

"So you're going to meet them tomorrow. No chance of your coming back here."

"Afraid not, hon. I don't think they'd charter a plane to bring me back anyway."

She even laughed a little.

"The boys miss you. They were enjoying that little bit of time they were having with their father."

"Just the boys?"

"You know what I mean. The truth is, I miss you more than I ever have in all your traveling, Coop. I am so ready for us to get a new start, I can't tell you."

Jesus.

When I didn't answer right away, she said, "Did you hear what I said?"

"I'm sorry, honey. I hear you. I'm ready for a new start too. More than you know."

"Take care of that shitstorm tomorrow and let's get going. Let's go home."

"Sounds great to me right now. Mel, I love you. Please always know that."

"I mean home, Coop, really home. Let's forget anything about staying in Australia. Maybe this trouble with WM-A will make that decision for us. Who knows? Goodnight, sweetheart. We'll be home soon."

I left the dirty dishes in the sink and got ready for bed. It was only seven o'clock but I was ripe for some much needed sleep. The phone rang but I didn't answer. This day's over. It'll wait.

CHAPTER 30

Sleeping was out of the question.

I was getting dressed for my morning meeting with Todd Ellingsworth when the phone rang. "Did you see it?" It was Gregory.

What "it"? Was he talking about the scandal on the news, the story I didn't watch? Was it about Gregory and Mel and me? Jesus.

"I've been gone," I said. "Mel and the kids and I have been in Fiji, so no, I guess I didn't see whatever it is you're talking about."

"Well don't believe everything you hear, okay? It's a shitty scandal sheet story about…"

Here we go.

"…Vicky. Mostly Vicky and some about me. All over the tube last night. They picked the story up from that rag in Canberra, *The Mirror*. Now this morning all the papers have it. Even a short article on the second page of *The Age.*"

Should I be relieved, I asked myself.

"Vicky and you? Why, what do they care about Vicky and you?"

"Good question. They are claiming that Vicky and I have been in a long-time affair beginning when she was still on the staff of the M.P. from Gold Coast, Del Bryant, and that she was having an affair with him at the same time."

"You mean like…"

"No, no, it's nothing like with you and Mel. Bryant's wife is divorcing him over what she calls his womanizing. She has accused Vicky on her list of known co-respondents. Says Vicky and Del had an affair while she was working for him and at the same time she was with me."

"Is that true?"

"Not really. She did once admit to me that the two of them had sex one night in his office after working late on some legislative project and having a few drinks along the way. She claims, and I believe her, that that was the only time. That was before she and I started dating."

"And you believe her?"

"Certainly. Listen, Bryant was a known quantity around the capital. His wife is right about him. He has been accused by several women of sexual harassment but always managed to get it covered up. Until now, that is. Beware the vengeful wife. My only concern is Vicky. She tried to quit her job after that but he almost blackmailed her into staying. Said he would tell everyone that she seduced him. She officially stayed on but didn't really work there anymore, didn't even go into the office most days, just enough to keep up some degree of appearances. She and I got together about that time. I hate that she is getting her name dragged through the mud for a one-time indiscretion. She is now being portrayed in the news as some sort of whore who broke up a marriage. Obviously I'm not happy that my name is now associated with the whole bloody mess. We're doing our best to help each other get through it but I gotta tell you, it's a shitstorm right now. We're barely hanging on and who knows what's coming next?"

That shitstorm thing again.

"I hope you don't mean…"

"Me too, Coop, me too. It's all bullshit anyway. Hopefully the whole truth will come out and it will stop there, or at least this will all just fade away with the next round of titillating stories. My new boss, Hawke, is not happy with me but he has his own rumors to deal with, his drinking and his own reputed wandering eye. I'm hoping I don't lose my new job before I am even officially announced."

Gregory and Vicky. Is that it?

"So sorry, mate," I said. "Hope it gets cleared up soon. That's a shame."

"It will. Just thought I owed you and Mel a call."

"Thanks for that. Mel's still in Fiji. Heads home tomorrow. Right now I'm getting ready for an early morning meeting with the lawyers at my firm."

"Lawyers?"

"I'm sure it's nothing but I gotta run. Again, I'm really sorry. Hang in there."

"You too, Coop. We'll be in touch."

Ellingsworth's secretary directed me to the legal department's conference room where he sat on one side of the table with Geoff Brown of his law staff on one side of him and Pamela Dorsett from the P.R. department on the other. He smiled and gestured for me to sit down across from them. The whole set up did nothing to relieve my feelings of vulnerability. Especially with Pamela there. I knew her as very capable but also very much a Muriel Mitchell-style feminist.

"Good morning, Coop," Todd said. He seemed more amiable than I had expected. "This is a hell of a mess, isn't it? That's too bad."

You could say that.

"Which mess," I asked. "Don't we always have messes to clean up? That's why we make the big bucks, isn't it?"

They gave each other puzzled looks.

Todd smiled again and said, "Look, Coop, you're in a jam and it puts the firm in a jam. You know that more than anybody. We're just here to help."

Now I smiled although it may have been more of a smirk. "I've heard those same words from legal before. It usually means trouble." It was an old lawyer joke but it fell completely flat. No more smiles from that side of the table.

Todd's tone turned serious: "I think we deserve better than that from you, mate. I think we have helped you a lot."

He had me there. He was right. I had more cooperation from his legal department than any place I had ever worked. "I'm sorry, Todd. I was just making a bad lawyer joke. So talk to me."

"Kevin told us all he knows about your precarious situation. We want to make it all go away."

Does that really mean make ME go away?

"You're in trouble, mate, and that means the firm is in trouble. Let's not make light of it but we do think we can work our way out of it. We're already moving on it. Look, let's be frank. It seems you have not always kept your dick in your pants, shall we say? Can we just talk frankly among us boys?" Almost instantaneously Pamala's face morphed from her professional forced smile to a scowl and back again. "If you will tell us honestly all you can, we can try to see if we are covering all the bases."

A baseball expression. *How would that translate into cricket talk? Focus, man, focus.* I sat back in my chair and decided not to play games. I needed to work with these people. Not much choice.

"Okay, I'm yours. It's pretty hard for me right now to know just who I can trust these days but to be fair, Todd, you have always played it pretty straight with me. I'll be as straight with you as I can. Tell me what you know and what you think you know and I will try to fill in the blanks. Let me start by confessing that you're right about my dick."

He smiled but the other two remained impassive. I found myself on the defensive again, my attempts at humor falling flat. "Let me also say, though, that it is really no laughing matter and I am not proud of it. I'm not some macho bloke who brags about his prowess."

"Really," said Pamela Dorsett, a statement, not a question. "I'm glad to hear it, Coop. I've admired your work over the last couple of years, but I admit I've had some doubts about your character with all that's been coming in."

Todd said, "Coop, you have been great for this firm. It has been a pleasure to work with you. We *all* respect and admire you. But we have a bit of a crisis on our hands, you do and we do. We need to find a way to quiet the storm."

"Agreed," I said. "If there's a way out, let's hear it. I'm certainly not seeing it. To be completely honest, I'm drowning."

Todd continued. "So what does 'out' mean to you, Coop. Tell us what you want."

"Does it matter at this point—what I want? 'Out' is all I know."

Pamela replied with another question: "Does 'out' mean out of the firm, out of your marriage, out of Australia? Again, we want to help, but help us by being clear about what you want."

"Okay, for sure, I do not want to be out of my marriage but that too may not be in my control. The number one thing I want is to keep my marriage and my family. As for the firm, if there is any way, I want to stay with B&C, and at this point, I guess my only chance with that is to get out of Australia and take the new job in New York. Again, I don't know if that is up to me anymore. Obviously, I am pretty vulnerable on all fronts."

"Your marriage is your business," Pamela said. "What you tell your wife is up to you. I personally would be pretty upset if I were in her spot, but like I say, that's between you and her. As for the firm, it will do no good for us or you if this gets out in public. I have talked with my counterpart in WM-A, and he agrees. They want to keep a lid on it as well. If that is going to be possible, and that's a big if. The only bet I would place is on the good old boys' culture you blokes have created. But I'm not a punter and I wouldn't even put a lot of hope in that. You're in pretty deep, I'm afraid."

I'll give her credit. I could see that she was trying her best to stay professional, but it was clear it was not easy for her.

Todd intervened to calm things down. "Coop, we've not only talked with Kevin, but as Pamela says, we also heard from WM-A. And we've talked with a Nicole Bartman from their Adelaide plant as well as Reggie Peters and some of the other plant management. [Shit!] Except for Nicole, they all spoke very highly of you. Nicole not so much. She's not happy getting dragged into the mess and she as much as said she thought you were a jerk."

I was sure Pamela repressed a smile at the comment.

"And the bartender in Sydney," Todd resumes. "Robin, I think her name is. She's the one Kevin told us about. I have to admit, she's also not happy about the possibility of her name getting out there but she strongly maintains that you are one of the good guys. I'll read you her exact words: 'He's a sweet bloke, no matter what. I felt so sorry for him stuck out here in Australia for years with his family back in America. He seemed so lonely.'" A lie I had used to help get her into bed. Successful then but so fucking pathetic now.

Pamela looked away while Geoff just stared down at the papers in front of him.

"I don't suppose her endorsement will help me very much," I said, again trying to lighten things a bit. Again, it didn't go over.

"Listen, Coop," Pamela said, "I want to do what I can for the firm, which I accept means doing what I can for you, but your snarky comments don't help anyone—not us, not you. This is a serious matter that affects all of us. You need to know that I'm working my arse off to cover yours and to protect the rest of us from this shitstorm. If I were you, I'd go a bit easy." Brown nodded but said nothing.

"I didn't mean anything," I said.

Pamela shook her head and gave me her best smile, which was quite nice indeed. "Exactly," she said.

Ellingsworth took over again. He explained that they had met with Nicole and Robin and both had agreed to a $50,000 settlement and signed a nondisclosure agreement with the stipulation that they would not ever be allowed to reveal any of the circumstances. Reggie was happy just to keep his job and happily signed an NDA. They had only been able to contact Gregory by phone, but he assured them that he had "no bloody reason" ever to speak of it, that he "loved and respected you and Mel" too much to ever speak of it, and that he was already in too much of a pickle of his own to ever speak of it.

I sat back and sighed. I stood and paced for a minute. Thank god. Todd smiled but the other two remained sober, and after a quick glance my way, averted their eyes and looked down.

I sat back down and said, "Thank you, Todd. Don't get me wrong, I am very grateful, but I still feel terrible. I'm relieved but I am also deeply ashamed and sorry for what I have put you and our firm through, how I risked not only myself but our business, as well as all these other people." Pamela nodded and I couldn't blame her.

I said, "And then there's the little matter of…"

"Your job. Knowing you as I do," Todd said, "I'm sure your job is no little matter to you. You're good at what you do, Coop, and everybody here and in New York knows that. They want this mess to go away but that doesn't mean they want you to go away with it. New York wants you in your new job as soon as you can get there. They want you out of here as soon as you and Mel can be ready to go. Best for all concerned. They have a lot invested in you and you have always—until now, maybe—delivered the goods. They expressed hope that you have learned some lessons but they look forward to your jumping into your new job there right away."

"That's great news," I said. I could smile for a moment. "Again, I am very relieved and grateful, but that isn't what I was going to say. I meant the little matter of my wife. She is my best friend and I cheated on her. She is not going to be happy even after I explain all this to her. I have no idea what I'm going to say to her."

Geoff Brown spoke for the first time all morning. "We need you to sign these, Mr. Houghton." He shoved some papers across the table. I wondered if I was being asked to sign an NDA myself, but they were just standard documents covering my transfer and move back to the states.

We all stood and shook hands, even Brown, sweaty palm and all. Pamela surprised me by holding my hand with both of hers and giving it a slight squeeze. I sensed pity. "One more thing," Todd said. "Just a heads up. Kevin is very pissed at you, more than I would have thought. I know you two were close both in and outside of work. I was somewhat surprised but my guess is he feels some degree of personal betrayal. Just thought you should know."

"I got some of that from him yesterday myself. I hope someday we can work it out but I don't think now is the right time."

"You're probably right. So anyway, take care and good luck."

"No worries," I said.

I went to my office and asked Doris to find a box for my things. She wiped away tears and stood. I sorted through my files for a few I thought I needed. When Doris handed me a box the look on her face made me want to cry as well. We hugged without a word and she went back to her desk. I put the files and some personal items in the box and looked around for what I might be missing. Just the big coffee table book with photos of Australia and Australians given to me by the Adelaide management team. It was too big for the box so I took it in one hand and pulled it up under my arm while I grabbed the box with the other and walked out. Doris tucked an envelope into the box and wished me luck. "You're a fair-dinkum boss, Coop," she said, and that was it.

I was stopped in the hall by Lou Sand, her cigarette dangling from her lips as she took the box from me. "Here, let me have that," she said. "You have enough of a load right now. I'll walk you to your car." Got my back again. They don't make any more Lou Sands.

"Yer an arsehole, you know that, mate?" she said, firmly but with a smidgen of humor.

"Never one to mince words, are you?"

"Yer in the shitter, now, as you should be. But you'll get out of it. You're too smart and talented for this to stop you."

"I wish I had your confidence right now," I said.

"You have had and you will have. I can't say I'm not disappointed in you. Even pissed at you. But I also can't say I'm too surprised. Smart, talented men don't always know what's good for them. Or what's right for other people either. Things come too easy for them. And they often treat women as if they owned them."

I couldn't argue and didn't. It was not the way I wanted to see myself but I was in no position to dispute her version. "Lou, as always, you're spot on. And let me tell you, I no longer have any bloody idea where I'll be a hundred years from now. At the moment I'm not sure about tonight."

She put the box on my back seat and shook my hand. No hugs from Lou. "You are basically a good man, Coop Houghton. I wish you were even better. I enjoyed our work together. But let me tell you something."

"Tell me, my friend. I trust your truth."

"Get some help. Help with your womanizing, I mean. You really do need to fix that and you aren't going to be able to fix it with just good intentions or will power. Get yourself some help."

"I suppose you're right."

"You know I'm right, shithead. And good luck in America, mate." She turned and went into our office building without looking back.

CHAPTER 31

Our house was full of empty. I lit a cigarette, grabbed a Bitter from the fridge, and wandered around, finally settling in my chair in the lounge just long enough to finish the beer and snuff out the smoke before I abruptly stood and went for another beer. I stopped and poured myself a scotch instead. I had escaped from the humiliation of public embarrassment and still had my new job in New York. All good. But...

Do I tell Mel anything or not? If so, how much? How far back? Do I tell her my second cousin made me jack him off when I was ten or eleven? Tried to make me take him in my mouth but I fought him off. Do I tell her that? Or even before that when Jerry Morse from across the street showed me what masturbation was? Or how, once into puberty, I did it myself incessantly, almost anywhere and everywhere, reaching orgasm for the first time when a friend showed me one of those little eight-page comic books I now know as Tijuana Bibles (which also may have given rise to my voyeuristic tendencies, now mostly manifest in watching her have sex with Gregory)? Or how my girlfriend Jane and I experimented in the eighth and ninth grades; Jane, who was pretty and sweet, the nicest and most popular girl in our junior high until I talked about our fumblings to the guys in the locker room after basketball practice and basically ruined her reputation forever? Do I mention that even while Jane and I were "going steady" I sometimes fooled around with other girls? Should she know that, while I never again engaged in locker room talk, the rest of the pattern has pretty much persisted to the present time?

Confessing all this to Mel now would only hurt her and very likely permanently hurt, if not completely destroy, our marriage. It would be selfish of me to tell her.

I felt the cool glass in my hand. The scotch was gone but some ice remained, ice which I began to crunch, my head leaning back into the chair. I have heard that old people say, as they look back, that they have no regrets about the things they've done, only about the things they didn't do. I have both. I regret what I did to Jane. I always will. Now in middle age, I regret a lot of things I've done. Mel only knows some of them.

I had no appetite for dinner. I fixed myself another scotch and took it to our bedroom. I was asleep before I finished it.

The phone rang sometime later. Mel said, "You sound like you were asleep. It's still early there, isn't it? I wasn't sure from this side of the date line."

I told her I had skipped dinner and lay down for a nap. I didn't mention the scotch. She said they were coming home tomorrow, a day early. "The boys say they really miss you, can you believe it? They say it's not so much fun without you."

"The boys said that? Incredible."

"They're right, you know. It's never as much fun without you."

Pause. "No fun here, either," I said.

"Coop, honey, I love you."

"I really love you too. I mean I really love you."

I tried without success to sleep again.

My senior year of high school basketball. Third game, after two poor show-ings on my part. Our first home game. Cross-town rivals. Took a pass on the opening tip and sprinted, with one dribble, toward our basket, my feet alive, rising, floating in the air, a finger roll over the front to the rim. Two points in the opening seconds of the game. That floating-on-air memory captured in the amber of my mind.

My feet never soared again that whole season. An uncontrollable spiral down to and out the bottom. Didn't even make the traveling squad to the final game. Guys I had played ahead of from junior high made that trip and played while I stayed home. Tacked my jock strap with a note to the team bulletin board so they would see it when they got back on the bus: "Coop Houghton hangs it up."

Now, all these years later, I can't let it go and ridiculously spend many wakeful hours trying to figure out what went wrong and who or what to blame. But, whenever I get to the end of this recurring nighttime reverie, I always come to the same trite conclusion: I didn't work hard enough. I have taken that lesson into every endeavor since. Work hard. Stay determined. Persist. Such clichés, but they have worked very well for me. Still, it's the one year of my life I wish I could take over. To this day. Or at least until now.

How do those lessons apply to the mess I'm in now? Fuck all.

Sometime I must have fallen asleep. The phone rang shortly after eight. I thought it might be Mel calling with her flight itinerary but it was Gregory. "Afraid the shit's hit the fan again, Coop."

CHAPTER 32

"It's Vicky, again," Gregory said. "I can't tell you how that part makes me feel right now."

"That part?"

"Vicky, I mean. It hit the papers and the TV news this morning. Follow-up shit to that other story only worse. Turns out that Vicky and Del Bryant had more going on than she told me. Turns out that she is a liar *and* a cheat. Turns out that she's pregnant with his kid."

"Jesus Christ, Gregory. You didn't know?"

Maybe nobody except Vicky knew or ever will know about most of it. About her and who or what she is or was or does. Maybe not even Vicky. How many times must we learn that people are not as simple as they seem on the surface. We can't know them without knowing their back stories and their stories are always more complex than we think. Even Mel, who always amazes me with her ability to size people up on short acquaintance, blew this one. She thought Vicky was so sweet and such a good find for our friend. We always think we need to know cause and effect so we can make things make sense. Why did so-and-so commit suicide? Was there a note? We think they must have had a reason, a clear cause. Or a childhood trauma, that once uncovered, would explain a person's whole life or even their death. So Freudian. But so much might just be random. Most of the time we never find out, perhaps because there never was a clear reason to begin with. Or it seemed like a good idea at the time. Who knows why Vicky did what she did, or is who she is?

I was still grappling with this riddle when Gregory said, "I didn't know any of it. I told you before, she had admitted to a one-time thing with him, but apparently it went on longer than that. I certainly didn't know she was pregnant, for one thing, and if I had, I

178

might have thought it was mine and would have been happy about it. Like I said, I can't tell you how well and truly humiliated I feel. Betrayed would be too mild. I'm pissed at her, sad for her, pissed at Bryant, pissed at those pricks in the press, and maybe most of all, pissed at myself. What's really weird is that when I first heard the truth about Vicky, I was shattered but—and you're the only one I could tell this—I was also a little turned on."

As shocking as this was to hear, and indeed it shocked me, at the same time I could relate. How sick it all was, we all were.

"You still there?" Gregory asked.

"Sort of," I said. "What the fuck is the matter with us is what I was thinking."

"I get it. But Coop?"

"I'm here."

"I said that was the part about Vicky."

"There's another part?" I wanted to hang up, pull the covers over my head.

"I hate to tell you but you and Mel are now involved. The three of us. Somebody's talking. It seems there's no privacy anymore. Eyes everywhere."

My stomach took another lurch. Who's talking? Kevin pissed about Diane and me? Gerald Lawson bitter about losing his job? His wife, Fran? She was capable of anything. "I have some thoughts on who it might be, some candidates. What are they saying—the papers, I mean?"

"Anonymous source or sources, as you would expect. They, whoever they are, report having seen us at that place out in Waverly our first night together and there are photos of us going into the hotel in Canberra. Some anonymous employee of the Travelodge says the three of us spent the night there in the same room."

I could hardly think but I managed to say, "All circumstantial."

"Right. But they won't quit there, the bastards. With Bryant and me involved plus all the political bullshit of the last few months in Canberra, the ratbag so-called investigative reporters are tasting blood. It starts with that Canberra rag, *The Mirror*, but then all the others pick it up and run with it. Like I say, nothing is private."

"What do we do, where do we go from here, Gregory? I'm a pretty good problem solver. I'm used to taking action when things are in a mess. But these are waters I don't swim in. You're the public figure. You're the lawyer. What the hell do we do, just lie back and let ourselves get raped?" I regretted the analogy the minute I said it. The best thing I could think of is that we, Mel and me, had the out of a quick escape to the States. It couldn't happen fast enough. I told Gregory.

"I reckon that might help a little, but mate, I don't think they're going to let go of this. You may find the paparazzi waiting for you when you get off the plane in New York. I hate to say that, but it could work that way."

Damn it, he could be right. "So what then?"

"Blast if I know. I'm going to call my friend, Jim Cairns. He's had more experience dealing with this kind of bullocks than anyone I know. We might be small potatoes compared to him."

That didn't give me the slightest comfort. I realized that Gregory, try as he might, was not going to be a lot of help. I would have to figure something out myself. At that moment I was coming up well and truly empty, but I had no one else to turn to. I have always tried to be the cause rather than the effect. How do I get ahead of this one? It was coming at me from all directions at once. I had no clue but I knew it would have to be me. Not right now. Right now was just raw feelings. Near panic. I needed to back away and come up with something. The only other person I could go to was Mel. I needed Mel but that was not without its own risks.

"You there, Coop?" Gregory said, breaking me from my reverie. "Listen, I know this is a lot to take in. I hate to say it but you had better read the papers, catch up on the news. Don't know what else to tell you, but please know that you and Mel are in my thoughts. I'll do what I can."

I went downstairs, made some coffee and tried to think. "Thinking stinks." I read that somewhere (Hemingway?). Turns out it's true, At least now. At least in this case. I was "gob smacked," as they say out here. Try as I might, I couldn't apply the skills that made me a successful consultant. Feelings took over, overwhelming any attempt at rational thought. I was scared. I'm normally not a crier but gave in and lay on the sofa on my back, allowing my eyes to well up, then rolled over face down and sobbed into a cushion. I groaned aloud, my voice muffled by the cushion. *Is this what they call a breakdown?*

Eventually I ran out of tears. I grew sick of wallowing in self-pity. I had to pick Mel and the boys up at the airport around 1:30 and needed at least the appearance self-respect. I showered and dressed and drove a short way toward the Toorak business section for lunch.

CHAPTER 33

I couldn't help it: Sheilas on the footpath in their light summer dresses, their mini skirts; even their long but form-fitting batik dresses caught my attention, grabbed my libido, a phenomenon that should have been impossible in my shameful misery. It seemed like they were all blondes and looked like Olivia Newton-John. *Mel, I honestly love you.* If she had been there, she would have pointed out that the blokes looked pretty good too, strapping blokes with their shirts unbuttoned enough to show the gold or animal tooth necklaces on their hairy chests. It was the mid-nineteen-seventies in Australia but still felt like the sixties. That's it. THE SIXTIES. The sixties were the only reason I could think of for the trouble I was in. Looking back, I know now that much of what we think of as "the sixties" really happened in the seventies. Especially out here. As it turned out, I experienced two decades of the sixties, twenty years of fucking around.

I meant to stop at one of the trendy cafes in Toorak but decided that didn't fit the occasion. I drove on into Prahran for some Greek food at a store front near the market. The gyro was perfect for my mood but the onions served to remind me of my reflux from last night, which reminded me of my emotional pain, which made the tears rise again. I sat there, a grown man trying to hide his weepy eyes, with other people eating their tzatziki and their Greek salads. Did they see? Had they read the papers, seen the news? Did they recognize me?

I hadn't yet read or viewed any news myself and didn't want to. Maybe at the airport while I wait for their plane to arrive. Maybe I should know something before Mel does. We would have to talk about things. I no longer had any choice. But what things? How much is coming out in public? How much do I come out in private?

Roger and Brett seemed delighted to see me waiting at the gate. Brett gave me a big hug and said, "We missed you, Dad. It was more fun when you were there." Roger was a bit more reserved but voiced general agreement with his brother. Waiting her adult turn, Mel melted into my arms.

"You have no idea," she whispered in my ear. "We all missed you so. You won't believe it but they both cried when you had to leave."

It was strange. I traveled a lot. It was part of our lifestyle. They were well used to my being gone, but something was different about this time. Maybe it was because we had a few days of pure vacation, relaxed quality time for the boys and me to hang out, something that was indeed rare for us. I would have been thrilled, full of warm family feelings had there not been fear in my bones, dread at losing the three of them, having little or no control of the future, the very imminent future.

Mel and I moved toward the baggage area arm in arm while the boys kept up a constant patter about Fiji, relating stories from both while I was there and in my absence. Mel just laughed at them while I had to grin in spite of myself.

I hadn't thought again about looking at a newspaper. It would have to wait until we were home. I would hide our copy of *The Age* until I had a chance to read it.

The process of getting the bags into the roomy trunk and the four of us into our WM-A Spirit sedan served as a further reminder of the jam we were in. Nice car. How much longer?

At home, I managed to scoop the paper off the coffee table as I wrestled Mel's suitcase toward the stairs. She was headed directly to the kitchen and didn't seem to notice. "A beer?" she asked. I answered in the affirmative as I climbed the stairs to our room and then called down that I was going to visit the loo.

The news was splashed across the top of the front page. This was *The Age*, the Australian version of the "Old Gray Lady," not a scandal sheet. It reported the story with its usual dignity but pulled no punches. Most of it was about the "love triangle" of Vicky and the two former parliamentarians, Gregory and Del Bryant; Vicky's pregnancy; and their half-truth comments and denials. References to Gregory's connections with Mel and me came near the end of the story, and the words "rumored" and "alleged" were used a lot, which evoked some small degree of relief. Mel and I could deal with that, I thought. Then the next paragraph, down near the very end, brought back the lump in my throat and turned my innards to jelly. "There have been additional anonymous reports," it read, "connecting Mr. Houghton to allegations of sexual harassment and misconduct with other women. Thus far all the women have chosen to remain anonymous. No charges have been filed." I wanted to throw up. The rest I could discuss with Mel, but that? Quite possibly the end of everything.

I hid the paper in my wardrobe, only a temporary postponement, but I needed some time to think and right now I needed to get back downstairs and pretend to continue to enjoy the homecoming.

The boys had started watching their regular afternoon programs on the telly but late afternoon news time was approaching so I shooed them upstairs to their room. Mel brought in my beer and her glass of red just as the news came on. "Let's turn that off and just relax," I said.

"I haven't seen any news in a week," Mel said. "Give me a couple minutes to catch up on the main stories and then we can have quiet time. I'd like some us-time myself."

Despite what she said, I moved toward the television to switch it off. "Good," she said, "switch from that crummy channel to the ABC. Just for a few minutes."

I had reached for the on-off knob but reluctantly turned the channel knob instead. What the hell? It's inevitable.

"Oh, my god, look. It's Gregory," she said.

Fucked.

Indeed, it was a headshot shot of Gregory evidently talking to an off-camera interviewer. "It's true that Ms. Markle and I had recently started a relationship. I had always admired her for her work with

184

the Honorable Member from Queensland, and when she and I both became free of our parliamentary duties, I asked her out. We were having a wonderful time before all this. Obviously I knew nothing of her recently reported pregnancy, which apparently is a result of a prior relationship with Mr. Bryant. I am referring to a their non-work relationship, another matter about which I was in the dark. I must tell you that I was devastated by that news. It hurt me deeply. Ms. Markle has tried to call me, but as I'm sure you can understand, I am not interested in talking with her right now. Therefore, I am unable to answer any of your questions about her plans going forward, nor those of Mr. Bryant, I'm afraid. I'm just trying to get my own life back together."

Mel had desperately grabbed my arm as soon as she realized what she was watching. "Oh, shit," she said, leaning forward, the better to take it all in, pulling me with her.

The camera now turned to the interviewer, a young dark-haired woman, probably in her late twenties, early thirties.

"If you can't tell us any more about Ms. Markle and Mr. Bryant, how about reports of your relationship with the Houghtons? Cooper and Melanie, is it?"

Mel squeezed my arm harder. I could feel her shudder. "Oh, my god," she said, as a series of clips came on showing the three of us coming out of the parliament building the day we cleaned out Gregory's office, walking in the door of the Travelodge, laughing together at dinner at the bistro that night. At least there was nothing of us inside his office or our room. Small favors. Mel tried to hide her eyes from the screen but had to watch through her fingers as she heard Gregory say, "Coop and Mel are my dear friends from America. Nothing more, nothing less. They helped me when I emptied my office the day after the election and we tried to have a nice farewell-to-Canberra dinner later. In fact it was a fairly sad occasion but we were making the best of it."

"Forgive me, but there have been rumors that the three of you were more than just friends. That there might have been some unusual, shall I say, connection?"

Mel let go of my arm, put her face in a pillow and began keening. "Absolutely not. They are a great couple and I shall miss them."

"You won't be seeing them anymore? Is that what you are telling us?"

"I wish it weren't the case, but Mr. Houghton has accepted a well-deserved promotion back in his home office in New York. They will be leaving all too soon. That was something of a farewell dinner you showed. Like I say, a sad occasion. I shall miss them."

"As we said at the top of the story, we have reached out to Ms. Markle and Mr. Bryant but they have not returned our requests for interviews. This is Bonnie Westervelt reporting from Melbourne for the ABC."

When I got up to turn off the set, Mel fell prone onto the sofa, her face still in the pillow, her back spasming in rhythm with her sobs. I could only thank god that they hadn't mentioned the rumors about me with other women. But surely it was coming.

"What's the matter, Mom?" said Roger, coming down the stairs for dinner.

"They just had a sad story on the news," I said.

"Must have been real sad."

"It involves a friend of ours," I said.

"Who? What friend? Do I know them?"

Mel got up and left the room, hiding her face from her son. She started up the stairs and passed Brett, who looked at her with a puzzled expression.

I said, "Mr. Gregory. I think you've met…"

"That guy from the parliament?"

"Yes."

"He lost, didn't he?" Brett said. "Is that why Mom is so sad?"

"More or less. Sure."

That seemed to satisfy him for the moment.

"Tell you what," I said, "I don't think Mom is in any mood to fix dinner. What say the three of us go out and pick up some burgers at McDonald's and bring them back here. We'll get a chicken sandwich for Mom."

CHAPTER 34

Our two young, true-blue Yanks were always ready for a McDonald's. The very thought had me ready to be sick and I was sure Mel would feel even worse, but the task at hand was to get them away from there and give their mother time to regroup. I called up the stairs to let her know what we were doing and we were gone. The route was more than familiar but I purposely managed to make a few wrong turns and ended up driving along the Yarra past the Botanical Gardens and back up or down (I couldn't be sure in my condition) toward the Shrine of Remembrance. My meandering eventually took us to the yellow arches in St. Kilda, way out of our way. Although the boys knew the shorter route, they didn't say a word. We all needed some time.

Mel was in the kitchen drinking at least her second glass of wine and fixing salad when we got back. She did her best to put on a show of gratitude for the chicken sandwich but we both knew she would do no more than take a symbolic bite and have a small portion of salad. She had set the kitchen table for a small but festive takeaway meal. After dinner we kept it light by watching back to back episodes of Monty Python followed by a half hour of Fawlty-Towers. I then led the boys upstairs and saw them to bed. I cautiously returned to find Mel sitting on the sofa, another glass of wine on the coffee table, a forced smile on her face. As I had the night before, I skipped my usual cleansing ale and went for the scotch.

We commiserated as much as we could before we broke down into laughter, by which time we had each had another drink or two. I put on some LPs and invited her to dance.

Tonight my dancing ineptitude, along with alcohol and our

precarious situation, led to our staggering around the lounge to Shearing's luxuriant sounds, then to faster and louder rock until we laughed ourselves silly and fell together onto the sofa. She was obviously ready to make love right then and there but I sat up and stared at the floor.

"Come here," she said, pulling me down toward her. When I continued to look away, she turned serious and asked what was going on.

"There's more," I said.

"What? I thought we were off the hook."

"There's more. Give me a minute."

I went upstairs and came down with the newspaper. She only needed a glance at the front-page headshot photos of each separate member of the lovers triangle to bring her upright and sober. As she started to read, she said, "This is the same thing we just saw."

"Keep reading."

The look on her face told me she had reached the part I dreaded. The situation was forcing my hand and the drink pushed me over the edge.

She spoke: "More? I'll say there's more. How much more, may I ask? Talk to me, you bastard."

I decided to barge ahead. "I don't know for sure what women they're talking about and I don't know who's doing the talking, but I'm going to tell you everything I do know. No lies, no cover ups. Okay?"

"If you say so."

I told her about the night with Nicole in Adelaide and the times with Robin in Sydney. We both tried in vain to keep away tears as I spoke. I told her about Fran Lawson, how I disliked and distrusted her but how I got trapped in her cabin in Fiji, how I resisted. I told her Fran's husband had spotted us with Gregory that first night at the pub in Waverly, the night she danced with him.

At that Mel got up and paced, looking more and more angry, or perhaps scared or both. Or was I projecting my own feelings onto her?

"I have a hunch that either he or Fran are the ones behind these stories," I said. "They're both bitter about the way he was sacked at WM-A."

Mel stopped pacing and glared at me. "You think I give a shit about them? It's you who's behind all these stories. You are stabbing me right now, you fucker. You're a liar and a horn dog. It was just you and me and Gregory, remember? That's all you wanted. I did it for you, you know. It was all your fantasy, never mine. I admit I enjoyed our times together and got a dear friend out of it. But don't forget, don't you dare ever forget, I only let it happen because it was what you wanted. That was *all* you wanted, no other women you said. You weren't interested in that, you said. You loved me and only me, you said. And everything you said was a lie. I guess anything you ever said has always been a lie. How do I know you are even telling me the truth now?"

"One more thing," I said. "I have to tell you one more thing."

"Oh, Christ, I can't wait."

"It's about Diane."

"Oh, Christ, don't tell me you fucked Kevin's wife too?"

"No, I didn't. Not ever. I swear. That's why I'm telling you."

"Telling me what, for god's sake?"

I told her about my whole conversation with Kevin, about finding out that WM-A was pulling its contract, that basically they had fired our firm and me with it.

"So your client fired you? Well, you deserve it, you prick. But what about us, the kids and me?"

I explained that I hadn't really been fired, that I was still in line for the promotion in New York, that they know at least some of what's going on here and want me to get out of Australia as soon as we can pack up and go. About how they hope I learned some lessons but still value my experience and abilities. I told her about my meeting with the B&C lawyers and the non-disclosure deals with Nicole and Robin.

"Fine, you're all assholes. All you good old boys covering up all the crap you leave behind. Muriel Mitchell has it right. So what's all this got to do with Diane. You said there was something about her in all this mess."

"Right. So she told Kevin that I have been hitting on her. For a long time, she says. It's not true, Mel. If anything it's been the opposite. I don't go to bed with friend's wives."

"Well, bully for you, a man of integrity."

I told her that Kevin had confided in me on the New Zealand trip about Diane's affairs, the ones he knew about. I told her about the dinner party at the Robertsons, about Diane's groping me under the table and in the bathroom hall. "Never, never, never," I said.

"So what?" Mel snarled. "So what's the big deal. After all this, why tell me about the one person you didn't fuck?"

"There's also Fran Lawson," I reminded her, knowing it would not gain me any points. She just threw up her hands and turned away, pacing again.

"I'm telling you about Diane because it was really her story, her lies, that, as far as I'm concerned, got Kevin to turn on me. I think Diane was the final straw for him, the one that got this whole chain reaction started. And she might also be the source for at least some of these stories."

"So you think it could be that Lawson woman or Diane Larned. Isn't that just great? The only two women in the whole damn world that you claim never to have screwed and they're the ones ratting you out."

"Believe me, I get the irony. But that's what I think."

"Well, good then. That's what you deserve. Two women you rejected are getting your ass. You've got that coming, you bastard." She went to the kitchen for some more wine. I poured another scotch.

She seemed to have moved from angry to humiliated and heart-broken by the time she returned. She was back to uninhibited sobbing.

"I'm so sorry, Mel," I said.

"How could you, Coop? How could you? You know how much I have always loved you."

"And I have always loved you, Mel. Always. And never more than I have the last several months. Never more that right now, in fact. That's even what I told Kevin."

"Then, how could you? The lies. How could you keep so much from me?"

I was all the way in at this point so I continued.

"No more, honey. I don't want to ever keep anything from you. I want you to know it all."

"You mean there's more?"

"I mean I've always been what you called a horn-dog when it comes to sex. I mean all the way back to when I was a kid."

"Wait," she said. "Before you get started with the sad story of your childhood, go back to Kevin. When you told him how much you love me, what did he say."

"Remember, he was pissed. He had just laid all those accusations from his wife on me."

"So? When you told him how much you love me, what did he say?"

"He said, 'Good luck with that.'"

"Exactly. He got it exactly right. Go on with your story."

I tentatively reached for her hand and she let me hold it. With retching pain and many pauses to gag and sob, I went all the way. I was manic in my resolve to hold nothing back, to spill out every last ugly truth. In the back of my mind were all the admonitions: don't complain and don't explain; what she doesn't know won't hurt her; you're only being selfish if you tell her; it will only hurt her. I was having none of that.

I went way back to tell her the story of my teenage second cousin making me touch him, and before that to my first experience playing with myself with Jerry Morris when I was only about eleven. My junior high years when I masturbated all the time and anywhere, when I got my first bare tit, when Jane and I experimented and I ruined her reputation and perhaps even her life. High school when Angela and I lost our virginity and when Nan and I made love. All the times I looked up girls' skirts and later masturbated. Watching the girl I grew up with across the street through her bathroom window, watching her from her waist up as she got ready for bed, amazed at her big beautiful naked breasts. Even the time I peeked in our own window to see our Australian babysitter with her boyfriend's hand

191

in her jeans. How the voyeur in me was probably behind my fantasy about watching another man fuck my wife, how I got off on watching her with Gregory.

Mel remained surprisingly calm during this whole barrage, letting her hand stay in mine, sometimes even gripping it in what felt to me like compassion. I had to let go when I got to the hardest part, however. I got up and poured us each another drink and began to pace as I talked.

I had to tell her about the other women I had sex with over time. I tried to ease into it with my college conquests. The sophomoric advice I got from a sophomore, Cap Wright, when I was a freshman. "Whenever you turn down one," he said, "you will always be one behind." I did my best never to turn one down. I told her while I went steady with a girl I claimed to be in love with, I fucked any others who would let me, even my girlfriend's married sister, my first with a somewhat older married woman; the second a hot, older, tough-looking married blonde I picked up at the campus hangout when she came from out of town to visit friends for the weekend. And when, as an upperclassman I was living off-campus by myself in the upstairs garret room, the sexy landlady came up and asked for a cigarette while her husband was at work. My hands shook as I lit both of us a Winston and she lay back on my twin bed to smoke hers, making sure to display her open legs and white panties until I moved to join her. We did it every chance we got for the rest of that semester, all the while my girlfriend wore my fraternity pin, engaged to be engaged.

With the one exception of junior high locker room bragging about Jane, I had never before told a single person about any of these incidents or transgressions. As hard as it was now to tell the love of my life, my best friend, the mother of my children, it was easy compared to what came next.

I sat back down and took the wine glass from Mel's hand, placing it on the antique chest we used as a coffee table. I then reached to take her hand but she moved it away. She had tears although, strangely enough, her damp eyes looked into mine with what looked like sympathy. But I knew I was about to well and truly break her heart. I told her about all the one-night stands and longer affairs I had engaged in since we were married, and there were many. My work travels and my influential positions provided numerous opportunities, with my nearly lifelong sexual obsession the only required motive.

In the midst of this most painful part of my confession, painful for both of us, I couldn't help it: there it was in the back of my animal brain: *"Never let a chance go by, go by, oh never let a chance go by,"* Stupidly right then, it did occur to me as a summation of my life in sex. I didn't dare share that thought with my wife.

As I plowed ahead, Mel pushed my hand away and curled herself into a fetal position on the sofa, I squeezed myself into a corner to give her room. I knew full well how I was hurting her but I couldn't help myself. Once I got started there was no place to stop until it was all out. She asked no questions, cried no tears, just curled herself up and held herself tight around the waist, around her guts.

"That's all. That's everything, Mel. I'm so sorry, so desperately sorry. I hate myself as much as I love you. I know that doesn't help anything, but I do. Through everything, I always loved you. How I could do that and still claim to love you? I don't understand myself but it's true. I know I can't expect you to understand it or to forgive me, but I swear I always knew I loved you through everything and that I love you now more than ever. But that's it. I'm sorry but that's it. I'm through."

Mel stood. She gave me a cold, stony glare through lidded eyes. "I have to pee," she said. I didn't know what to expect, would she even come back or go straight upstairs to bed, or to pack her bags, or to pack mine? But she used the downstairs powder room, then poured herself another glass of wine before she returned to the sofa. Still standing, she turned her eyes to mine, her cold look still there.

"I had sex with your brother," she said.

It took a moment for it to sink in. Did she really just say that? Then I gagged.

"What are you telling me?"

"I fucked Roger."

"Jesus Christ, Mel. Jesus Christ." She was talking about my

brother who had been killed in Viet Nam. A brother I loved dearly. A brother I missed every day. The brother whose death also devastated Mel at the time. The brother after whom we had named our firstborn.

"When we were living in Stamford—before the kids were born—remember, you were always on the road. As you know, he usually visited when he came to New York. Before he went in. Then when he was home on leave. I liked him. I liked him a lot. You know that. Loved him, even. I was alone, sometimes for weeks at a time. I was young and alone and lonely. He was your brother but he was my friend."

"Your *friend*, for god's sake?" I jumped from the sofa and stood, looking down at her. The look hadn't changed. Cold and determined. "When, where, how many times?"

"What does that matter, you prick. Not many. Maybe three."

"Christ." I couldn't believe what I was hearing.

"If we're going to do this thing—this confessional thing—we're going to do it all the way," she said. "So okay, the first time was after we had been out for dinner and had a few drinks. We came back to the apartment and sat on the couch in the dark watching a movie. When we stood up to go our respective beds, we just latched on to each other and that was that. We fell back on the couch and it was all over in a minute. Your brother was what I believe is called a premature ejaculator. And it didn't get any better the next two times we tried. Other nights. Other times when we knew how wrong it was and tried so hard to resist. Your brother loved you and so did I. I *did* think I might be pregnant once. We talked about abortions even. I was so dumb, I knew nothing, hardly knew what an abortion was. It turned out I was just late."

"Holy shit. So are Roger and Brett even mine then?"

She slapped me. Hard.

I jumped up and went to the stereo. I unceremoniously ripped the Shearing record from the turntable. Threw it at her. She didn't flinch as it hit the back of the sofa next to her head. "He was there a lot and I was lonely," she said, defiance in her eyes. I grabbed the record again and tried to smash it over my knee but it gave and didn't break. Then I stomped on it until it did. I yelled into her stoic face, "Our song, remember?"

"The sex wasn't even very good," she said.

"Oh, my god. The sex wasn't very…"

I picked up some of the pieces of the record and sat down with them in my hand. Now crying, she looked at pieces in my hands, and I began to cry too.

"Jesus Christ, Mel, who are we?" I said.

She reached out for me and I took her in my arms. I could hardly breathe. "Who are we, Mel?" We just held each other and wept. I finally pulled away and went to the bathroom. When I finished peeing, I washed my hands then leaned on the counter and looked in the mirror, trying to take in the sadness I saw. I was looking at someone I had never seen before. But then nothing was as it was anymore.

Mel looked up at me as I came back to her. I saw the same sadness there, but then she surprised me again. She grabbed my hands and pulled me down.

"All that made me feel sick," she said, "but also horny."

Strangely, I knew what she meant. "Me too," I said and we fell to the floor, knocking over wine glasses, wine spilling on the coffee table and some on the old dark carpet. Raw fucking with most of our clothes on, my pants half down, knees rubbing against the roughness of that thin carpet. Was it pain crossing her face from the rub of the floor on her sacrum or just passion or both? As we removed the rest of our clothing, the desperateness eventually mellowed into deeply felt love-making. When it was over, we peeled apart and continued to lie there on our backs, a last look into each other's eyes before we both just stared up at the ceiling, still panting. That is where we fell asleep.

CHAPTER 35

I woke to kitchen noises and an awful hangover. "Mel?" I called, still on the carpet, naked.

She, wearing her clothes from the night before, looked in and said, "You'd better get dressed before the boys come down. It's their first day back at school. Vacation's over."

You got that right. God I hurt. I pulled on my underwear, pants and shirt, leaving my shirttails out and went to the kitchen. Mel laughed at my hound dog appearance. "I feel the way you look," she said.

She didn't say a word about our revelations of the night before, offering me a cup of coffee with a slight smile. She continued to busy herself fixing breakfast for the kids. I just stood, leaning back on the counter, downing the black coffee. When she saw me put down the empty mug, she came over, and without a word, hugged me. It took me a moment to respond, my arms at my side until I wrapped my arms around her and clung. Neither of us said a word. She finally let go and I started for the stairs, passing Roger and Brett as I went up to our room. They each gave me a puzzled look but only greeted me with a "Hi, Dad."

I turned around and returned to the kitchen. "Back to school, eh?" They groused a little but their mood picked up as we sat around the kitchen table and chatted about Fiji. It had all the appearance of normalcy but I felt pain in both my head and my guts. Mel asked me if I wanted something to eat—"Weetabix or an egg?" With my stomach in revolt, I declined.

Finally the boys left for the tram ride to Melbourne Grammar and Mel and I stared at one another. She cleaned up the dishes, then poured us both another coffee before joining me at the table.

"So, who are we?" she asked, repeating my question from last night, a question for which I had no answer.

"I don't know."

"I know you're a bastard."

"And you?"

"I suppose. So where do we go from here?"

"I don't know."

She finished her coffee and stood. "For starters, I'm going up to take a shower."

"Shall I join you?"

"Let's not go into that right now," she said, pausing before she added, "If ever."

There it was on the front page of *The Age* as I sat down on the sofa, the sofa that was the scene of so much drama the night before. Now there was more.

A photo of Mel and me coming out of the Canberra Travelodge with Gregory. The lead paragraph said an unidentified woman and her husband had come forth with allegations of attempted assault against me, "the American managing director of Brock and Case, a well-known international consulting firm." Assault! The source went on to implicate me in further sexual misconduct with two other unidentified women who had refused comment. It was also claimed that the paper had reached out to me for a response without success, a complete surprise, and as far as I knew, a totally false claim. The whole of the story was reportedly linked to the broader context of the "Canberra Triangle investigation." They even managed to bring in the Cairns-Morosi story. None of this seemed up to the standards of *The Age*, adding to my disappointment and rage.

I turned on the television and dialed in the ABC morning news show. They were in the middle of a segment with a chef cooking up one of his favorite dishes, but as they went to a weather summary ("unrelenting heat wave"), they teased with "Stay tuned for more on the breaking scandal."

Mel, in her post-shower robe, was standing as if paralyzed at the foot of the stairs. The phone rang.

"Don't answer it," she screamed, but by that time the receiver was in my hand. I did pause before offering a tentative hello. Mel stared at me as I covered the mouthpiece and silently signaled her that it was Gregory. She sat down on the bottom step, her face in her hands.

"I'm so sorry," Gregory said. "Mel and you don't deserve this. I'm so sorry you had to get thrown over the side of the boat with me and my problems."

I paced as far as the phone cord would allow. I told him that I accepted his apology, that we knew that he had no bad intentions, that we cared for and trusted him. Once having covered that, I went completely silent. What else was there to say? I was a confused blank.

After a long gap, Gregory said, "Jim quoted the title of Henry Ford II's biography to me." *Jim? Who the fuck was Jim?* "' Never complain, never explain,' he said."

The whole of last night's and this morning's frustrations burst out: "Who said? Who the fuck are we talking about and what the fuck does that mean?"

"I told you. I told you I was going to contact Jim Cairns for how to deal with the press on this kind of shit. According to him, if you read Ford's book, he had a lot of issues in his own personal life that became public and he claimed to live by that motto."

"What fucking motto? You mean that crap about don't complain or explain?"

"That's what Jim told me."

"Christ, Gregory, is that all you've got? Is that what I'm supposed to tell Mel?"

"I'm just passing on some advice from a guy who's been there, is all I'm saying."

"I'm not Jim Cairns, for Christ's sake. I'm not some public figure like him or like Henry Ford or whoever. Or even like you, for god's sake. And I don't want to be. We don't want to be, Mel and me. Don't you get it?"

I hadn't been angry at Gregory before—felt sympathy for him, in fact—but now I was pissed, pissed at everything that was falling on me, pulling at me. I was ready to hang up on him when he said, "Forgive me, I love you both. It's true, you have not been public figures. Until now, that is. That's to your advantage. But, if you don't want to be even more in the public eye than you are now, my own best advice is to get out the country, go home. You're going anyway. Go now and let this thing here blow over."

"You may be right," I said. "Listen, the ABC just came back on with more on the so-called sex scandal. We'll ring you later."

Mel looked up as the news readers started in. The report consisted of previous stories warmed over, the same shots and clips focusing primarily on the Canberra triangle, not us, thank god. Our series of short clips was replayed as part of a longer montage about the political participants, including, again, Cairns and Morosi. A panel of pundits then offered their interpretations and speculation on the political fallout. Mel and I were left out, thankfully. We were just footnotes to the main story and I could only hope it would stay that way.

We looked at each other blankly. There were too many questions and no answers. Nothing to say to each other beyond more apologies, so we said nothing. Mel went to kitchen and began to scramble some eggs. I turned off the telly and joined her. We ate in silence, once in awhile stealing a glance at the other before instantly averting our eyes.

Finally she asked, "Is this worth saving, Coop?"

My immediate and certain response was yes.

"You sure? I'm not so sure."

"Mel, I fucked up. For a long time, for most of my life, I have been fucked up where sex was concerned. I may need help getting…"

"*We* need help. That is if we both think it's worth it."

"It's worth it, Mel. I have never for a moment, not any time through all the shit I pulled, not known that I loved you and only you with all my heart. That you have always been the best thing that ever happened to me. That may be hard for you to believe but…"

"I believe you. The same for me from way back when. I said I liked your brother, still miss him, but I always only loved you and I always knew it. Same with Gregory."

The thought of her with Roger gave me another deep stab. I had picked up the shards of the Shearing album from the lounge carpet earlier and regretted the loss of that song, our song, lost to us forever. "So it's worth it, then," I said.

"It's going to be hard, if not impossible," she said. "The strange thing is I feel we're closer right now than we have been for some time and yet I don't trust you worth a flying fuck."

I reached for her hand but she pulled it away. It was going to be hard indeed.

CHAPTER 36

I got myself cleaned up and stayed away from the television the rest of the day. It didn't help that I didn't have a job, an office to go to, a project I was working on. Mel and I were physically and emotionally exhausted from the night before. She went back to bed and I lay on the sofa and tried to read a book I had once started but my frazzled brain and muddled thoughts prevented me from any chance of focusing on the page. I did eventually doze a little, waking up when the doorbell rang along with a determined rapping.

I peeked through the closed drapes and couldn't believe the scene. TV trucks and what I assumed were a flock of reporters were just outside our gate. One reporter had made it past the gate and was at our door. I tried to ignore the clamor, returning to the sofa and my book, hoping if we could just wait them out, they would conclude that we were not at home and would go away. I know now how naive I was about such things.

When the bell-ringer/door-knocker persisted, I gave up and cracked open the door. "We have no comment at this time," I said, "and would appreciate it if all of you could respect our privacy."

"But Mr. Ho…"

I closed the door, not slamming it exactly, but firmly enough that I thought it conveyed my message.

"Who's that?" Mel called down.

"No one important, go back to sleep if you can." But just then the phone rang. Oh shit, now they're going to be calling all the time. I reluctantly picked it up, thinking to tell them the same thing I told the bloke at the door, but before I could say anything, I recognized a familiar voice.

"Coop, this is Joel Lesser." Lesser was a Managing Partner in our New York headquarters. He apologized for not knowing the exact time difference, "Or even which day it is there. Hope I didn't wake you."

"No, Joel, this is good. A relief to hear your voice. Things aren't so good here at the moment."

"So I understand. That's the reason I called."

"So the news got over there already."

"Some. Maybe not everything, but enough. How are you and Mel holding up?"

"Barely."

"So, listen. We want you to get the hell out of there right away. How soon can you be in the air?"

"Jesus, Joel, I don't know. I'd be glad to be gone yesterday but Mel and I have to get packed and organized to leave."

"No time for that, my friend. You need to get on a plane now. Leave the rest to Mel. Our firm over there will help her with anything she needs, but I want you out of there and in my office ASAP."

"I hear you. I'll do what I can."

"Let me know what I can do to help."

I hung up. "Shit." I didn't realize I said it loud enough to be heard upstairs.

Mel called, "What was that all about?"

I tried to sound calm. "You need to sleep, remember? It was just Joel Lesser. Wants me in New York."

I could hear her feet hit the floor in our room. She was in her robe and downstairs in a flash. "Joel Lesser? What does he expect, for god's sake? We have so much to do."

"Me, Mel. He wants me. Right away. Like now. Like today if could make it."

"But…"

"I know, I know. I don't know how we're supposed to make this work. He wants me to leave you to pick up the pieces, finish packing and all. Says that B&C here will help you with whatever you need."

"That's ridiculous."

I tried to hold her, console her, but she was not interested. Not from me. Not right now.

"And what about us?" she asked. "Where does that leave us? We said we needed help. It's we who need to pick up the pieces, not me—the pieces of our life, of our future, if we have one."

I sensed she was in no mood for me to offer suggestions. "You're right, sweetheart...Mel... I just don't know."

This time the banging was at the back door. I said, "Reporters. Peek out the front. The fucking paparazzi are everywhere. I already sent one guy away from the front door. Now they found their way to the back. I locked it. You look out front, I'll check the back door."

It was Roger and Brett. They looked beat and angry. I halted them as they tried to head up to their rooms without a word. Mel turned away from the front window, befuddled. They were not due home for a couple more hours. "What's this about?" Mel asked.

Brett answered first: "It's messed up."

Mel's eyes searched each of theirs. She said, "Messed up? What's that supposed to mean?"

Roger hurled his rucksack at the foot of the stairs. When he finally lifted his head, he was looking straight at me. "The Headmaster sent us home. Said it would be best."

"Why best?" Mel asked. "You belong in school." Her eyes followed from Roger to me.

Roger turned to his mother. "It's all over the school. All the kids knew more about everything than I did, than we did. They teased us, made jokes, dirty jokes about us, about you two. They got on us bad, especially Brett. I didn't like it but he got it worse than I did. The Headmaster called us in and told us we had become a 'distraction.'"

Brett chimed in, "That's what he said, a 'distraction.'"

Roger sat on the bottom stair and glared up at us. "We didn't know anything. You didn't tell us anything. What the fuck is the matter with you guys?"

A first. We had never heard either kid use language even approaching that. It was not the time to wash his mouth out with soap however. We had no choice but to accept his anger.

"And those assholes out there," he said, turning his glare to the front of the house. "They were worse than the kids at school. They pushed us and kept throwing wild accusations about you two, asking us what we thought. We pushed them away and finally got to the back door. A couple of them followed us."

"Are they still there?" I asked.

"I don't know. You let us in and then I don't know."

Mel asked them nicely to come into the lounge and sit. "We need to talk."

"You think?" Roger said.

Mel did her best to calm them down. She acknowledged the mess. She acknowledged that maybe we should have said something earlier, that we had no idea everything was going to blow up like it did, that we hoped to keep them out of it. They settled down and listened but when she uttered the standard "It's complicated," Roger stood up, looked down at his mother and screamed "Bullshit. That's just more bullshit."

Poor Brett watched in shock and broke into sobs. Mel moved to sit in his chair with him and hold him. She was crying herself.

"So now what?" Roger snarled.

Mel looked up, still holding Brett, and said "New York wants your father there as soon as possible."

"Good," said Roger. "So when we going?"

"Not 'we'. Him. Just your father for now."

"Can't we go too? I don't want to stay here any more. Brett and I can't go back to that school. They keep reminding us that Melbourne Grammar is where the new Prime Minister went to school. As if we didn't know that by now. Malcolm Fraser went there so we are disgracing their precious history."

"Roger, that's a crock. Don't worry about it," I said. "You don't have to go back to Melbourne Grammar. You can help your mother get everything packed and ready to go. I want you all there as soon as you can make it. My firm will be helping."

"So you're not coming back for us," Roger said, bitterness in his tone.

"That would just take longer, postpone your own departure. You said you wanted to leave as soon as possible."

Roger stood, grabbed his rucksack and marched up the stairs. "Bullshit," he called back, "More bullshit."

Brett looked stunned, tried to dry his eyes but returned to sobbing.

With both of the boys upstairs, I contacted the transportation department at my office then joined Mel in the kitchen. She was fixing dinner and drinking her glass of red. I poured myself a scotch, resolving that it would be the first and last of the evening. We avoided our normal toast to "London Town," even though I couldn't have loved her more. As I started chopping for the salad, she looked at me with somber eyes.

"I think it'll be good," she said.

"Good?"

"At first I was upset that you were going without us. It felt like one more betrayal. Plus we said we need to get some help, that it was worth it, we thought."

I wasn't at all sure where she was leading.

"Now that I've had a little chance to let it soak in..."

"Some chance," I said. All I felt was the continuing chaos.

"A little chance, I said. I've been out here thinking that this may be for the best. I mean you taking off right away."

"Transportation has me on Qantas first thing in the morning."

"Good luck with that. Glad it's not me. But what I'm saying is maybe it will be good for both of us. Time to sort things out."

"Us? How does *us* sort things out when *us* is on opposite sides of the world?"

"I mean each of us...individually. I know I have a lot to think about, soul searching to do. I imagine you do too."

Understatement. *Long, long flight. Too much time for thinking. Soul searching. Do I even have a soul? Did I ever?*

Dinner was pretty much a silent, somber affair despite Mel's efforts to keep it light and upbeat. The boys kept their heads down and left as soon as possible for their rooms. With my early morning call, I followed soon after, deciding to skip the evening news. Mel did not join me. However, when she came up in the middle of the night, she did wake me. She made a desperate attempt at love-making, her hand fumbling its way into my pajamas, but it was futile. She gave up and hugged me gently. Then she spoke the last words I would hear from her before I left for America: "Be safe."

CHAPTER 37

I learned when the driver picked me up in the morning that a long, tedious plane trip would now be even worse. The normal route had me flying to Los Angeles on Qantas with a fueling and maintenance stop in Honolulu, followed by a non-stop L.A. to Kennedy. A United Airlines pilot strike meant that I would now go by way of Honolulu and San Francisco instead, where I would catch a Delta flight to Atlanta, with a final connection to LaGuardia.

Flights from the U.S. to Melbourne are bad enough but mostly take place all through one seemingly endless night. Going the other way it feels like you go through darkness and daylight again and again. More to the point, it meant that leaving this morning, I will, if I'm lucky, arrive in New York sometime mid-day tomorrow. With all that was going on in my life, it seemed I was in for a daunting test of endurance with way too much time to brood. If I could have turned around and crawled back into the warm bed with Mel, I would have, despite what I may have had to face there.

There had been no time to prepare myself for jet lag by changing my sleep patterns, nor did I get off to a good start when I asked for a cup of black coffee before we even took off. Just one, I thought, to clear my head for some serious thinking, then none after that for some serious sleeping. I wasn't a good sleeper in planes, trains or automobiles, but I was armed with effective sleeping pills given me in the past by our firm's doctor. I would save those for later.

After takeoff, I sat back and tried to read an article by Australian social scientist, Fred Emery and his English colleague, Eric Trist. The paper was titled "The Causal Texture of Organizational Environments." I have long tried to see past the surface of the problems as clients present them to me so as to wade into the underlying systemic issues, to deal with field as much as figure. While I worked hard *not* to make theory the basis of my client relationships, my knack for developing my own working theories made me a better consultant. My hope now was to use the paper by Emery and Trist as a way to occupy my brain, to get something else in my head other than the swamp in which it was presently submerged. I started by reading the abstract: "Environmental contexts of organizations are themselves shifting at an increasing rate under technological change. The causal texture of the environment is considered by an extension of systems theory. Laws connecting parts of the environment to each other are often incommensurate with those connecting parts of the organization to each other, or even those governing exchanges. A typology is suggested which identifies four 'ideal types': (a) placid, randomized environment; (b) placid, clustered environment; (c) disturbed-reactive environment; and (d) turbulent fields. Illustrations are provided in 2 case histories."

Duh. I might have known better. My own "disturbed-reactive-turbulent field environment" continued its siege even as my eyes stayed on the page, on a sentence or a word that once had my attention before it wandered off back into the my own disturbed-reactive-turbulence. I dreaded the apparent inevitability of wallowing in my own case history for the whole bloody trip.

I swore to lay off the complimentary booze, following at least one item on the list of jet lag admonitions. I managed it for an hour or two until lunch was served when I accepted the gracious offer of a glass of champagne from the flight attendant, a woman of an age suggesting that she had been at this for a while. I was grateful for her, for her lack of youthful beauty, for not being a further distraction, for the fact that I didn't have to smile and be flirtatious. I was sick of myself and my proclivities. The very thought made me nauseous.

The delicious seafood omelet and salad caused me to switch to a delightful Australian Riesling for my next glass. Perhaps the wine would help me with a postprandial snooze. Not what the experts recommend, but so it goes.

With my seat-back reclined, I closed my eyes and tried my best not to think, which, of course, was futile. I was immediately plunged into an anarchic review of my tangled web of turbulence. My brain lurched from Mel and Gregory, to the media outside the house, to our kids, to Adelaide Nicole and Sydney Robin, to Virge, to Kevin and Diane, to Fran Lawson and her husband, to New York and what Joel Lesser had in store and more, all in no order, all in one gut-tightening knot. My attempt at quiet, sleep-inducing meditation only resulted in my becoming irritated and restless. The hell with it. I have always claimed to live so as to be a cause not an effect. Enough of this Hamlet crap. Time to take arms against my sea of troubles. Time to end them. I cranked my seat back to its upright position, reached under for my briefcase to extract a lined tablet and "went to work." Use what you know how to do.

I began to sort the tangle into a list:

Mel and me
Roger and Bret/Mel and me
My job (B&C Australia and America, Kevin, WM-A, etc.)
Gregory
The Canberra triangle
The press, bad publicity for me and my firm and our clients
The women: Nicole, Robin, Diane, Fran, et al.
The move to NYC

I knew there was more but my turbulent brain stopped me there and I wrote:

Other

I knew better than to attempt the obvious by proceeding to solve a list of problems in priority order. I knew from my work with organizations that problems don't get solved in such a neat and orderly way. I knew that important problems came in the form of a mess. The key was not to find the highest priority problem but (switching metaphors) to find the one domino that would, when knocked over, knock over the most other dominos. That key domino may not be the highest priority problem at all. My father taught me the same basic lesson when he took me fishing as a boy, and taught me how to undo a backlash on my reel. He was a genius at finding the one piece of line to grab first, the one that was key to unraveling what he called "the rat's nest." Eventually you had to deal with other tangles along the way, but you applied the same principle each time.

I found myself in the middle of a rat's nest, the biggest rat's nest of my life. But I sat there with no idea of which thread to grasp. As is always the case, each problem I might try to solve was connected to one or more of the others and fixing one might screw up the others and vice versa. Real life's game of whack-a-mole.

I set it all aside for the moment to reflect and ordered a scotch. The announcement that the movie was starting soon was a relief. Blinds were drawn, darkness prevailed. Perhaps the film would be a distraction. Perhaps I might even fall asleep. Perchance to dream.

The movie was one we had seen recently, *Barry Lyndon*, a film I wasn't sure about. I am not a movie buff; I go for entertainment and did not find that film very entertaining. I had some appreciation for the fine cinematography, stunning scenery, outdoor scenes that seemed almost like landscape paintings by old masters, and indoor scenes similarly artistic like still-life tableaus. Unfortunately for me, they had about as much action as still life. When Mel and I and Gregory left the theater in one of the Melbourne suburbs, I compared the experience to visiting an art museum, art being another subject for which I have no claim to expertise. Like huge pieces hanging on a museum wall, the movie scenes required a sort of standing back, creating a separation from the actions or feelings of the characters in the scene. Mel said she hadn't thought of that but that I was probably right. Gregory complimented me on my prowess as a movie critic and said he found the film too slow moving for his taste as well. Obviously, though, one of the three of us, Mel, was a fan, which set the three of us up for a pleasant evening of languid lovemaking.

All of which, I thought, made it the perfect movie for me to watch on the plane. If nothing else, maybe it would finally help me get some sleep, which it did not. I found the story to be of slightly more interest this time around, perhaps because I was already familiar with it. I saw and heard things that I missed on first viewing. I closed my eyes in the slowest parts, but my own troubles reemerged.

Indeed, eventually the Lyndon character and his unraveling resonated all too well with my own. It hit me so hard that when I heard the narrator soon after the climactic scene of the movie say the following, I added the quote to the list I had made: "Fate had determined that he should leave none of his race behind him, and that he should finish his life poor, lonely and childless." I had even greater difficulty sticking with the film after that. The very thought chilled my bones. Was this my fate as well? Not me, I determined. I was a cause not an effect, remember? But no doubt I was shaken and more than ready when the lights were back on and the announcement came that we were about to land in Honolulu.

Morning in Paradise. We had flown through at least one of the nights. Right after disembarking, I started to walk the concourses. I needed to stretch and exercise both my body and my mind. We were in Hawaii where the airport concourses are often open to the warm and fragrant air, but there was no paradise feel to it as far as I was concerned.

I couldn't get the movie out of my mind as I passed gate after gate, past people in boarding queues, people sitting and reading, people trying to snooze. How I envied those who were successful.

I still thought it was a pretty boring movie but the parallels with my life were unnerving to say the least. Ryan O'Neal was wooden in the role, I thought, his character so often passive, even passively evil. All his suffering was caused by himself, his ego, his ambition, his promiscuity, his overall self-centeredness. It was not lost on me that I was my own Barry Lyndon, that I was the domino, the piece of fishing line snarling up the rat's nest.

I was both cause *and* effect. I was a closed system.

This came as a blinding glimpse of the obvious. But what to do about it other than kill myself, which I wasn't up for? It was an important insight, but as I knew from my consulting practice, insight does not necessarily lead to behavior change. Nevertheless, the recognition was a starting point.

I continued to walk and think before eventually settling into a seat in the Qantas first-class lounge and taking out my tablet once again. I wrote my own name to the side of the list with arrows to each of the other items along with arrows connecting them to each other as appropriate. I was the system consultant at work. But no solutions leaped from the page other than removing myself from the picture somehow short of suicide. I remembered reading Arthur Miller's premise that the playwright must only conclude a play with the suicide of his main character if his character has no other way out. I was not Willy Loman. Or Barry Lyndon.

Time to get back on the plane.

Monty Python and the Holy Grail was more entertaining. I was glad when, after another lunch and glass of wine, it was announced as the film for that leg. We loved watching Monty Python reruns in our lounge in Toorak. It was one thing the whole family enjoyed. Again, I had already seen the film with Roger in the balcony of a theater in Albury, Victoria, where we all found ourselves on the drive back from a happy family vacation. Mel stayed with Brett and got in a little shopping. At the theater, Roger and I were reduced to tears of laughter more than once and experienced at least some small regret that we couldn't share it with the others.

I put aside the quasi-systemic diagram of a mess I now had on my notepad and sat back for a fun ride. As with *Barry Lyndon*, I saw things the second time that I missed the first. In the scene near the beginning about killing the witch, John Cleese does a hilariously long-pause take. What I hadn't noticed before is how Eric Idle starts to crack up and bites his scythe to disguise it. Roger would have loved it.

Oddly enough, this was the movie that put me to sleep at last. I conked out about half-way through and woke just before landing in

San Francisco, sorry to have missed the film but grateful for some rest at last.

I was sick and tired of my clothes and my body and was happy to find showers available in the terminal. My carry-on bag had a shaving kit and a change of underwear. Unfortunately, I had to put on the same wrinkled outer garments, but I did feel better.

Now I had to switch to Delta to Atlanta before another plane to LaGuardia. As soon as I boarded I broke down and took one of the sleeping pills our company doctor had given me. The flight attendant asked me if I would like a drink before takeoff and I accepted her offer, ordering a scotch on the rocks.

The next thing I knew she was nudging me awake. "We're about to land in Atlanta," she said. "I'm sorry you missed your drink and your meal. Time to wake up." God, what is it from San Francisco to Atlanta, four hours or so? A complete blank. "But," she said, "you will be glad to know you won't have to change planes here after all. Everyone will have to get off and re-board, but we're sticking with the same aircraft." I dozed again in the gate area but made it back on for the final leg of this endless trip.

CHAPTER 39

I had cleared customs in a daze back in San Francisco so in New York I had only to take the escalator down to baggage claim where several drivers held signs with their clients' names. Mine was not among them. After all this transit time and all the hassles resulting from the strike, I accepted the delay as a minor issue and bought a *Times* to read while I sat out what I was sure would be a short wait. It was early morning and rush hour traffic may well have held up my driver. It was a relief to read a newspaper without fear of my name and photo being in it, although the normal turmoil of the baggage claim area was anything but relaxing.

A half hour went by, and then an hour. There must have been a mix up. Perhaps it had something to do with the fact that my arrival airport had been changed from JFK to LaGuardia. I left the terminal and stood in the taxi queue. Might as well just take a cab in. One hitch in that plan was that normally the driver would first take me to my hotel where I could take another shower and get into my suitcase for a change of clothes before hitting Brock and Case headquarters. Since I hadn't been told which hotel I was staying in, I went directly to the office, wrinkles and all. Not the best impression to make when showing up for my new position.

I rode the elevator to the third floor and Joel Lesser's office suite. His secretary looked uncertain as I explained who I was and my reason for being there. "Oh, dear," she said, and led me to the break room where Joel looked as confused and surprised as she did.

"Jesus, Coop, I'm sorry," he said, grabbing my hand to shake it. He was obviously caught off guard. "It is today, isn't it? I guess we were confused about all that date-line stuff. I wasn't expecting you until tomorrow. I mean, have a seat, man, I'll get you some coffee. How was the trip?"

"A mess. You don't want to know."

"The fact is, you look like hell," he said. He told his secretary to check on my hotel reservation.

Nothing had happened since I landed in New York to bolster my confidence.

"I feel like hell if you really want to know," I answered. I took a shot at explaining the ramifications of rerouting around the pilots' strike but sensed his mind was elsewhere. I managed to get a laugh from him when I related my sleeping adventure from San Francisco to Atlanta, which seemed to relax the tension a bit. His not mine. We made more polite small talk, finished our coffees, and he invited me to join him in his office. His secretary had checked, and she assured me that I had a reservation at the nearby Berkshire hotel.

Joel didn't ask me to sit in the comfortable conversation grouping at the far end of his office. He immediately sat behind his desk and motioned for me to take a seat in one of the two chairs across from him, from which I could take in the third-floor view of other people's midtown office windows. My muddled brain began to wonder what that building was that I was looking into—who owned it? Did the building have a name. What business was it? Who was that working anonymously in the office I could see into? I had worked in these B&C offices for years and never asked those questions, but at that moment I was struck by the anonymity of New York City. It felt so lonely.

"So, first," Joel said, breaking into my reverie, "tell me, from your point of view, about all that monkey business in Australia."

Monkey business. No easing into it, is there? Focus, Coop. Time to focus.

I explained it all as well as I knew how, attempting to put myself in as good a light as possible while not giving the impression that I was soft-pedaling the truth. I concluded with: "That monkey business, as you called it, has turned into one helluva serious shitstorm and I'm glad to be here and out of it. I'm looking forward to diving in to my new job, focusing on something I know I'm good at. I'm a fish out of water with all that stuff back there, the political connections, the media, all that bull. What I'm saying is that I can't wait to get to work again."

He frowned before he gave me a forced smile. "Coop, I'm afraid you're not out of the woods here as much as you think. Neither are we, meaning the firm." At that moment his secretary brought in more coffee and handed him a file folder. Even she appeared to share the discomfort emanating from Joel and me.

He opened the file folder, glancing down at it only for a matter of a few seconds as if giving himself a briefing. "The fact is, as I'm sure you know, way over here in the U.S. we don't usually get a lot of news coverage of day-to-day goings on in Australia. Unfortunately, this may not turn out to be the normal case."

"You mean it's made the papers here?" I slumped back in my chair.

"Not exactly. Not yet anyway." He went on to tell me that a very few small articles about a love triangle involving Australian politicians had appeared in the back pages of various papers but nothing too egregious. Again he added a "yet." "However, we have had some press inquiries. We have been asked to comment on pending stories. So far we have not done so but we may have to at some point."

"Stories about me?"

"And others."

"Like our friend Gregory Michel, I suppose."

"Some of that, yes, but that's not the real issue over here. It seems people take that kind of stuff among politicians for granted, and it's all so far away."

"The real issue?"

"Look, Coop, these scattered reports from Australia seem to have flushed out some stuff closer to home."

I was totally confused.

"Women—American women, I mean—have started to come out of the woodwork. So far they are only so-called 'anonymous sources.' They aren't willing to be identified."

"And these unidentified women are saying what?"

"Damn it, man, to put it mildly, they are calling you a woman-izer. Apparently, from what we are being asked to comment on, they include women right here in this building, from secretaries to your professional colleagues. And there are others from who knows where?"

I was completely on the defensive and gave a weak reply: "Jesus, Joel, it was never that bad. No worse than anyone else. You know as well as I do that that stuff has always gone on to some extent. Who hasn't flirted with a secretary? Maybe even you."

"No comment, but this goes way beyond flirting. Some of these women—some of them accomplished, successful women, I might add—have accused you of way more than flirting. For example, they say that you abused your position, that they were intimidated, that they were afraid for their careers, that you used them for sex."

"Jesus. No way. Not true. I'm not saying I'm perfect—far from it—and, believe me, after what's happened in Australia, I'm ashamed and more than full of regrets—I've learned my lesson—but I never had non-consensual sex with anyone, ever, not ever. The so-called sexual revolution changed things, you know. Any women I had sex with wanted to have sex with me. It was always a mutual decision."

Joel was obviously uncomfortable with the whole subject, as, was I. He briefly stood and paced and spoke more loudly than his normal tone. "Damn it, Coop. Come on. You don't understand. All that doesn't matter anymore. What you call consensual doesn't cut it. They're not accusing you of rape, at least not yet. They *are* saying that consent doesn't mean the same thing when you have power or even influence on their careers. And besides, some of it doesn't even rise to the level of intercourse. Some of it is simply what they are calling 'harassment,' that your so-called flirting sometimes crossed the line, went beyond the line to inappropriate touching, even too many touches on the shoulders or a pat on the butt."

"You gotta be shitting me."

"Sometimes it may have been only verbal flirting but became too persistent; you wouldn't let up."

I could barely breathe now let alone speak.

Joel sat down and tried to calm himself. He spoke slowly now in a more modulated tone but his voice was still shaking. "You're a good man, Coop. Obviously we think a lot of you around here. Your contributions to this firm are well recognized. Otherwise you would never have been given the opportunity to run the Melbourne office, to be the national face of Brock and Case. Otherwise you would never have been considered for the promotion back here."

I was desperate to seize the opening. "I appreciate the vote of confidence, Joel. As I said at the beginning, I'm pumped up to get started. I feel bad about all the distraction I've apparently caused and I take full responsibility. But I want to get past it and back to making the kind of contribution to the firm that I always have. I'm confident that I can do that. Now what can we do to deal with the distraction and move on to what we're all here for? What can I do to help?"

"There are potential lawsuits involved," he said, ignoring my plea. "Legal is trying for settlements where they can."

"Settlements?"

"Non-disclosures."

"I'm familiar with hush money."

"Some have indicated they don't want to settle. That they want you to be held accountable. And not just *you*. Brock and Case."

"Why the firm?"

"For 'fostering a culture.' That's what they call it. For fostering a culture of sexual harassment and misconduct, for encouraging this kind of shit to go on. This is the first I've ever heard of such a thing, Coop. But it's the seventies. Women's lib and all that. Gloria Steinem, feminism and all that crap. Burning their bras. Like you say, the sexual revolution. Jesus Christ, Coop, who knows where it's all headed? And right now it could all fall in our lap. Just the publicity alone could kill us."

"So how do we get ahead of it? What do the PR guys say."

"Coop, this goes way beyond what PR can do."

"So what, then?"

"Coop," he began. He kept starting his sentences with my name. Every time he did it, it sounded more menacing. "Coop, you need to resign."

There it was.

"Resign? Holy fuck, Joel? Resign? You can't be serious. You just gave me that speech about how important I was to this firm, how deserving I was of this promotion. I came all this way to hear about my new job, to get myself ready. You can't be serious."

Joel gave it his best calm voice, but his red cheeks betrayed him: "We need you to resign today." He took some papers from the file and pushed them across the desk to me. "Read these over and sign them, please. They may take you a while. Among other things, they cover your severance package, a very generous package I should say. Most people would call it a genuine golden parachute. And there's some legal stuff."

"Stuff?"

"We will cover any legal expenses associated with the settlements and possible civil proceedings. Those in which the firm is involved, that is. Any others I'm afraid you're on your own. And the standard non-compete stuff."

Christ, they've thought of everything. They may have slipped up on the date of my arrival this morning but they've been planning all this for days.

I felt helpless, powerless, impotent, humiliated, embarrassed, and deeply ashamed. Scared and angry as well. I was being ordered to resign. I had been dismissed and that was that. I signed the papers then and there and stood.

"It's a helluva thing," I said. "I thought we were better than this. I love Brock and Case. I always gave it everything I had."

"We *are* better than this, Coop, and so are you. We hate to lose you, but with…"

"No more, Joel. No more. Let's leave it there."

I took his proffered hand and gave it a limp shake.

"One piece of advice, friend to friend." he said. "If I were you, I'd get away from New York, at least for a while. Someplace quiet, out of the way, where the paparazzi will be less likely to hound you."

"Thanks for the tip," I mumbled. (Was I being sardonic or grateful? I honestly didn't know any more.) "If only I had someplace to go." Definitely sardonic. And true.

"Maybe we can help with that. Let us know. In any case, we will be doing our best to smooth this whole thing over, keep you out of it as much as we can. Satisfy these women to shut them up. Maybe someday the time will be right to bring you back."

I gave him a half smile and walked out of his office, went down in the elevator and out the door of Brock and Case for what I knew would be the last time. I was out on the streets of Manhattan, the concrete jungle.

CHAPTER 40

I checked in at the Berkshire. I had no idea how long the firm would handle the hotel cost and no desire to find out. But where would I go? Going back to the Melbourne circus would probably be worse than staying in New York. And what would I do there anyway? Unemployed and under siege in Toorak was not an appealing thought. I needed to get Mel and the boys on a plane to somewhere, somewhere in the States, but where?

It was the middle of the night in Melbourne. Not a good time to call. I sipped a scotch from the mini bar, reflecting on my options, which ranged from almost none to totally none. As if by default, I dialed the number Virge had given me for wherever he had settled. Somewhere around Atlanta, I supposed.

We made short shrift of small talk before I dove directly into my labyrinth of problems. He said very little, only occasionally offering a quick phrase with his amazing capacity for empathy.

"Come here," he said when he sensed I was winding down. That was it: "Come here."

"What does that even mean?" I replied.

"Lie low, right? Come here with us and lie low."

"What would I do?"

"You would lie low. Take some time and figure things out."

"Not sure there's much left to figure with."

"Take some time. You have a pretty good organism as your operating system, Coop. In time you'll come to trust it again."

"There's Mel and the..."

"Of course. We can figure that out too."

"How would I know where to live, where to look for a place?"

"All in due time. In the meantime, stay with us. Judy will be delighted."

"Now you're going too far.

"No, I mean it."

"Look," I said. "I know you mean it and I love you for it. But it all seems like too much."

"Think about it then. Promise me you'll think about it."

"You got it and thanks. I'm a wreck right now. Not worth fuck at thinking about anything. But I'll think about it. I will."

I hung up and thought of crawling under the covers until the next morning even though it was just after noon. I also considered going down to the bar and getting drunk or going out for a bottle and bringing it back to the room. Not my style, really. The night Mel and I spilled our guts was the only time I had really let myself get blasted in forever, maybe since undergrad days when that was the whole object of a night out. The very idea of feeling that way again turned me off completely. Why would anyone voluntarily do that to themselves? Maybe if they were me right now. But no, it would only make things worse.

I decided to go out for lunch. A walk around Manhattan might be good. I have always loved to walk the streets of this city. *Revisit old landmarks. MOMA is nearby. The Carnegie Deli? A corned beef sandwich for lunch? Too much grease for the way my stomach feels. Maybe the new World Trade Center. It's been open a couple of years and I've never been to the top. Windows on the World they call it. Fuck it, let's just go out and see what happens. Can't stay in this room and think.*

I did indeed walk for a while. Some of my best thinking comes on a vigorous walk, but today I was trying not to think. Ended up passing MOMA, didn't go in, crossed Madison, joined the Times Square squalor, mindlessly unaware of my surroundings. I finally settled for a slice of pizza at a food truck. I folded and finished it as I walked back to the hotel, where I did, in fact, crawl under the covers which is where I had an attack of pizza-induced reflux, thus avoiding sleep once again. When I was able to calculate the time change, I dialed the many numbers required to get through to Mel, only to hear our phone ring at that end until I gave up. I wished I could leave a message but this was not like reaching a secretary at my office. My office? What a concept.

I went down to the lobby bar and ordered a scotch and a burger. I finished the scotch and half the burger before hitting the street once again. Already growing dark, February in New York was a cruel reminder that I was no longer in Australian summer. No longer home. Where was home? No office, no home.

Times Square again, the street chess and three-card-monte hustlers even in the cold. The whores. Then more whores over on 8th Avenue along with the peep shows. Out of some kind of morbid curiosity, I entered one of the peep show houses. It felt empty, like I was the only customer. Slatternly and bored, women in scuzzy attire looked out at me from open booths. What were they offering? I could make some guesses but they showed little interest in me, or in anything else for that matter. I went into a booth and put a dollar's worth of coins into a slot. There were several sordid "movie" titles to choose from but the default selection already playing was of a naked fat woman engaged in intimacy with a horse. It was like rubbing my nose in my own coarseness, sickly emblematic of who and what I had become. I didn't stay for the happy ending, pushing back the curtain, hurrying past the "girls" with my head down. Out onto 8th, I felt like just one more piece of the flotsam.

I am 8th Avenue!

CHAPTER 41

Thank god Mel answered when I rang her the next morning. I told her how I had been treated since landing at the same time yesterday. *Was that just yesterday?* She said little as I related the conversation with Joel, about his take no prisoners approach to my total dismissal. This finally evoked a response, "You were fired, truly fired?"

"Officially I was asked to resign. No, not asked, *ordered* to resign. But face it, I was fired, sacked." I felt myself getting too heavy. I made a futile attempt to lighten things up: "A little like what Kerr did to Whitlam."

"Not exactly," she said.

"But no worries. They did give me a very nice golden parachute. We won't have to worry about money."

"Great. That's just great. They pay you off to shut you up. But it's the 'we' part of 'we don't have to worry' that matters, isn't it? Is there still a 'we'?"

"Oh, god, I hope so, Mel. Remember, we said it was worth it. We were worth it. Remember?"

"It seemed right at the time."

"And now?"

"Like I said, I don't know anything anymore. I don't even know who I am any more, or who you are, or we are. Or if there even is a 'we.' Poor Beth Robertson."

"Beth? What about Beth?"

"Poor Beth has sort of taken me under her wing. Such a wonderful, selfless woman. I feel like she's the only one I can talk to right now. All my other so-called lady friends are urging me to jump ship, and they don't mince words. Throw the bum out. Leave him now."

As painful as that was to hear, I said, "Mel, I can understand why they would say that. In fact I would expect it. I almost feel the same way—about myself, I mean, not us. I hope and pray that Beth doesn't agree with them."

"You don't pray, Coop."

"You know what I mean."

"I'm not too sure what anything means anymore. But no, Beth is not saying the others are wrong. She says they may be right. The difference with Beth is that she is not judging, not judging me, not judging you. She's not trying to pump me up either, no false optimism, no cheerleading. Just listening. Just supporting. Just loving. She wants me to do what my heart tells me to do. She does say that marriages do sometimes survive affairs. Some, she says, do just that. They survive. Some learn and grow from it and become better. I don't know what I would do without her."

I found myself immediately pulling for Beth. "As always, she seems to show wise understanding, Mel. Deeper than a knee-jerk throw the bum out."

"But you *are* a bum."

"Guilty. Absolutely guilty. And deeply ashamed. I hate what I have done to you but I also hate myself for doing those things in the first place. That's not who I want to be, for both your sake and for my own."

Mel let my words hang there for a moment before switching back to Beth. "Obviously I'm the not first person who's confided in her. She has lots of stories. Not gossip, no names, but all meant to give me some perspective. And things also haven't always been peaches and cream between her and Michael."

I resisted my natural urge to pry into the juicy tidbits about the Managing Director emeritus of World Motors of Australia. Possibly consider it for leverage. I let it pass. All I said was, "I can imagine it wasn't. Not with that blow-hard."

"That's not what I mean. She didn't say anything against the man. It's obvious that she loves him. All she said was that he was a dashingly handsome captain in the British military when they met in India. The Sandhurst grad who had his pick of the ladies. The same was still true when he made colonel and they decided to get married. She says she has no idea if he has ever had an affair or even affairs. But she has never been sure that he didn't. She decided years ago not to probe to find out. Didn't think it could help to know. She loved him and she was going to keep him no matter what. And yes, to your point, she did say he is sometimes a bit of a pompous ass and she wants to keep him anyway."

I laughed despite my general emotional emptiness, a condition now partially ameliorated with Beth's slight encouragement. "Good stuff, Mel. You always said you wanted to grow up to be Beth."

"But I'm finding growing up is hard to do."

"Isn't the song about 'breaking up?'"

"That, too."

I shouldn't have mentioned it, but it brought another subject to mind. "How about Gregory?" I asked, not sure of the answer I wanted to hear.

"He called once and asked me to dinner but I turned him down. We talked then for a while. He's still dealing with all his issues. The press is all over him. He's still getting over the shock about Vicky and Del Bryant. She turned out to be a very different person than the one we thought we met. That's even more true for him Much more dark and calculating, apparently. I think he wishes he was the father of the baby but knows better.

"And, yes, I'm sure you're wondering, it was clear he wanted more than dinner. I told him I couldn't, not any more. That I was dealing with too much. But the fact is I am not in the least bit interested. I'm pretty sick of men right now. I'm sick of him right now, meaning Gregory. The man we knew has been replaced by a whinge-ing, pathetic specimen of something I don't recognize. Everything is someone else's fault. Maybe I'm just finally seeing his true colors. I guess I still care about the guy but I really want nothing to do with him. He may have picked up on that because he simply said good-bye at the end of the conversation, no hint of anything in the future. Which was fine with me."

I was relieved and changed the subject. "Okay, then, how are the boys?"

"Still not back in school. They never want to go back there. Fortunately, the press has left our front yard. They're back to focusing on what they call 'The Canberra Triangle.' I guess we're not as newsworthy, thank god. But Roger and Brett are still getting either the cold shoulder or verbal bullying from some of their old classmates, boys they thought were friends. I talked once with the headmaster and he is not too encouraging either. He hasn't fully ruled out their return but he kept saying that, for their sake, for Roger and Brett's sake, it might be better if we considered other options."

"Courageous of him," I said.

"They do miss you, I have to say, even if they don't use those words. They want to know what you're doing. Are we going to New York soon, they ask. Some of it is just wanting to get out of here, I suppose, but they do miss their father."

This is brought tears to the back of my eyes. "And you?"

"I miss the Coop I have been in love with all these years. Do you remember him?"

"Barely. But maybe you can fall for another Coop. I have to find him myself, Mel. I hope *I* like him better too."

"I will admit I have some of that myself."

"Mel, as for moving to New York, you can tell them that it's out of the question." I told her about Joel's advice to get out of town to someplace quieter, away from the paparazzi. I told her about Virge and his invitation.

"Go," she said. "You should go. Virge and Judy will be good for you."

"And you?"

"Me in Atlanta? Never part of my life plan, but who knows? I never planned any of this. I may never plan on anything again in my life. We'll have to see. Beth tells me to do what's in my heart. First I have to find out what that is."

"Please do. I've done nothing but make that same search since I got on the plane in Melbourne. But I wish with all *my* heart that we will find it together."

"It would be hard. Harder, I think, than either of us knows now. All I can say is I'll have to wait and see."

"All I can say is I'll have to take that for now. Thank you so much for talking about all this with me. I didn't know what to expect."

"And who knows who I will be the next time we talk."

"I'll take that chance. It's all I have. And I mean 'all.' Thank Beth for me."

"I thank her every day. Good-night, Coop. Call again sometime."

"I promise."

CHAPTER 42

A few days later I sat in the Cash's living room; Virge, Judy, and I sipping tea the afternoon I arrived. Their house—an older, smallish home in the old Atlanta suburb of Decatur proper—held the promise of reflecting their warmth once they had time to settle in. Too early for roses and the Bermuda grass lawn still a tawny shade; it all made Virge itchy to get started. Just as I remembered from their place in Connecticut, their old eclectic furnishings showed a touch of comfortable class. "Cozy" was the obvious word for the whole enterprise.

As I spun out my story, they listened attentively, sympathetic without encouraging any self-pity on my part. Having already told Virge some of it by phone from New York, I only briefly touched on my conversation with Joel and his demand for my resignation. I spent more time on my own angst on the long flight over, my grasping at straws in my attempts to make some sense of the whole bloody mess. I related my mindless wandering of the Manhattan streets including my demoralizing shuffle among the dregs of 8th Avenue. Finally I gave them my banal conclusion: I was both the cause and the effect of everything that was happening. Not the only effect, obviously. I couldn't begin to calculate the collateral damage. But clearly, I was one of my own victims.

Judy looked at Virge with a slight smile: "Sounds a little like *you* when you flew home with your broken noggin."

"Don't remind me," he said.

"But we got *him* put back together okay," Judy said. "I think maybe we can even salvage something with you."

The conversation switched briefly to Virge's new job with the

CDC. He worked for the Director, National Center for Health Statistics (NCHS), creating new models for tracking and predicting health outbreaks. "It's a lot quieter here than at B&C," he said, "but I'm not just sitting around on my bum. I hold a dual appointment as associate professor of research and statistics at Emory University. Both the agency and the university dangled offers of administrative positions for considerably more money than I'm making now. Judy and I celebrated the offers by splurging for a dinner out, talked it over, gave thanks for our good fortune, then went to sleep and let it the idea pass. I love things just the way they are."

The cozy house, the yard, the soon-to-be-blooming roses, the work, and most of all, Judy. It was obvious to me that Virge had found his ecological niche. I couldn't be happier for him. Or more envious.

Judy must have picked up on my feelings. "It hasn't all been a bed of roses," she said, and asked to know more about how Mel was feeling. I told them about our call. "I never met this Beth person, but I love her already," Judy said. "I think she's got it just right."

Virge was more subdued when he said, "Like Judy said, we haven't always had it so good. We have our own fidelity issues to deal with, you know." I looked at Judy who first put her head down then looked up and laughed.

"You think it's hard dealing with your man running around with other women.?" she said. "Try it when it's another man, or men. But we're making it. With help we're making it."

Virge saw my oblique glance his way. "I'm sure you knew, Coop."

"Didn't know for sure but had my suspicions."

"Well," he said, "suspicions confirmed. That's how I got my skull bashed in."

I said, "Of course there were rumors to that effect but I tried to avoid jumping to conclusions. I was too wrapped up in just worrying about you."

Judy said, "Me too...for a while. Then, when he was out of the woods, I wanted to know what the sonuvabitch did to get his head bashed in."

"Coming out of the closet to your wife of twenty some years, your best friend, the mother of your kids," Virge said, looking at Judy. "It's hell."

Judy said, "Something like the hell you said you and Mel went through the night you both spilled all the beans."

"But you two got through it. I can tell just being here with you both that you got through it."

"Still getting through it," Judy said. "It doesn't happen all at once. I've had to come to accept the sonofabitch the way he is. He's bi-sexual, let's face it. He tried to promise me he wouldn't mess around with men anymore, but I realized at some point that was ridiculous. He is who he is, what he is. All I ask now is not to be lied to. I want to know what's going on. Not to probe but to understand. We've both tried to focus on understanding. So far it's helped. I think we're more intimate than ever. All marriages change all the time, I guess. I like the marriage we have now more than the one before. But I think it'll take years to embrace it totally."

"And so far," Virge said, "no other men. But who knows?" He looked at his wife with a twinkle. "I've got some cute guys in my classes."

She gave him a nasty look and said to me, "I even love the sonofabitch now more than ever. Why, I don't know. But he's right about the cute guys. Some of them have caught *my* eye too." The two of them cracked up. I smiled through some slight embarrassment at both their confessions and their open display of affection. I also projected my own situation and felt doubts and misgivings that what they were saying could work for Mel and me. At least not in their totality.

After a few moments' pause—for their laughter and my reflections—Judy said, "Who knows anything, Coop? One day at a time, one foot in front of the other. You and Mel have yourselves to worry about. We're not trying to give you any glib answers. Heavens knows we don't have any ourselves. We like where we are but no guarantees we will next week. Our only guarantee to each other is that we will keep trying."

CHAPTER 43

I stayed with Virge and Judy for the three-day fish limit while I searched for a place to live. I had no idea what I was going to be doing, just knew I had to stay away from New York for the time being and that I wanted Mel and the boys to join me soon if that were possible. For what I hoped was the short term, I found a rental apartment in Buckhead, the Toorak of Atlanta, the area where I thought we might settle, if settling down was even in our future.

I hoped to find some work as an independent consultant but was in no hurry. I worried some that my forced resignation from B&C and the reasons for it might follow me and tarnish my chances with any new clients. Again, I was flying in the dark. I really had no idea how all that would pan out. In the meantime, I would settle in, look at houses in Buckhead, and try to talk Mel into joining me.

My calls to her evolved into updates. Mel informed me that I was back in the Australian papers, stories that referred to me not so much by name now. I had become "the American expat," the one who had returned to the America, perhaps thus "escaping any accountability for his actions against his female victims." Apparently sexual misconduct short of rape was not an extraditable offense.

The papers cited four different sources, one unnamed and three named, as being particularly unhappy about that. The unnamed source was a woman who said she had once worked under my management at B&C (almost surely Pamela Dorsett, she whom I found somewhat challenging in my meeting with the firm's lawyers). The woman was reported as saying that a "widespread abusive culture had developed" under my leadership. "A man who himself was the very role model for such behavior." She said she been "against the cover up made possible by financial settlements with the wronged women." She went on to say that the firm now had a chance to prove it would "no longer engage in its misogynistic ways." Still she said, I should be held accountable in some way. (*How about getting fired?*) This all seemed so much more hard-nosed and merciless than she came across in our meeting.

Kevin's wife Diane was the second source, stirred by Kevin's suing her for divorce. He blamed me as "only the most recent among her many affairs." She in turn claimed that I was the real villain, pursuing her against her will.

I interrupted Mel's update with "Mel, I swear…"

"I know, Coop. I know. Would it surprise you to know that I believe you? Diane's a piece of work. I've always known that even if you didn't."

Mel finished with the story of two more closely connected sources, both anonymous. One a man who was not at all happy about being sacked by WM-A (Gerald Lawson) and his wife (Fran the Formidable). He claimed to have been let go because he blew the whistle on me, on his direct observations of indiscretions on my part, just as his company was about to hire me to an important executive position. He also blew the whistle, coining the phrase a second time, regarding his suspicions of his wife's many affairs as well, one of which he said may have been with me. She, in turn, said her husband was a wimp and a liar but added that I indeed tried to get her to have sex with me while she was vacationing in Fiji.

On this side of the Atlantic, meanwhile, B&C seemed to be doing a good job of keeping the American angle out of the New York papers. I was not kept officially up to date, but I was sure that the settlements, and their costs, must have been piling up. I did hear through what was left of my grapevine that one of my accusers who was resisting settlement finally gave in when B&C threatened to report certain issues in her own past, things about her which may or may not have been true. While my conscience was no clearer, and none of this helped assuage Mel's misgivings or rebuild her confidence in me, my fears of public exposure were ebbing.

Finally in late March, Mel told me she and the boys were leaving

Australia. "B&C is on me to get moved," she said. "They say they can't keep me here any longer. They need us to get out of this house so that another expat family can have it. They're kicking us out of the country."

"Believe me, I get it. The feelings are all too familiar. So maybe you'll come live with me?" I asked, making no effort to disguise my anxieties over her answer.

"To tell the truth, I don't know anyplace else to go. I have no other life over there."

It was not the total answer I hoped for but I would settle for it at the moment. "That's wonderful. Shall I find us a house?"

"Why don't you have a look around and narrow it down some. I'll help when I get there. And one more thing."

"Yes?"

"I miss you. I miss us. Whatever us *is* now. Not the us of the last few years but some new version of the old us. I know we can't go back there but maybe we can find a new us that feels something like that. I told Beth that I thought that was where my heart was and she said go for it."

For the first time in months, I felt joy, joy flooding my mind, flooding my heart, even my body. She couldn't see my welling tears but I'm sure she could hear them in my voice. "My god, how I have longed to hear words like those," I said.

"Let's not kid ourselves, Coop, we're not there yet, but like we said, we're worth it. We swore to that and I'm coming to work on it with you. In Atlanta, Georgia, of all places."

"Mel, I think we can be happy anywhere. We could be happy in Gary, Indiana. But from what I have seen so far, Atlanta is a great place. Energy all over the place. A lot is happening here right now, business-wise but also culturally. I think you will like it. And I think we can be happy here."

My life took a great leap forward when I met their plane at Harts-field in mid-April. We did the hugging thing, but it all felt tentative, especially with Roger and Brett. They acted almost as though I was a distant uncle they had only seen a few times in their lives. Mel's kiss was on the cheek. Nevertheless, they were "home" and with me. Thing were going to work out, I was sure. Life could begin again.

On the way to the apartment, I filled her in on the fact that Virge had tried to line me up with a teaching job in the Emery business school but they had no room in their budget for further faculty. They suggested I meet the dean at Georgia State which I did. Alicia Bonfort was a sophisticated, attractive and friendly woman, obviously very bright and accomplished. Her short black hair and flashing black eyes seemed to reflect high energy. I learned later that she was highly thought of among upper levels of the Atlanta business community and a leader of charitable activities in the city.

I was grateful when she said was impressed with the quality of my resume but not too surprised when she also admitted she had done enough digging that she was aware of some of what she called my "extracurricular activities." "I take some of all that with a grain of salt," she said. "I know how things work and I'm sure you've learned some lessons."

As was the case at Emery, she also said she couldn't offer me a full-time, tenure track position, but if I was interested, she could use me to teach two classes as an adjunct professor. "It's not much money," she said, but I accepted on the spot. Teaching MBA classes in strategic management and organization behavior would get me back in the game, plus I would have time for some outside consulting if and when it turned up. I would also have time for Mel and the boys and me to get reacquainted, to rebuild my family.

There was no better time for them to arrive in Atlanta. The whole city was in bloom, even downtown was alive with blossoming trees—cherry blossoms, pear blossoms, but most of all the dogwoods. In the city, I gave them a quick circle tour of Georgia State, a plain, ordinary urban campus, but even there the trees were impressive. When we got out as far as Buckhead, the posh homes presented magical landscapes of azaleas and even more dogwoods. Mel gave me a big smile. "It's not Gary, Indiana," she said, "but I guess we might be able to make do here."

They moved into the apartment with me but Mel loved the place in Buckhead that I had at the top of my list. We closed on it within the week. Soon thereafter we got the boys into a good private school. Everything was coming up dogwood and peach trees.

CHAPTER 44

The initial euphoria of having my family together again faded with the blossoms. For one thing, Mel wouldn't sleep in the same bedroom with me let alone have sex. "Too soon," she said. "We promised to get help and sex is the biggest thing in our way. You don't get off that easily, no matter how sweet you try to be now. You hurt a lot of people, most of all me. There has to be more."

And then there were the boys. They knew too much, thanks to the media, about their father's betrayal of their mother not to feel some of that same betrayal themselves. They remained remotely polite with me, avoiding me as much as possible while trying to be very protective of their mom.

Virge and Judy invited the two of us to their house for dinner. Virge proudly toured us through his rose garden. I had hopes that seeing them as I had when I first arrived, seeing how they had worked on their issues, the progress they had made, might help Mel see a way forward. They did recommend their marriage counselor and we agreed to contact her. They also said some of the same things they had said to me about embracing the opportunity not for rebuilding the old marriage but for building a whole new one, maybe even better than the old one. Judy spoke of accepting her husband the way he was. Mel was very attentive and asked a lot of questions.

On the way home, though, she talked about everything else: the cozy home, Virge's roses, how nice it was just to see him thriving. But when I asked about the marital advice, she remained cool. She said maybe we should see their counselor or maybe we needed to shop around some.

"Shop around?"

"Do some of our own research. Get some other recommendations. She may be great, the best, but the truth is, I'm not so sure I want the same counselor poking around into our lives that our friends have." I let it go. I wanted her to feel confidence in whomever we chose.

My work at Georgia State, on the other hand, offered something of a respite from the tension and mixed signals at home. At some level I was aware that an adjunct position at a middling institution was a come-down (no Harvard or MIT), but it was better than dodging the detritus and dog shit of 8th Avenue, and at least for the time being, I was lucky to have it. It had its satisfactions. My teaching got off to a good start and I found I seemed to have a knack for it. Maybe, like Virge, I had found a congenial new niche. Both classes met at night since most of my students were working full time, eager for an MBA to advance their careers. This was highly motivating for all of them as far as maintaining high grades, which for some, meant studying and for others meant trying to bluff their way through. Although I was new at teaching, I had long experience with both types.

Dean Bonfort was full of compliments on my good start. She asked me frequently what she could do to help but offered no advice. She said I didn't need it. I asked for nothing until my students requested meetings with me and I had no office in which to hold official office hours.

"Of course," she said, and apologized for overlooking the obvious. Office space was at a premium, she said, and while it was normal for adjuncts to hold office hours in their classrooms just before or after class, she would try to find me some space of my own. The next week she showed me a small room off her own office, more or less her private antechamber. "I know this is much smaller than you are accustomed to," she said, "but I'm afraid it's the best I can do right now. Will it serve?"

"It will be perfect, Dean Bonfort, and thank you for giving up some space for me."

"Not to worry," she said, reminiscent of Australia. She flashed me her winning smile and patted my arm. "This way I'll keep you close by so I can pick your brain. And please, call me Alicia."

I did sense a small problem developing with one of my Strategic Management students. Kayla Clayton was a stunning black girl who worked in some kind of management job for Goodwill Industries. She had all the signs of one of those who was doing her best to bluff her way through. All students in the MBA program were part of a cohort that stayed together from course to course, so her peers were already well acquainted with her before they got to me. Early on, I divided the class into project teams in which they were to study a major industry and give a group presentation on the strategic challenges and opportunities within that industry. I immediately detected a resistance from Kayla's group. When I allowed some class time for work on their project, the team seemed to work around her rather than with her and she seemed quite happy to let them. She smiled at their intense chatter but said almost nothing.

Each member was to take one aspect of the task for the presentation. When it was her turn, Kayla covered her topic with smiling enthusiasm combined with very little content, some of which was not even relevant, some of which sounded as though taken word-for-word from an encyclopedia, and the rest of which seemed merely made up as she went along. The others on her team mostly looked down at their notes or out to the rest of the class with knowing smirks. Her group as a whole did an outstanding job and I gave them an A, not wanting to punish them for Kayla's short comings.

Next was an individual assignment, a written analysis of a fairly complex case study. Kayla's paper looked to be a collection of plagiarized paragraphs linked by meaningless filler. I was ready to give her a failing grade, but being new to the institution and new to teaching, I thought it best to talk it over with my dean.

Alicia chose to meet me in my little den instead of her office. As always, she was fashionably dressed: a mid-length navy skirt and flashing green stockings, which I presumed were pantyhose. We sat knee to knee as she read over Kayla's paper. I did my best to ignore it when one of Alicia's nylon clad knees bumped mine. Once, however, it was so noticeable that she laughed and excused herself, patting me on the leg as she turned to the side and crossed her legs with a soft swish. I may have even blushed, but not her. "Behave yourself."

she said, flashing a smile while I turned my head to the side, embarrassed despite myself.

When she finished reading, she said, "This is not our first go-around with Ms. Clayton. What do you have in mind?"

I wasn't sure of what I was being asked, but I said I thought I needed to give her an F. Alicia nodded as if to confirm my judgement, but said, "We don't normally give F's in grad school, Coop. Mostly As and some Bs. C is basically the equivalent of an F. But even there, let me caution you. Kayla will not take a C lightly. She will protest and let you know how well connected she is." Spotting my blank look, she added, "Kayla is loosely related to the mayor's family, as she reminds us at every opportunity." Maynard Jackson was the first African American elected Mayor of Atlanta, and a major face of the progressive image this southern city wanted to project to the world.

I was perplexed. "So you know this and so do her fellow students. How do I avoid losing their respect as well as my own if I just slap an A on this kind of work?"

"I'm not telling you what to do," Alicia said. "It's your decision. I'm just supplying you with data. It's up to you and I will do all I can to support you."

This was not at all what I wanted to hear, but I thanked her for consulting with me. "Any time," she said, uncrossing her legs as I looked away again. Once more she patted me on the knee as she rose to leave. "I'm sure you've been faced with sensitive problems before, Coop," she said. "You've been around. I think you and I need to find the time to have a drink somewhere after we leave the office someday. There's a lot I would like to share with you. Bring you up to speed, so to speak."

Why is it beginning to seem as though there is a double meaning to everything she says to me? Am I imagining it?

I scribbled a C+ on Kayla's paper, then went on to read the others, most of which exceeded my expectations (or biases) for Georgia State working grad students. When I finished the stack, I left for home, wondering what to expect *there* today.

As always, driving up Peachtree was a chore but it would be no better on the freeway. I was truly enjoying the city itself but not the traffic, although it gave me plenty of time to try to process the day. Given my history, especially my recent history, I was not comfortable about either the Kayla or Alicia situations. Now, before I got home, I was faced with a decision: do I tell Mel about my feelings or not. I was committed to regaining her trust and had vowed openness and honesty. Telling her would accomplish the latter but perhaps not the former. I was still undecided when I parked in our garage, but chose to let things pass when I saw her with the boys in the family room.

CHAPTER 45

The next evening I left the case analysis papers on my classroom desk to be picked up by the students before class. When they took their seats, they buzzed with each other about their grades, some comparing my red margin notes and comments. Kayla did not join them, merely stared at the paper and then at me, before turning it face down and plunking it on the arm of her desk. Her look was a mixture of anger and smug amusement. It didn't help me concentrate on my teaching.

At the break, she came directly to me and said, "What is this? This is the worst grade I've ever had on anything."

"I'm sorry to hear that," I said.

"I need to talk with you. I don't understand."

"How about during my office hours tomorrow at five?"

"Can't do it then. What about right after class tonight?"

I really didn't want to do that but I felt pressure to seem somewhat accommodating so I agreed. For the rest of the class, I couldn't help but find myself glancing her way too often. She was always staring my way as well, a "dare me" stare.

When class ended, I suggested she and I just stay in the classroom for our conference, but she insisted on meeting in my little office. She claimed that otherwise people in the class might be watching and listening.

"Ah, I see Alicia keeps you close by," she laughed when we entered the room. "Nice."

"Meaning?"

"Oh, nothing. Just nice is all." Her grin implied more.

I did my best to lay out the whole picture for her. Before focusing on her paper, I commented as diplomatically as I could on my observations of her work with her team and her part in their report. I then got fairly blunt when I pointed out what I thought was not her own writing in the paper, to which she got very defensive. I proceeded to those parts of the paper that sounded more like her own work but didn't add anything of substance.

She argued some, but mostly fell back on a plea based on her hurt feelings, feelings that I was picking on her unfairly. With tears, she promised that if I would just raise her grade to a B, she knew she could do better.

When I politely refused, she dried her tears and switched tactics to indignance, letting me know quite clearly just who she was, what connections she had. "If that's the way you want to be," she said. She abruptly stood and threw her paper in my trash bin before turning her back to me and leaving, her shoulders thrown back and her hips swaying dramatically.

I needed a double Scotch when I got home, but I still didn't tell Mel about Kayla. I was afraid of how she might take it. Would she think I was the one on the make again?

CHAPTER 46

Alicia called me at home the next afternoon. "We need to talk. Can you meet me for that drink we talked about?" I hadn't talked about any drinks at all, but that wasn't worth mentioning.

"Kayla?" I asked.

"Meet me at The Clock at five-thirty."

When I told Mel to hold my dinner because I had to meet the dean, she shrugged with indifference. She did that a lot lately.

The Clock was a sleek bar/restaurant done in concrete contemporary, similar to the dizzyingly high atrium lobby of the nearby Hyatt Regency. Alicia Bonfort was nowhere to be seen so I took a seat at the bar and ordered a single malt. I felt the need for fortification. Before I was served, she swished in and motioned me with some urgency to a corner booth. The bartender acknowledged the pantomime and nodded with a smile. "I'll bring it to your table," he said.

Alicia had dressed with her usual colorful flair, this time with bright yellow stockings to go with her slightly more creamy short skirt and matching silk blouse. fitting for a gloriously warm and sunny-day-going-on-evening. This lady could obviously hold her own in fast circles. I had changed from my work-at-home clothes into a green polo shirt and dress khakis.

I slid into the L-shaped booth opposite her but she motioned me to come to her side. "We can talk more privately this way," she said. Jesus, what kind of trouble am I in? In any case, it could be bad.

When I took my place, she patted my thigh, something I was coming to expect. "Have you been a bad boy again?"

"God, I hope not. What's up?"

"Listen, I kind of like bad boys. That is, provided they're discreet. I was just hoping you could be discreet."

At that moment I choose discretion by saying nothing. I had no idea where this was leading but my hopes for any kind of successful outcome were dwindling.

After she ordered an aquavit, she said "I warned you about Kayla, didn't I."

"You did. So this *is* about Kayla."

"Of course. What else did you think it was about? You are bad, aren't you." The pat on the leg.

"I didn't know. I guessed it might be but you had said before that we should meet for a drink sometime. I had no funny ideas, believe me."

"Nor did I, believe me. So, Kayla. Just as I suspected, she's upset. She came to see me today and made some threats. She wants you fired, for one."

"Fired? Over a C+?"

"Yes and no. She's pulling out all the stops this time, playing both the race and the sex cards. She claims, as the only black woman in the class, that you have had it in for her from the beginning. That you didn't like her, respect her. That you were always putting her down."

"Alicia, I don't think I've said two words directly to her before our meeting after class last night. As for her being a black woman, of course I recognized that she was very attractive. That's it. Nothing more."

Alicia shifted slightly away from me as she said, "About your meeting with her. I told you she played both the race and sex cards."

"That I didn't like or respect her because she is black and a woman. I get it."

"There is more to it than her gender. She claims you came on to her in your conference with her, in your little office space. In fact she said she wanted to just stay in the classroom after class to talk with you but that you insisted on meeting in, in her words, 'his cozy office next to yours.'"

"She said that? I swear it was just the opposite. She's the one who insisted on my office. And she made some remark about it being so close to yours."

"Remark? What did she say?"

"I don't remember exactly. Just that she said it with a smirk on her face. I think maybe all she said was 'Nice,' but I had a feeling it meant more than that. But I made no effort, no gesture, said nothing that she could have interpreted as my coming on to her."

"You don't know Kayla's powers of interpretation. She obviously had looked into your background somehow. She most certainly did more homework on you than she ever did for a class. She accused you of being a habitual womanizer who offered to raise her grade in exchange for sex in some form."

"In some form?"

"Well, to put it bluntly, she said a blow job. Right then and there in the office."

"Christ."

"I know. That didn't sound like your style."

"My style?" I asked, astounded. What the hell did that mean? Not only Kayla's ridiculous accusation but what was Alicia saying about my style? She just chuckled at my question, which only added to my confusion over her meaning.

"So anyway, that's what she claims. And it may not make any difference whether or not it's true."

"Goddamnit, it's not true and that sure as hell does make a difference."

"Maybe to you, and maybe even to me. Knowing her and knowing you at least a little, I believe your story, not hers. But that may not make any difference when it comes to her threats. She wants me to fire you immediately or else."

"Or else what? What can she do?"

Alicia took a sip of aquavit. "Get *me* fired," she said. "I'm the one who hired you, says Kayla. I'm your boss and I'm the one responsible. I'm the one who sets the tone for the culture. She won't come after me, she says, as long as I take care of the problem, by which she means you."

"Come on, Dean, that's ridiculous. How the hell can she get away with getting *me* fired let alone a dean?"

"I told you who she is, her connections. Even then, I doubt that she can get me fired but she could make life hell for me by trying. I don't want to see my name all over the *Journal* or the *Constitution*. I wouldn't think you'd like that either. Or, even worse, at a trial."

"Oh, come on. A trial? Excuse my language but what the fuck?"

"Your language is appropriate. She's saying she will take you to court, sue you. Unless."

"Unless?"

"Unless you are immediately dismissed."

"Fired."

"That's what that means."

"So what are you going to do?"

"I'm going to talk to her again. Try to talk her out of it. And you're going to be there with me when I do it."

"Is that wise?"

"The opportunity to confront your accuser. You have that right, you know. It may or may not work but she may find it more difficult to make her story credible with you sitting there in front of her." Alicia had moved back closer to me. I was waiting for the leg pat but got a big smile of anticipation instead. I think she was waiting for my enthusiastic response to her suggestion.

"Not so sure," I said. "Sounds uncomfortable all the way around."

"You think *that* sounds uncomfortable. You ever been the subject of media scrutiny?"

"As a matter of fact…"

"Oh, of course. So you know what really uncomfortable feels like."

"Like shit and like it will never go away."

"So it's pay me now or pay me later. What say we first try just a little discomfort now, hopefully head off more later?"

"I'm not sure it will get the job done, but yeah, okay, I'll try it with you and Kayla."

"Coop, I want to keep you. [*Scary thought.*] I think you are off to a good start toward becoming an outstanding graduate school professor, maybe full time tenure track when and if I get the budget. I've thought that from the beginning. Also, in case you haven't noticed, I like you. I had hopes that we might become friends."

Not sure, at this point, of the desirability of either of those possible futures but let it go.

"Can we order dinner now?" she asked. "Mostly Scandinavian menu and all delicious." I had assumed earlier that we would be having dinner together, but now I said, "Alicia, thank you. I'm sure it's wonderful, but with all this crap going on, I don't feel much like eating. Anyway, my wife will be waiting to hear how things turn out. I'll grab a little something at home, but again, I thank you for the invitation."

Her body language made it clear to me that this was not what she wanted to hear. She suddenly became very distant, literally as she slid a slight but definitive distance away, but also in what she next said. "If that's the way you want it. I have a husband too, you know. I'll let you know about the meeting."

I left as she took a last sip of her drink and gathered her things.

CHAPTER 47

I knew Mel was not in the least bit waiting to hear about "how things turned out." She knew nothing about any of my Alicia and Kayla complications. I had chosen not to tell her. Now maybe there was no escaping it.

She was in the family room reading a letter, her empty wine glass on the coffee table in front of her. She barely looked up. Indeed, the letter was in her lap but she was looking at a newspaper clipping that apparently came with it. There were tears in her eyes. I sat and reached to embrace her but she shoved me away.

"You better get yourself a drink," she said, drying her tears. "A good, strong one."

When I came back with my double scotch on the rocks, she said, "It's from Beth. Poor, dear Beth."

"Hearing from Beth usually makes you happy," I said. "What's going on?"

"She's shattered, that poor, sweet lady. It's Mike. Now, like all of you other bastards, he's made the papers. Women are coming out of the woodwork, accusing him of unwanted sexual advances. But some of it goes back for years, apparently. They were ready to ride off into the sunset of retirement, enjoy the golden years, and all that bull. Now she doesn't know what to think or do, just the way I felt when she helped me so much. She says she feels like I did when I told her I didn't know who I was or who we were anymore."

I didn't say a word, just reached for her hand, which she pushed away. I remembered that Mel had recently told me that Beth said she would rather not know if Mike had ever had affairs, a form of "what you don't know won't hurt you." I didn't say anything however. Mel was in no mood.

"Remember when I always said I wanted to be Beth when I grow up? Well, no more. Look at what it's got her. I still love her but don't want to *be* her. I'm also sick and tired of this *me*. I need to grow up to be myself."

"Good for you," I said, and reached for her hand again, another futile try.

"Be careful what you wish for, Coop. You may not like me as a grown up. You may not be able to live with a grown-up me."

She handed me the newspaper clipping. "Read it and weep," she said and walked to the kitchen for more wine, leaving me alone.

It was an Op-Ed piece from the Melbourne *Age* written by Muriel Mitchell, the feminist writer who fired several well-aimed shots Jim Cairns' way, back when he and Junie Morosi were all over the news. The headline read "Male Privilege: Enough is Enough." It began with a rant about the male sexual abuse that, she said, had run rampant in Australia for years, in all walks of life. She circled back around to the Cairns-Morosi, harping on the multiple attacks on Ms. Morosi's character: that she was nothing but an opportunist bent on manipulating Cairns and others; that she obviously had no qualifications for her government position or salary. Mitchell quoted an editorial which had once claimed "Junie Morosi is an immoral adventuress who has slept with a variety of notable politicians."

Mitchell wrote:

Demean the woman, always demean the woman. Paint her as the siren diverting all the poor males from their noble pursuits. No matter that Ms. Morosi was a more than competent professional doing her job, probably better than Cairns himself.

Now look at where we find ourselves today. Two more members of parliament (ex-members, thank god) guilty of using their power and influence to attract or attack, depending on your point of view, another capable young woman, leaving her to choose abortion or single-motherhood. Of course nearly all the males in parliament are against the abortion option, leaving the young woman no publicly approved choice in the matter. Whereas, as Gloria Steinem has said, "Women are now stumbling all over each other to accuse our male politicians and business moguls of fostering egregiously abusive cultures." Stumbling, however, is the problem. Almost none of the women are willing to go on the record, to be named in public. Some have signed settlements forcing them to keep mum. Others are just plain afraid, afraid for their jobs, their careers, and maybe most of all, their names and reputations. Why expose themselves to being publicly humiliated the way we have all witnessed with Ms. Morosi? Why indeed, when the men will undoubtedly all get their second chance, while in the meantime, the women never had a first chance, at least not an equal one. Why indeed? If they were to come forth now, they would lose whatever opportunity they had in the first place. Why indeed speak publicly when they would likely lose whatever chance they ever had at a normal life, even beyond the workplace? Why indeed, when they would have their names and reputations dragged through the mud?

Meanwhile the men go on with a slap on the wrist, if that, shortly before being resurrected, often in better shape than before. 'Twas ever thus.

Finally, one last, and to me personally, sad addition to this trail of tears: One of the finest women it has ever been my privilege to know has just now been dragged into this swamp—one of the most gracious, generous people with whom our city, our state, our Australia has ever been blessed. Although a long-time hard-working member of the Women's Electoral Lobby, she would never be what you would call a feminist as such, or an activist as such—or, like me, a bitch— but she has done more for women, for victims of abuse, for poor aboriginal girls, for people of all genders, races, and persuasions than anyone else I can name. Never basking in the limelight, never taking credit, never even asking for thank yous. It's just who she is. She would think it odd that we even noticed. I will not use her name. She always wanted it that way when she deserved kudos, and now deserves them for her own sake. That is, now that she has been sucked into this cesspool, with her husband exposed as one more long-time philandering mogul. As Steinem says, 'Women have two choices: Either she's a feminist or a masochist.'

And, dear reader, guess what's going to happen next. I have reached out to my friend but she has not returned my calls. No wonder. I'm sure she has enough pain and sorrow without my particular brand of intrusion right now. But not to worry. When I think the time is right, I will ring her again and tell her that she is still my hero. My sources tell me that this news about her beloved man came as a complete and shocking surprise to her. Even though there have long been rumors, she not only didn't know, she didn't want to know. Imagine her devastation.

Accountability? Consequences? He will undoubtedly get some awkward pub-licity for a while but will retire any minute now with the kind of golden hand-shake that the good old mates in his position always get.

I love you, my friend. We all should, for she is us.

Enough with the masochism, it's time for the women's movement to move. We must make our collective voices heard. We must no longer let them silence us. Not with their money. Not with their threats. Not with their shaming. We must hold hands as one and scream. Men will say we are screaming like little girls, and we must say 'Yes' and then we must scream like girls. Little girls and big girls. Whole armies of resistance will rise against us. But never mind. No one will give us power. We must take it. 'We shall overcome.' We must overcome.

CHAPTER 48

I turned from the clipping to Mel. Both the column and her mood caused me to hesitate to say anything. She looked at me with indifference.

"So?" she said.

"So, I don't know," I said. "All I know is that I share your feelings about Beth."

"Beth needs to get mad, but she's too sweet."

"Right."

"So I need to be mad for her, which is not so hard. I was already mad anyway. Mad at you, for one. Mad at Gregory, mad at the press, mad at all politicians and other bigwigs. Mad at what my kids are going through. Mad at me. And mad at that bitch."

Having just come from a meeting with a bitch, a meeting about threats from another, younger bitch, and the bitches of my acquaintance in the Mitchell column, I was drowning in bitches. I didn't know which bitch Mel had in mind, so I asked.

"That Mitchell bitch. And all those feminist bitches," Mel answered.

That threw me. I would have guessed that Mel would have aligned herself with the columnist and her call for feminists to band together. Again, the best I could muster was a blank look.

"They're all so fucking self-righteous. They have no idea what real women feel and what they go through. I don't believe they even like women. And she pretends to be Beth's friend, Beth's advocate. Do you really think that Beth's identity will stay a big secret? So all that bitch does is add to Beth's humiliation, just like all the other blood-sucking paparazzi. And those other women she writes about—women you and I know—you think when they read that paper they felt liberated, ready to rally in the street with all the other bitches?"

I couldn't have been more confused. Her stance seemed all top-sy-turvy. I actually was sympathetic to Mitchell's message despite the shrill. Even as a man, I was ready to join her call to action. I was sure Mel would be too. But like a bemused fool, I chose to rush in. I had been looking for an opening, and instead, forced myself in where there wasn't one.

"I'm not sure what I'm about to say will do either of us any good," I said. "In fact, I'm pretty sure it won't. But I promised you. That night we laid it all out, I promised I wouldn't hold anything from you, that I would tell you the truth."

"So, good god, get on with it. What now?"

"I've been dealing with my own bitches," I said.

"That's my word, not yours. You can't use it. You don't know how."

After another mental/emotional duck on my part, I went ahead and told her about my new entanglements with Alicia and Kayla.

"You shit," she said. "You're all full of truth-telling and yet this has been going on and you didn't say a thing until now. What's to say you're telling the truth this time? You've probably been waving your dong again, just like always."

"Waving my dong? Please, not that again."

"You're a bloody dong-waver. Everything you told me. You finally got caught waving your dong in Australia. That's how we got in this mess. But even all that didn't stop you. Now we're back into it because you can't help waving your thing."

"No, I swear…"

"You swear shit. You expect me to believe anything you tell me anymore."

"I didn't lie to you. Until I met the dean today, I was assuming, hoping, that none of this was going anywhere. That nothing would even happen. That I wouldn't let anything happen ever again. So I wasn't lying to you or covering anything up. I didn't tell you until now because I wanted to shield you. Why stir things up when there is nothing in it?"

"Shield me? And how is a shield different from a cover up?"

I gave up. "I don't know, Mel. Right now, right here, I don't know a damn thing. You tell *me*. Like you have been saying since back in Australia, I don't know who you are anymore. Or me. Or us."

She stood abruptly and looked at me like I was a hopeless case. She went to the side-board to fill her wine glass before turning and glaring at me.

"I'll tell you this much about who I am, or at least who I'm going to be. I'm going to be the biggest, baddest bitch of them all. Muriel Mitchell will have nothing on me. Not Gloria Steinem. None of those bitches. But I'm going to be my own bitch, not theirs. For one thing, I'm going to be a bitch for Beth. As for who you are? You'd better figure that out for yourself. Maybe you'll be this badass bitch's husband, but if you are, get yourself ready. Because ready or not, here I come. I don't know if you can take it. And I don't know if I want you to. I don't know if I want to be married to a man who can take being married to the bitch I'm aiming to be. You'll be at the front lines of bitch-hood. What kind of man would that make you? What kind of dong-waver would settle for that? And from what you just told me, you're about to get fired again. Then you'd be the out-of-work, dong-waving husband to a bitch. So does that answer who we are if there is a we? We're going to be a couple with the all-time bitch married to the unemployed, dong-waving husband. Sound good?"

"Not the dong-waving part. I don't know if I ever was a dong-waver but if I ever was, I'm not anymore."

"But the all-time bitch part?"

"I love the all-time bitch part."

"Me too," she said. "I'm ready for it."

"Me too" I said. "She makes me hot."

We risked waking the boys up.

CHAPTER 49

We met in Dean Bonfort's office, she and Kayla Clayton and I. Alicia did her best to make it appear as though we were all colleagues working together for a solution: Kayla and I on a sofa, Alicia in an easy chair across the coffee table from us. Bottles of water and a dish of hard candy on the table. She offered us coffee or a soft drink. "Or I'm having tea, if you'd rather," she said, holding up her mug with the obvious tea bag. I said I was good and Kayla grabbed a water.

Kayla did not make eye contact with me. After what I hoped was a surreptitious glance her way to confirm this, I determined that it was a good thing and I would not look at her either.

The dean started. "We are all adults here and we share a common goal. Mr. Houghton and I want all of our students to succeed and that includes you, Kayla. And I'm sure you share that goal as well."

Kayla rolled her eyes.

"I'm hoping we can find a win/win here," the dean went on, ignoring the obvious tension, attempting to plow right through it.

I took a deep breath and rode into the breach. "Look, there is no win/win here. You two are both master manipulators and I respect mastery of most anything. On the other hand, I would have no self-respect if I sat here and let this farce go on. I am guilty of nothing here except letting you two get away with this bull. I declare us all losers, or a lose/lose/lose if you prefer. So I'm resigning as of right here and now."

I was not going to go gentle.

"Kayla," I said, "I know all about how important you are, how well connected. So sue me. You've already tried blackmail. I really don't give a damn. I may go down but I'm taking you with me. You're a liar, a cheater, and a manipulator who thinks she can get by on her good looks and by abusing her relationship with a good man like the mayor. Alicia, you're not much better. Just another manipulator, a good-looking cock-teaser who has all of Atlanta conned into believing you are this upright intelligence devoted to the public good. I guess your husband must buy your act too, even as you're trying your best to get in my pants. Who knows how many of our leading citizens have let you in there? I'll give you credit for one thing though. You've shown me what it feels like from the other side of the desk. I thank you for that insight. I have a growing respect for women. I'm learning. Anyway, I'm trying to learn. In fact, I go from this cozy little get-together to an appointment with my wife and a counselor. But based on what I know now, the two of you give women and feminism a bad name. You play right into the old stereotyped scripts.

"Well, you can both forget about me now. Or, like I said, sue me. I'm out of here."

I laid a copy of my resignation letter on the dean's desk. I didn't take the time to check their expressions or hear their comebacks whatever they might be.

I felt free for the first time in months as I drove to meet with Mel and the counselor. Maybe burning bridges can do that. Free you up, I mean. But now I had a major bridge repair project in front me. Maybe even a new bridge to build. I knew I had screwed up many times, that I *have been* screwed up for too long a time. I knew the marriage Mel and I once had was over. I knew if we had any chance of making it, it would have to be a new marriage, a second marriage but to each other. Mel had been a character in my story for too long. It was her story now and I hoped that I would always be in it. She will be my cause and I will be her effect. Knowing and loving my wife as I did, knowing that it was going to be difficult, knowing that we (especially *I*) needed help, I nevertheless felt a growing sense of confidence that we could get to the other side of the bridge together.

No worries, mate, she'll be right.

Truth? I was worried.

ACKNOWLEDGEMENTS

Thanks to all the pros, semi-pros and just plain folks who helped me with this book. I will surely leave some out but here goes:

To Rowland Johnson, Rick Bailey, and Jennifer Ward Dudley for your feedback on a work in progress. In each case your comments led to changes for the better.

To the Destin Writers group: Pat Hager, Doug Pugh, Patricia Prince, Ann Borger, Bill Koster, George Shershanovich, Jane Mayes, Janet McMillan, and Ellen Ryan. Such a supportive yet challenging mix of talented snowbirds.

To Patricia McNair, writer/mentor/masterful teacher, and my fellow participants in her Interlochen workshop for help with the first couple of chapters.

To the pros at Mission Point Press for everything from editing (Tanya Muzumdar, C.D. Dahlquist), design (Heather Shaw), and marketing (Doug Weaver, Jodee Taylor). They are so good at what they do.

To the beautiful country of Australia and its generous and fun-loving people—especially friends Mike and Sue Leonard, Neil Watson, and mentor/teacher Merrilyn Emery. This novel is not roman-à-clef and none of my Aussie friends or acquaintances appear even in fictional disguise. Well, maybe one, but only you know who you are.

To my family and most of all to Pennie, who lit my fire over fifty years ago and even now keeps the flame alive.

ABOUT THE AUTHOR

Now in his 80s, Dr. Richard Ault is something of a literary Grandpa Moses, having published two novels this year with plans for twenty more or so in the future. His previous book, *The Names in the Hat*, is about a timely subject at this point in history: the reinvention of democracy. He is presently working on a novel dealing with cancer, a disease once suffered by him and now his wife. Before taking up fiction, Ault was principal author of *What Works*, a book about consulting, and wrote several articles and book chapters on that subject. Like the main character in *Dismissal*, he was a consultant to a large multinational corporation in 1970s Australia. Unlike that character, this novel is not about him.

Dick and his wife, Pennie, share their time between northern Michigan and northern Florida.

Made in the USA
Middletown, DE
18 May 2023

30860576R00156